THE PERIL OF PRIDE

Cover by Fresh Design

Print ISBN 978-945419-83-6

Ebook ISBN 978-1-945419-84-3

LCCN 2021930273

THE PERIL OF PRIDE

THE SEVEN DEADLY SINS (BOOK SEVEN)

GRETA BORIS

To my Fawkes Press Team, especially Jodi Thompson, for all the encouragement, education, and patience you've shown me from the first of the Seven Deadly Sins to the last.

Of that tormented realm the Emperor
Out of the ice stood free to middle breast…
If he was fair of old as hideous now,
And yet his brows against his Maker raised,
Meetly from him doth all affliction flow.
O how it made me horribly amazed…

From the Ninth Circle of *The Inferno*

The Divine Comedy of Dante Alighieri

1

I hit the second roof hard and rolled across the concrete. A flash of orange disappeared over the next ledge. I glanced around me, saw no one, and followed the flash. One more roof top, this one only large enough to create a rain shelter over the San Bernardino County Correctional Facility's side door. From there we could lower ourselves to the parking lot without the help of bedsheets, which was a good thing because we were out of them. We'd left the last one tied to a pipe.

When I dropped to the ground, adrenaline shot through my veins like meth. It was cold, for Southern California anyway. It couldn't have been much over forty, but I was sweating. I crab walked across the parking lot toward the street, dodging from car to car.

It was like a dream, a very familiar dream. One I'd imagined, planned, obsessed over, then finally given up on years ago. But then came the virus. For most of the world, the disease totally sucked. For me, it had its advantages.

I slid into the shadows next to the man I'd thrown my lot in with, for better or for worse. "This one?" I jerked my chin to the car we leaned against.

"Not here. Don't want to take a cop's car." Chuck gasped out the words. Swimming upstream through ductwork then rappelling down the laddered roof tops was strenuous, but he seemed to being having more trouble recovering than he should. He had the virus, but he'd been hiding it from the guards so our plan wouldn't be derailed.

"Where then?"

Chuck had traded cigarettes for a cell phone while we were inside. He stared at it now. "There's a gym a mile and a half away. It opens at five."

"How do we get there?" I plucked at my orange jumpsuit. Not exactly camouflage material.

"Quickly," he said, and led me to a culvert that ran next to a muddy creek bed.

We didn't see anybody, but it was at least three-quarters of a mile before I stopped sweating. Then the chills started. I'd been alternating between sweating and shivering for two days. I wondered if I had the virus too.

I jogged ahead to keep warm, but I couldn't keep it up for long. I'd run around the yard in circles, and on the basketball court, but running straight, running to get somewhere, that was hard. Especially now. My spirit was willing, but my flesh was weak, as my Mom's boyfriend, Hal, used to say before he beat me.

"There it is," Chuck hissed. Sure enough, a sign for California Body Works glowed in the distance.

"What time is it?" I was thinking out loud, didn't realized I'd said it.

"Let me check my Rolex." Chuck made a big show out of pushing up his sleeve and staring at his bare arm. "Oh, darn. I must have left it on the yacht."

I slapped his back, and he staggered forward. "Probably 4:30, 4:45, something like that," he said. "I'll check the phone after we find a good spot."

We posted up between a stand of bushes and a metal fence on the side of the parking lot and waited for the cars to come. It was a slow trickle at first, but before the sun rose, there were a good twenty cars in the lot.

Chuck couldn't stay still. His leg was shaking in time with a song in his head, and I had to stop him from launching himself at every vehicle that pulled in. He kept saying he wanted to be on the road before the cell doors opened and the guards noticed we weren't in the grub line. There was wisdom in that, but I was waiting for the perfect car.

Our disagreement caused a couple of tense minutes before the Honda Civic rolled in. The color was indistinct in the dim light of the streetlamps, dark blue or gray maybe. The paint was oxidized on the roof and the front hood, and there were dings on three out of four door panels. It was perfect; so was the driver.

He squeezed his bulk into the charcoal-gray morning and stretched. He had a tangle of brown hair that looked like it hadn't been cut or combed since the world shut down. He definitely wasn't an athlete, or a fitness junkie, probably a computer nerd with a New Year's resolution.

He opened the hatchback, rummaged around, pulled out a towel, slammed the hatch down and headed for the gym. I counted to five hundred to make sure he hadn't forgotten anything, then scooted to the driver's side of the Honda and opened the door. Computer nerd hadn't bothered to lock it. He was probably hoping someone would take it off his hands. I was happy to oblige.

Chuck appeared at my side with a piece of tin he'd liberated from the dumpster at the end of the lot, thinking we'd have to break in.

I grinned at him. "Patience pays, my man."

I slid into the driver's seat. Chuck got in the back. Hot wiring new cars is almost impossible, but this wasn't a new car. We were pulling out of the lot in under five minutes.

"Jackpot," Chuck said as I turned onto a side street. I didn't plan to hit the freeway until I had to. They always watch the freeway.

"What?" I asked.

"This guy left a gym bag full of clothes."

A half hour later, we parked at the end of a cul de sac of seen-better-days homes. I changed into a pair of computer nerd's black sweatpants and a green T-shirt with a fire-breathing dragon across the chest. Green is my lucky color. The clothes were a little short and a little loose, but they were okay.

Chuck looked comical. Computer nerd's clothes were three sizes too big on him. He had to thread a bungee cord through the belt loops of the black jeans to keep them up. He'd tucked in an over-washed black T-shirt like it was a button down. If he hadn't, it probably would've reached his knees.

Luck seemed to be with us. It was trash day. I pushed Chuck's jumpsuit at him and picked up my own. We separated, each targeting a different house. We lifted the lid on the can out front, took out two or three bags, placed our peels inside, put the garbage back on top, and headed to the car.

Chuck held up a twenty he must have found in one of the jeans' pockets. "There's a coffee shop next to the freeway. We can switch plates and grab some caffeine before we head south."

South. I wanted to go south as bad as he did, but I knew he'd bring it up first. Chuck was a monkey mouth. As long as I'd been his cell mate, he'd never stopped talking about Orange County. According to him, the land flowed with milk and honey. Problem was, all the wrong people owned the dairy farms and the bee hives.

"Don't know if that's smart just now," I said.

Chuck's mouth got skinny. "That was the plan."

"The plan was to get out. We never said what came next."

"But I told you—"

"Yeah, I know. You told me lots of things. You told anybody who'd listen lots of things, which makes me think Orange County is exactly where they'll be looking for us."

He stopped talking—a minor miracle—until I parked in the coffee shop's lot. "I'll get us coffee. You look for plates," he said then.

That was fine with me. I never mastered the vente, grande, stupidee fancy coffee ordering thing. I just wanted a cup of joe. While he went in, I switched plates with an old Volkswagen on the side of the building, then walked to the front.

The sun hadn't warmed up the day yet, but there were a couple of millennials sitting at outside tables, tapping on their laptops anyway. I glanced over the shoulder of a black-haired chick and my gaze rested on her screen. Instagram. What a waste of friggin' time. She was scrolling through selfies, and pics of food, and dogs, and kids, and—

It hit me.

We should check Instagram. People spread their lives out on the internet like my grandma used to hang bed sheets on the line.

Chuck came out with two paper cups. I shook my head. These shops may have fancy names and fancy prices, but they still serve joe in paper cups like everybody else. Before I could take a sip, the black-haired chick stood and ran into the coffee shop. She left her laptop behind.

As I watched her walk away, I thanked my lucky stars—one, two, three times. Then I snagged the machine from her table and walked as quickly as I could to the Honda.

Chuck had to jog to keep up with me, one hand holding up his jeans. "What are you doing? We don't want to attract attention."

I didn't answer him, just slid into the car and started the engine. He got in next to me, and I handed him the computer. "Don't let the screen go blank. We'll never get back in."

He wanted to ask me questions, but a coughing fit kept him too busy, which was fine with me. I drove around the back of the coffee shop, hoping to hang onto the internet connection. He'd stopped coughing by the time we rounded the building but seemed exhausted by the effort.

I parked under a tree and took the laptop from him. It was still logged into Instagram. "Why don't we see what's happening in Orange County?"

Chuck growled something I didn't understand, but he looked as interested as I was when I found the right page. "Check this out." I flashed the screen at him.

He sucked in a breath.

I poked him in the side with my elbow. "Huh? Huh? Was I right, or was I right?"

"So, what are you thinking?"

"I'm thinking we have a change of plans."

He chewed his bottom lip. "I don't know."

That irritated me. Checking Instagram had been a stroke of genius. "If you want to go someplace else, you can hitchhike." I tossed the laptop out the car window and started the engine.

"Whatever." Chuck was too sick to argue, but he cut his eyes at me. They were narrow and hard like a cat's. I don't trust cats. My grandma told me sometimes they jump in cribs and suck the life out of babies because they smell milk on their breath. His eyes made me cold all over again.

2

FIONA

"Did you get his puffy jacket?" Fiona said.

Devon held up a Thomas the Tank Engine suitcase. "I packed everything that was on the list. Want to check?"

She did, but she didn't want to insult him. "No. I'm sorry. It's just—"

"The first time you'll be apart overnight except for our fifth anniversary, and that was only one night."

"It is."

"I'm aware." Devon grabbed her by the shoulders and planted a kiss on her forehead. "You've mentioned it thirty-three times in the past two days."

"I haven't."

"You have. Makes me think you don't trust me."

Fiona gazed at her husband appraisingly. It was amazing. No matter how intimately you knew someone, the right circumstances could completely change their appearance. Devon was one of the most responsible people she knew. He was brilliant, a successful family law attorney, son of a university professor and an anesthesiologist, a loving husband and father.

But this morning, he'd painted a cartoon grin on his usually solemn face. His flannel shirt was rumpled, and the buttons strained over his middle. When had he began to develop a paunch? His jeans were stuffed into hiking boots so new they squeaked. And the smooth, brown, cheek she loved to kiss was fuzzy with the beginnings of a vacation beard.

Her husband looked like one of Caleb's Build-A-Bear stuffies come to life. Children might cling to plush toys when they were feeling frightened, but she did not. Teddy bears provided no real security.

Devon's eyes widened comically. "Why are you looking at me that way?"

"You look like you're going to Country Bear Jamboree."

"There are still bears in Big Bear." His smile widened.

"Exactly." Fiona emphasized this point with her hands. "Real bears, not Disney characters."

Devon hefted a backpack onto the bed. "I'm prepared. Look."

She wandered over.

He pulled out a flashlight the size of a car battery. "Flashlight." He shoved it in again, then yanked out two large water bottles. "Hydration is important in the cold. People often don't feel thirsty in low temperatures, but they need to drink."

Next, he showed her sunglasses in two sizes. "To prevent snow blindness," he said. Then he waggled a can of bear spray at her and nodded sagely. "See?" And finished the backpack tour by proudly displaying a first aid kit and several protein bars. He must have Googled "What to bring on a winter hike."

He'd obviously hoped the bag would set her mind at ease, but it had the opposite effect. "You're taking Caleb hiking? He's three." Her voice rose several decibels.

Devon held up both hands, palms forward. "No. Not hiking, but some of the sledding trails are secluded. We'll have to walk a ways to get to them."

Fiona crossed her arms over her chest trying to contain her fear. "Why not take him to the public runs? They're all set up for kids. It seems so much safer."

"Public is exactly what I'm trying to get away from." Devon zipped up the pack. "I want him to experience nature. To see snow in the woods the way I saw it as a kid."

Fiona turned a laugh into a cough and covered her mouth with her hand. Devon grew up in a suburb of Chicago. There'd been snow in the winter, but she'd never seen a forest when they'd visited his parents. A couple of trees between houses maybe, but nothing that could be called "woods."

He hefted the pack over his shoulder, grabbed Caleb's suitcase and his own duffle bag, and walked out of the bedroom.

Fiona followed. "I get that, Dev, I do. But he's only three. He's so little."

"I not little," a very little voice piped up. Caleb popped out of his room and skipped to his mother's side. He looked like a mini-Devon with blonder hair and paler skin. He wore a blue flannel shirt, new jeans, and a pair of tiny hiking boots.

"Where did you get the outfit?" she said.

Caleb stopped and stared down at himself as if he'd forgotten what he'd put on. "Daddy buyed it."

"Nice."

Caleb took her hand and pulled her toward the living room. "When are you coming to Big Bear, Mommy?"

"Hopefully, Monday or Tuesday, sweet 'ums. I have to work this weekend because Aunt Olivia is going away, too."

"I'll miss you." Caleb's lower lip dropped on one side.

Devon scooped him up, buried his face in his son's stomach, and blew a belly fart. Caleb squealed.

"We're going to have some guy time, right, buddy?" Devon said when Caleb's feet were on the floor again.

"Right."

The tickling and pep-talk had done their magic. Caleb sounded confident again.

"We'd better hit the road," Devon said. "I'm supposed to pick up the key by three."

"Don't drive fast on those roads. There's black ice." Fiona cringed as soon as the words left her lips. She remembered her own mother throwing out cautions as she drove off on teen adventures and thinking she'd never do the same. Motherhood changes your DNA, however. She couldn't help herself.

She followed Devon and Caleb to the car, buckled her child into his car seat, and kissed her husband. "Call me as soon as you get there."

"Will do." Her husband slammed the door of the Audi Q7, and rolled out of the driveway.

She watched the car until it disappeared at the end of the street, then turned back to her quiet house. Something rattled in the kitchen as she closed the front door. Her heart banged out a couple of extra beats before she recognized the sound as the ice maker dropping cubes inside the refrigerator. She laughed at herself under her breath. This was as good for her as it was for Caleb. Fears were hills to be climbed, and the view was always better from the top. That's what her therapist said.

She wandered into the kitchen, poured herself a cup of coffee, turned her back to the counter, and gazed through the doorway to her empty dining room. Why had she been looking forward to this?

TWO HOURS LATER, Fiona entered the Fish Bowl. Her gaze was momentarily caught by the Pacific Ocean sparkling through the picture windows. The blue view had earned her studio its name.

"Yay, you're here. I have a couple of things to go over with you before I take off." Olivia spoke without taking her eyes from the iPad in front of her. "I have a shipment coming in tomorrow—leggings and long-sleeved tops. Good for winter." She tapped at her keyboard. "I cleared a space on the shelves for them. And—" She paused as she finished typing, swiped a program closed, and looked at Fiona for the first time since she'd entered. "And the small medicine balls you wanted are coming in too."

Olivia was nothing if not efficient. Fiona had hired her to run the small boutique connected with the Pilates studio when she was pregnant with Caleb. Liv quickly became indispensable.

"Great. What time are you leaving?" Fiona squeezed behind the counter and deposited her purse on a shelf beneath. She was a bit concerned about running the Fish Bowl without her partner but knew Liv would burn out if she wasn't forced to take breaks now and again. She was dedicated. So dedicated, she sometimes made Fiona feel like a slacker.

"Not until eight or nine. Davy is sleeping now," Olivia said. "He wants to drive through the night while there's no traffic."

"What about you and Brian?" Brian was their thirteen-year-old son.

"Brian can sleep through anything, and me? I'll be up all night worrying about Davy falling asleep at the wheel."

Fiona took her own company tablet from a desk drawer and turned it on. "I guess you can sleep when you get there."

"I don't know about that." Olivia shook her head. "Brian has an entire agenda laid out. After we check in at the B&B, we're going to rent snowshoes and walk around Lake Mary. When we're done snowshoeing, we're going ice fishing." Olivia bent to drag her things out from under the counter.

Fiona perched on a tall stool. "I thought this was a snowboarding trip?"

The answer was muffled by the wooden cabinet. "It is, but we only bought single-day passes. They're not good until Sunday."

When Liv stood, her cell phone rumbled inside her tote bag. She rummaged around until she found it, then held it to her ear. "Yeah."

A frown creased her forehead as she listened. "But we're leaving tonight." She listened for several seconds longer, the frown deepening. "All right, well, thanks anyway." She disconnected the call and stared at the phone screen.

"Something wrong?" Fiona asked.

"That was the dog sitter. Her cousin's wife's sister is having a baby in Hesperia, so she can't watch Crackers."

"What does her cousin's wife's—"

Olivia held up a hand to stop the question. "Don't ask me. I didn't understand the connection. Something to do with watching her cousin's kids so they could go to the hospital."

"Are they letting extra people into the hospital now?" The virus that had shut down most of the globe was beginning to wane. Many businesses, like the Fish Bowl, had been allowed to open with limited capacity.

"I guess."

"Well, I can watch Crackers." The words popped out of Fiona's mouth before she'd thought about them.

Olivia narrowed her eyes. "Fiona. You're supposed to be taking a couple of days for yourself."

"I'll be working anyway."

"I know." Olivia tipped her head to the side. "Work is one thing, but you don't have to take on Crackers, too."

"I love Crackers."

"I'm sure you do, but he's still an added responsibility."

"He'll be company."

Olivia sighed. "Are you sure?"

Was she? She'd been looking forward to relaxing evenings home alone, bubble baths, a mystery novel she'd recently bought but hadn't had time to read, chick flicks. Dog walking hadn't been a part of her plans, but Olivia needed a break. She'd been looking forward to this weekend for weeks.

"Of course. He'll keep me safe while the boys are gone." Fiona nodded at the dog bed that was a permanent fixture in the lobby. "And I can bring him into the studio during the days."

Olivia stared at her for a long second. "You don't have to walk him. You could just throw a ball in the yard."

"I want to walk him," Fiona said and found she meant it. "There's a hiking trail near my house I've been wanting to investigate, but Devon isn't into exercise, and I've been afraid to go alone. Crackers will be the perfect companion."

Olivia brightened. "He loves to hike."

"It'll be good to have him there at night, too." Fiona's voice dropped. She hadn't realized until that moment how much she'd been dreading the hours after the lights went out.

Not that she was afraid. She wasn't. Not exactly. A better word was anxious. It wasn't logical. Her half brother was locked up, probably for life. He wouldn't be bothering her. But past experience had taught her how dangerous human beings could be.

"Besides," she continued. "Caleb has been after us to get him a dog. It will be good to see what it's like having one in the house."

Olivia climbed onto the other stool. "Are you hesitant about the responsibility? It's a lot of work."

"I'm not the problem. It's Devon."

"I thought Devon liked dogs? He always plays with Crackers."

"He does, but you know him. He has to get a doctorate in canine behavioral psychology before we can adopt one. He's researching breeds right now."

Olivia laughed. "Mutts are easiest and healthiest."

"Oh, he would agree with you after four weeks of investigation. But what combination of breeds?" Fiona turned her palm up. "German shepherd and…?"

"Lab?" Olivia offered.

"Labs are great, but they are prone to hip dysplasia just like shepherds. He's pondering hounds now."

"They make good search and rescue dogs." Olivia should know. Crackers was trained in search and rescue.

"Caleb will be in high school before Devon makes up his mind." Fiona opened her email. "I've got Crackers, and you should get going. I bet you're not done packing."

"Tell Devon, from me, that there are some things you can't learn virtually." Olivia slid off the stool. "Dog ownership is kind of like parenting. Books are okay, helpful even, but experience is essential."

"I tell him that every day. I'm actually a little worried about him having Caleb all to his lonesome."

Olivia raised her eyebrows in question.

"Devon overthinks things. His response time is slow. Caleb moves fast. I keep trying to tell him being a dad isn't like being a lawyer. You don't have to prepare a brief to convince a three-year-old to put away his Lego blocks. It doesn't matter if he likes or dislikes your decisions."

"Amen," Olivia said. "Brian has recently discovered the joys of debating. A simple statement like *Brian, pick up your socks* would turn into a three-hour discussion if we let it." She raised her blue eyes to the ceiling and spoke in a pretty fair imitation of her son. *"If a sock falls in the living room and no one is there to see it…"*

Fiona laughed. "Oh, my gosh. I didn't even think of that. You're right. We're raising a future adolescent."

"Exactly." Olivia shouldered her tote bag and walked toward the exit. "I'll see you around eight." She paused and turned. "You don't have to watch Crackers, you know. I could drop him at the vet's."

"Would you stop?" Fiona said. "I want Crackers."

"It's just, I don't want to be one of those people."

Fiona laughed. "One of what people?"

"The people you take care of. Because you do, you know."

"I do what?"

"You are a born caregiver, but I want to be equals, friends, not a burden."

Fiona felt her face grow warm. Devon had said something similar to her not long ago. She'd complained because he'd missed dinner again, and they'd argued. His parting comment—before he stormed off to the bedroom—was, "You act like everything and everyone in your life is your responsibility, Fiona. Sometimes, I feel like another task on your to-do list. If I didn't, I might spend more time at home."

"We are equals. You'll be doing me a favor by leaving Crackers with me." Fiona paused. "I'm a little nervous about being home alone at night." She hadn't wanted to make that admission, but it was the truth.

Olivia searched her face for a long minute. "Okay," she said, and the door closed behind her. Fiona stared at her friend's blond head through the glass as it disappeared down the outdoor staircase. The loneliness she'd felt when Devon and Caleb drove off that morning crept up on her again.

What was wrong with her? She was a grown woman, a strong woman both physically and emotionally. Her therapist had fired herself and suggested Fiona keep her number only in case of emergencies. She'd said Fiona had come through the terrible events following her father's death with flying colors. So why was she so on edge?

Her phone dinged with a text message. She glanced at the screen. It was Devon. *We're here, safe and sound. I'll call after I put Caleb down tonight.*

This was followed by three pictures, the last was her grinning son laying in the snow, spread-eagle, with the caption: *Our little angel.*

Her expression matched Caleb's as she viewed the image. This trip would be good for all of them. Fiona copied a shot of Caleb and Devon in a goofy pose and opened her Instagram app.

She pasted in the picture and typed: *Sledding in Big Bear for the first time, and Mom gets a weekend alone!*

Alone. She'd forgotten was that was like, which was probably why it made her nervous. She and Caleb were together constantly. As much as she loved being a mother, her son needed his father too. Devon had admitted he felt both a little jealous and a little left out, which was encouraging.

She'd tried not to micromanage him after the comment he'd made about feeling like a task on her list, but she was concerned about how little time they'd spent together lately. She wanted Devon to *want* to be with Caleb, to *want* to be with her. Hopefully they'd do some quality male bonding while she took care of things at work. Then Monday or Tuesday she'd head up the mountain and finish out the week with them.

The front door jangled, interrupting her thoughts. A tall, lean woman in yoga pants entered. "I'm here for the four o'clock Reformer class."

Fiona opened the reservation app on her iPad. "Name?" She took the woman's information and sent her to the back room. "I'll be there as soon as our other student arrives," she said.

A busy evening of personal training and small group sessions followed a busy afternoon of the same. It was dark by the time Fiona locked the studio door behind herself and headed to the parking lot. A frisson of nerves bristled the hair on her arms as she hurried across the dimly lit asphalt to her car.

Watching Crackers for the weekend was a win-win. Liv could get away, and Fiona would have company. She clicked open the driver side door and slid inside.

Do we ever grow out of our need for security blankets? She buckled her seatbelt, case in point. The compression of the strap across her chest was comforting. A large furry animal to cuddle, especially one with fangs, would be even more comforting.

3

DEVON

The road twisted and narrowed until it became a single track of frozen ground. The blanket of snow covering everything made it difficult to know where the lane began or ended. It also covered the patches of black ice Fiona had warned him about. Devon thought of her each time his tires lost traction. Thankfully, Caleb snoozed through the slipping and sliding.

Fiona would hate this. She liked to be in control of her environment. She enjoyed walking outside and greeting neighbors on her way to the mailbox. She felt secure when familiar things and familiar people surrounded her. Devon had wanted to leave the known world behind, at least for the week.

However, after this long stretch of empty road, he began to think he'd left it too far behind. When a snow-dusted wooden structure appeared through the pines, he exhaled with relief. This had to be it. The image on the B&B site had shown a log house nestled in the pines, very picturesque. The reality was a bit more run down, but any shelter was welcome at this point. The flurry of snow on the other side of his windshield was beginning to obscure his vision.

Devon settled the car into what he hoped was the driveway, turned off the engine and listened. He heard exactly what he'd hoped to hear

—nothing. The silence was heavy, an almost physical thing, and it was a balm to his soul.

The past month had been a nightmare, one he hadn't been at liberty to share with Fiona due to attorney-client confidentiality. No divorce case was pleasant, especially when there were children involved, but this case had been the worst of his career.

The wife, Emily, was a stay-at-home socialite and Devon's client. The husband, Myron, was a trial lawyer. He'd been abusing her for years but was savvy enough to keep the damage invisible to everyone but the various doctors who'd treated her. He'd even made sure she rotated through the urgent care physicians. Only once had one expressed concern, but Emily had covered her husband's misdeeds with lies.

Devon hadn't had anything he could use in court. Myron had convinced Emily he'd not only get custody but punish their three children if she disrupted the status quo, never mind the damage he'd inflict on her. She was terrified of him.

It wasn't until a neighbor had witnessed him gut-punch Emily, watched her fall to the floor, and saw three brutal kicks land in her abdomen that Devon had what he needed to win the suit.

He threw open the car door. He hoped the beautiful quiet would silence the words that had rung in his mind since. After he'd won full custody for Emily and had criminal charges brought against Myron, the man had waylaid him on the courthouse steps. There'd been suppressed rage in every taut line of his body. Vitriol, like corrosive acid, dripped from his mouth. *Do you know what it's like to lose a child? No? You'll find out.*

So Devon took his son and headed for the far reaches of San Bernardino County as soon as he was able. It wasn't a permanent solution. And, honestly, he didn't think Myron would follow through with his threats. Domestic abusers didn't pick on guys their own size, in Devon's experience. But the tension and the worry had taken their toll, and he needed a break.

He trudged around the car and opened Caleb's door. His son's head lolled to one side, a thin line of drool extending from his mouth to the car seat cover. Devon smiled. How did kids manage to look adorable doing totally non-cute things? "Hey, bud. We're here."

Caleb's eyes opened, long lashes fluttering for a moment. A look of confusion flashed across his face, followed quickly by recognition, then excitement. "Is there snow?"

Devon unhooked his straps. "Take a look."

Caleb slid from his seat into the white world. His eyes grew wide. "Snow," he whispered.

Devon popped the trunk and lifted the bags of groceries he'd brought. "I should get these inside," he said, but he was talking to himself. Caleb had run up the small embankment toward the house, stumbled over his feet and fallen with a clomp.

"Snow," he said again, throwing handfuls of it into the air.

"You need to get your mittens on," Devon said. "Snow is cold." He tromped past his son to the cabin, dropped the bags on the porch, and fished the key out of his pocket.

The lock clicked, but the front door stuck in place. Devon gave it a shove with his shoulder, and it popped open. The interior smelled musty, and it wasn't much warmer inside than outside, but it looked okay.

There was a living room to his right, the far wall of which was taken up by an oversized stone fireplace. To his left was a doorway leading into the kitchen.

The room was long and narrow. It had a small dining table by a window that looked out on the front yard. The cooking area was at the rear. Devon deposited his groceries on the counter, deciding the refrigerator was superfluous at the moment, and went in search of a thermostat.

He found it down a paneled hallway and turned on the heat. An encouraging rumble came from somewhere in the house. A moment later, warm air began to flow through the vent at his feet.

"Daddy." He heard a pathetic cry. Caleb stood in the open doorway, red hands raised. "My fingers hurt."

"I told you, you have to put your mittens on. Come here." He and Fiona had different parenting styles. Devon believed a child should understand why they were asked to do things. Caleb's frozen fingers had taught him a valuable lesson. One he wouldn't forget.

Caleb trotted to him, and Devon held his hands over the flow of warm air. His son whimpered. "You'll be okay in a minute," Devon said.

After two more trips to the car to retrieve the rest of their bags, Devon closed the front door. "Let's go see the bedrooms."

Caleb's hands must have recovered, because he darted away from the heat, down the hall, and into the closest room. A moment later, he was out, then quickly vanished into another doorway. He repeated this process several times, reminding Devon of a prairie dog popping in and out of its holes.

"This one is mine," Caleb called from the first room he'd entered.

Devon followed his voice. The room contained twin beds. It was a small, wood-paneled space that would have been dark if it weren't for a wide window on the far wall that opened onto a Christmas-card scene. A shining alabaster hill sloped away from the house, ending in a copse of silver-tipped trees. The sky was the palest of blues, striped by a constantly shifting pattern of snowflakes.

Caleb stretched out on a navy-blue bedspread, his short legs and arms as wide as he could spread them. "I'll sleep here."

"Then, I'll take this bed." Devon sat on the twin a few feet away. Between the beds was a small nightstand topped by a heavy wooden lamp carved into the shape of a bear.

Caleb's forehead furrowed. "You're not going to sleep in the big bed?"

Devon shrugged. "Maybe when Mommy comes." He patted the mattress. "I'm gonna bunk in with you tonight."

Caleb jumped up and fisted his small hands. "Yes."

"Want me to teach you how to make snow angels?" Devon asked. His son's eyes narrowed, and his mouth tipped down on the left side. "If you put on the mittens and the hat Mommy packed, you won't get so cold."

Caleb thought about it for a long moment. His mouth returned to its usual rosebud shape, and his hands clenched again. "Yes."

Snow angels were a hit. The hill outside the house was covered with them. Devon had sent Caleb into their bedroom to take off his wet clothes while he looked for firewood. The heater had taken the chill off the house, but he wanted to build a blaze in the stone fireplace for atmosphere. There was no wood in the metal basket in the living room and none in the closet next to it. Maybe there was dry wood outside somewhere.

He didn't bother with his jacket but did grab the waterproof gloves he'd lain on the table in the entryway next to yet another lamp shaped like a bear. This one reared up on hind legs and leaned against the rod the shade was attached to. Devon had noticed a similar lamp in the living room atop the bookcase near the fireplace. The owner of the cabin must have carved them or gotten a deal at local gift shop. They appeared to be all over the house, each one in a different menacing position.

Devon walked outside and after circling the house twice, he found a short plywood door under the back steps. On the other side of it was a crawlspace that had been turned into a woodshed.

Ten minutes later, Devon had a nice pile of cut wood stacked against the fireplace wall. "Caleb," he called, "want to help Daddy build a fire?"

Was it okay to show an almost four-year-old how to build a fire? He knew what Fiona would say, but didn't families in rural communities teach their children these kinds of basic skills early? A healthy respect for fire could save a child's life. Besides, he didn't plan to allow Caleb to touch anything. He just wanted to him to watch, to understand how it was done. He would also explain the dangers involved.

Caleb didn't answer.

Devon brushed sawdust from his hands and stood. "Hey, Caleb. What're you up to?"

Again, no answer. He was probably *reading* one of his picture books. He couldn't actually read, but Fiona had read them aloud so many times, Caleb had most of them memorized.

"Buddy." Devon stepped into the bedroom they were sharing and stopped. Caleb wasn't there. His heart knocked out two extra beats, then he remembered. His child had recently learned the game of hide and seek, only sometimes he didn't announce he was playing. He liked to stow away behind a door or under a bed and scream "boo!" when an unsuspecting parent ambled by.

"Where, oh where, is Caleb?" Devon said in a sing-song voice. "Have you seen him, Mr. Bear?" He addressed the stuffed toy propped against the pillows. "No? Hm. I'll have to eat all the mac and cheese myself."

Devon dropped to his knees and peered under the bed. No Caleb. He rose and glanced behind him to the closet. "It's a shame he's gone missing," Devon continued. "I brought rocky road ice cream, his favorite. Maybe you can help me eat that, Mr. Bear. I know how much you like"—he tore open the closet door—"sweets." The word thudded to the floor.

The closet was empty.

Devon's heart thumped again. "Caleb." Fear colored his tone with anger. "Caleb, this is enough. No more scaring Daddy. You come out now, you hear?"

If Caleb heard, he didn't obey. The silence Devon had been longing for cursed him now. He ran to the window and peered at the darkening day. The snow, a bright blue-gray, lay placidly between him and the pine woods.

He had a sudden understanding of why so many terrifying children's stories, from *Little Red Riding Hood* to *Hansel and Gretel* to *Snow White*, took place in the woods. Anything could hide in them. Especially at night when the trees cast long moonlit shadows and branches reached across narrow paths.

A creak and a slam somewhere in the house startled him from his thoughts. He spun, expecting, hoping to see a small shape come bounding into the room screaming *boo*! There was nothing.

Devon strode through the house, flinging open doors as he went. "Caleb," he bellowed. "This isn't funny anymore."

Not in the master bedroom or closet. Not in the bathtub or behind the bathroom door. Not in the living room, hiding behind the easy chair with its awful, crocheted afghan.

The sound came again. The kitchen. He was sure it came from the kitchen. "Caleb," he said in a softer tone.

Do you know what it's like to lose a child?

"No," he said aloud to Myron's hateful voice and entered the kitchen. The only possible place Caleb could be was the pantry. Devon hadn't opened that door at the end of the room yet, hadn't bothered putting away their few dry goods, but there must be space for a child inside. There had to be.

He crossed the kitchen and pulled the door open and stared. It wasn't a pantry. Twin benches lined the left and right walls of the room. Hooks were drilled into the wall above them. A plaid jacket hung off one, a few moth-eaten beanies off two more. A pair of rubber boots leaned by a Dutch door at the far end.

A Dutch door that led to the outside world. It opened an inch or two as if by an unseen hand, then pulled shut with a slam.

"Caleb."

Devon bolted through the door and down the icy steps into the cabin's backyard. A picnic table peeked out beneath a snow comforter. A grill leaned precariously under a mound of white, but these things hardly registered. His gaze was captured by footprints, tiny footprints, that spanned the distance between the house and the woods.

Not bothering to get hat or gloves or jacket or phone, Devon ran. "Caleb." His son's name knifed through the frigid evening. Snow muffled sound, but cold made sound travel farther by bouncing the waves into warm air pockets that projected them forward.

Devon knew this because he'd spent two weeks studying cold weather survival before heading to Big Bear. He'd thought the information might come in handy. He liked to prepare himself for new situations, but the information wasn't helping him now.

Why hadn't he studied about the thought processes of three-and-a-half-year-olds? Why hadn't he researched what young children do when you send them to their rooms to take off wet clothes? Why hadn't he kept his eyes on Caleb instead of trusting him to listen?

"Caleb," he yelled again.

He didn't pause when he reached the treeline but plunged into the darkening woods. After only a yard or two, he stopped. Was that a footprint or a rock or a clod of dirt? There was so little light it was difficult to see the prints of Caleb's small hiking boots. He should have gone back for his phone.

He knelt and squinted ahead at the spaces between the trees. There were shadows in the ice—Caleb's tracks. It must be Caleb's tracks. He moved ahead, more slowly and carefully this time.

The cold bit into his flesh and froze the tears in his eyes. He hollered his son's name in a rhythm, every thirty seconds the same notes, the same timbre. It was a song of desperation.

Endless minutes later, he heard a whimper. The sound shot through him like an arrow. "Caleb," he called, then stilled himself and waited.

"Daddy?"

"Caleb? Where are you, baby?"

"I'm here, Daddy. I gots lost." The whimper expanded into a sob.

Devon rounded a fat pine and saw a patch of red in the dying day. He ran. A moment later his arms surrounded his shivering child. He buried his face in Caleb's hair and savored the scent of baby shampoo. "You're okay now, son."

When they reached the house, Devon wrapped the ugly afghan around his child and sat him on the living room floor while he built a fire. When the fire was crackling, he ordered Caleb to stay put, and hurried into the bedroom for his pajamas.

Devon pawed through the suitcase until the familiar dinosaur-print flannel PJs came to hand. A sob caught in his throat. They were so small. They had feet. What had Devon been thinking, sending his son into the bedroom by himself?

As he pulled off Caleb's clothes and scrubbed his red skin with a rough towel, he prepared the questions he wanted to ask in his mind. He helped his son into the PJs, snapped the bottom snap, and said, "Why did you go outside when Daddy asked you to go into the bedroom?" He asked the question in a calm measured tone, despite the torrent of emotion still churning inside him.

Caleb's lower lip went crooked. "I needed help, but you was gone."

"What do you mean, I was gone?" Devon said.

"You wasn't in here."

Devon was about to argue, then realized he must have been outside getting the wood. "I went to get wood."

"You didn't tell me."

A picture of what must have happened began to play in Devon's mind. "So you went into the kitchen to find me?"

Caleb nodded sadly. "You wasn't there."

"So you walked out the backdoor?"

"I looked for you."

Devon closed his eyes. His son's face made his whole chest ache. What if a wild animal had found him before Devon had? There were mountain lions in the forests here. There were bears. There was cold, maybe the most lethal killer of all.

He snapped the final snaps on the PJs, wrapped Caleb in the blanket again, and pulled him into his lap. "Let's make a deal. Okay?"

Caleb's head moved up and down against his chest.

"When I was in Boy Scouts, we had a buddy system. Do you know what that is?"

The boy's head moved in the opposite direction.

"It's when you and someone else agree that you'll always stick together."

"Even when you go potty?"

"Maybe not potty, but if you do go away, you always tell each other where you're going and when you're coming back."

"Why?"

"To be safe. If Daddy hadn't found you in the woods tonight—" He couldn't finish that thought, but he didn't think he had to. Caleb had obviously been terrified.

Neither spoke for a long moment. They watched the spikes of light in the fireplace grow brighter as the room darkened around them. Caleb broke the quiet. "Are we buddies?"

"Absolutely."

"We stick together?"

"Like glue."

Caleb giggled. "Like bubble gum?"

"Yup."

"Like sticky tape?"

"Yes."

"Like Hug-a-Boo-Boo bandages?"

Devon squeezed him tighter and kissed his neck. Caleb squealed. "Like goopy-goop-goop?"

"I think you made that up."

After a dinner of mac and cheese and hotdogs and three readings of his favorite Thomas the Tank Engine book, Caleb's eyes began to close. Devon scooped him up, carried him into the bedroom, and nestled him under the blankets. Two little arms reached into the air for a final hug. "Where you going?"

"Back by the fire," Devon said. "I'm going to call Mommy."

"Supposed to tell me." Caleb yawned out the words.

"I just did."

His son's eyes closed, and he whispered, "Pancakes for breakfast?"

Devon swept the bangs off his forehead. "Sure. See you in the morning, buddy."

"Night, buddy." And Caleb was out.

4

FIONA

The doorbell rang. At least, Fiona thought it had. She couldn't hear much over the blaring of the television. As soon as she'd gotten home, she'd turned on the TV and every light she walked past on her way to the kitchen to pour herself a glass of wine. It made the house feel less empty.

She grabbed the remote, lowered the volume and heard the chime of the door clearly. Her gaze fell on the mantel clock. It was only 6:45. Olivia was early.

She padded to the front door. "Coming," she yelled at the wood. "You're early. Good. Maybe you'll—"she opened the door and shut her mouth.

"Hi, Fiona. Long time."

Although she liked, even admired, the slender, black woman standing on her porch, dread crept over Fiona at the sight of her. "Detective Sylla." She stumbled over the name.

They stood eyeing each other for a long moment before Fiona realized she was being rude. "Come in." She moved aside, and Sylla stepped into the house.

She hadn't seen the detective in four years, not since she'd come to tell her they'd caught the person who'd murdered a real estate agent in the Laguna Beach home Fiona inherited after her father's death. "Can I get you a glass of wine?" She nodded at her own glass.

"No, thanks. I'm on my way to dinner with a friend." Sylla's British accent gave her an air of mystery. Fiona had always wondered what a Brit was doing working for the Orange County Sheriff's department but had never asked. They didn't have a personal relationship.

Fiona noticed the detective's clothing for the first time. She wore jeans, a slouchy sweater, boots, big hoop earrings and... was that eyeshadow? She'd never seen the woman out of her work clothes. She actually looked pretty.

They walked into the living room, and Sylla settled on the couch while Fiona perched on the edge of an easy chair. "It's nice to see you," she said. "But I'm sure you're not here to be sociable."

"I wish I were."

Having a cop come to the door was always nerve-wracking. Fiona ticked through the possibilities for the visit in her mind. Sylla wasn't here about Devon and Caleb. She was an investigator, not CHP, and Dev had texted Fiona to say they'd made it up the mountain. Fiona hadn't broken any laws lately, so that left only one thing—her half brother. Her mouth felt dry. She took a sip of wine and waited.

"Your brother escaped from San Bernardino County Jail last night. I wanted you to hear it from me before you saw it on the news."

There it was. Fiona had dreamed about this moment. It had been her recurring nightmare for a full year after he'd been caught. She set her glass down hard. "He wasn't in San Bernardino. He was in San Quentin." She said this as if it would disprove the investigator's statement.

"The state mandated San Quentin decrease its population by fifty percent due to the virus outbreak. According to AB 109, nonviolent prisoners can be relocated from state pens to county jails. So they released some, they moved some."

"Since when is murder nonviolent?" The calmness of Fiona's tone belied the emotion swirling inside her.

Sylla inhaled and exhaled slowly. "It's not, but they had to jump through a lot of hoops to meet the state's demands. I guess your brother—"

"Half brother," Fiona interrupted her.

"*Half* brother wasn't violent while he was there. He was also at higher risk for the disease, being a bit older and—"

Fiona held up a hand, cutting her off again. "Okay, okay. So they moved him. How the hell did he escape? Aren't the county jails secure?" Anger had broken through her stoicism. Her voice trembled.

"Yes, generally speaking, but they don't have the security levels of a state prison. Anyway, we think your," she paused, "half brother and his cellmate saw the cell phone video of an earlier escape from Santa Ana and mimicked it."

Fiona couldn't believe what she was hearing. "Wait, there is a video of a prison break on the internet?"

Sylla stared at her hands for a second before replying in a monotone. "Right. Apparently, the San Bernardino escape was staged almost identically to the Santa Ana escape seven years ago."

"How? How did they do it?"

"They climbed through a ventilation shaft to the roof, tied bed sheets together, and lowered themselves down. They managed to end up in the open parking area, so no fence. Easy to run from there."

Fiona couldn't speak. There were so many questions running through her head, she didn't know which to ask first. "What are you doing to find them?" She settled on the most important.

"Everything we can. He'll be caught, Fiona. Trust me."

Fiona stood, unable to sit still any longer. She walked to the cold fireplace and wrapped her arms around herself. "He'll come here."

"Maybe." Sylla inclined her head. "But if he's smart, he'll head for the border."

"He's not stupid, just insane."

Neither woman spoke for a long moment, then Sylla said, "Is your husband at home?"

Fiona gave a quick shake of her head. "He and my son are in Big Bear."

"Perhaps you should call him?"

"No." The word erupted from someplace deep within. Fiona tempered her voice. "No. I think it's good they're away. I don't want Caleb here if…"

"You could join them."

"I'm the only one at the studio until Tuesday. We've just reopened. I can't shut down again. Not if I want to stay in business."

"I've ordered security checks on your house, for your sake but also because it's a possibility he may head here." Sylla stood and gazed at Fiona. "It's a long way from San Bernardino to Dana Point. We're sure to catch him."

You couldn't hold him when you had him. Fiona kept that thought to herself. None of this was Sylla's fault, and it didn't pay to shoot the messenger if you were relying on the messenger to protect you.

Forty-five minutes after the detective left, Olivia and Crackers arrived. Fiona's gaze roamed the street as she let them in. No police, not unless they were in an unmarked car.

Olivia was talking, "...two cups of dry food. I brought one can as well, but just give him a little scoop or he won't eat the dry." Her friend walked to the kitchen. Fiona watched Crackers disappear into the rear of the house, then followed Olivia. The dog was most likely looking for Caleb. He and her son were crazy about each other.

Liv was unpacking a bag onto the counter when Fiona joined her. "I brought his favorite water bowl. He won't drink out of metal ones, and I didn't want you getting slobber all over your dishes."

"Want a glass of wine?" Fiona said, hoping she wouldn't rush off.

Olivia eyed the bottle sitting next to the plastic tub of kibble. "I'm supposed to get straight home."

"Half a glass?"

She groaned. "Okay. What do you want to bet Davy won't be ready when I get back anyway? We have too much stuff to fit into the car even with the roof racks, but he's determined."

Fiona took a stemless wine glass from the cupboard, splashed some wine into it and slid it onto the counter in front of her friend. "Come sit where it's comfortable."

Olivia sank onto the couch where Sylla had been sitting less than an hour ago. Fiona took the place she'd taken earlier. She swirled the wine in her glass but didn't speak. Bad news, like bad food, churned inside, wanting out. It didn't seem fair to her friend to spew it at her, however, especially not when she was getting ready for a much-needed vacation.

She searched for a topic of discussion, sure her silence seemed suspicious. Before she found one, something wet slapped into her lap. She started.

"Crackers, that's not yours." Olivia leaned forward and took a stuffed squirrel away from her pet. "Sorry." She made a vain attempt to wipe it dry with her free hand.

"It's okay. I'll wash it," Fiona said and stroked the dog's shiny ears. "He's just looking for Caleb."

"You might want to close Caleb's door. All those toys are tempting. Crackers isn't great at sharing." Olivia launched into a story about how he stole another dog's ball at the dog park and led the entire pack on a merry chase. It saved Fiona from having to talk at all.

Ten minutes later, she stood at the door holding the collar of a very confused Black Lab mix while his mistress drove away. After another perusal of the street, she closed and latched the front door, returned to the living room, and slid to the floor with her back against the couch.

Crackers nosed her face, gave her a gentle lick, then curled up beside her. "It's you and me, buddy," she said. He thumped his tail in response, and Fiona didn't feel quite so alone.

THE CALIFORNIA KING seemed huge without Devon in it, a desert plain, an open sea. Before Detective Sylla had come by, Fiona had imagined cuddling under the comforter and watching a romantic comedy—something her husband wouldn't participate in on general principal—until she fell asleep.

The night wasn't going as planned. She'd put a movie on but couldn't concentrate. Sylla's news spun through her mind like a twister, removing all else from its path. It was only a forty-minute drive from San Bernardino to her home at this time of the night. Not far. No matter what Sylla said. He could be here now. In the street in front of her house. She'd searched for the promised police presence and hadn't seen it.

Fiona hadn't been able to decide whether to leave the lights on or turn them off when she got in bed. If she left them on, her house felt like a fishbowl—naked to prying eyes. If she turned them off, she couldn't see if there was someone inside, hiding in a dark corner. Lose-lose situation. She compromised by leaving only the kitchen and hallway lights on.

She flopped over on her side and looked at Crackers, who snored softly on the floor by the bed. He was her comfort, her early-warning system. She reached into her bedside table drawer and pulled out her other comfort—a Sig Sauer. She ejected and reinserted the magazine. It was loaded, as it had been the last ten times she'd checked it.

She'd bought the handgun when the corpse was discovered in the upstairs bedroom of the Laguna Beach house. She'd also taken shooting lessons at a nearby range, and while she was no Navy Seal, she was reasonably proficient. She'd kept it in her bedside table until she'd had Caleb. As soon as he could crawl, it had been locked away in a gun cupboard.

Devon hadn't protested, as she'd expected. He didn't like it—she could see that by the tightness of his mouth whenever the gun was visible. Although he never talked about it, she guessed he'd seen firearm tragedies in his line of work, but Fiona was careful.

She set the gun in the nightstand again but left the drawer open so it would be handy. Her phone rang as she rolled onto her back. She glanced at the screen. It was Devon. "Hey, honey. How are you guys?"

"Great, we're great." It was so wonderful to hear her husband's voice. She choked up for a moment. "Fi? You there?"

"Yes, here," she said. "So, from your picture, it looked like Caleb loved the snow."

Devon paused. "He does. Had to drag him inside when the sun started going down."

His tone was a bit too enthusiastic. Fiona wondered if father and son had a disagreement. Every once and a while, Caleb relapsed from the curious threes into the terrible twos again, especially when he was excited. "Temper tantrum?" she asked.

Again Devon hesitated. "No," he said. "He was fine. Bribed him with a bowl of rocky road."

She could tell from his voice she wasn't getting the whole story but decided to let it go. When they'd fought, Devon had also accused her of micromanaging his parenting.

"How was your day?" Devon said.

"Fine." It was her turn to lie. "I'm dog-sitting for Olivia and Davy."

"Caleb will be green with envy when he finds out. He loves that dog."

She glanced at her sleeping companion. He was pawing the air now, chasing a dream rabbit. "He's a good one. We should consider a lab-shepherd mix."

"I'm working on it."

"I know, but I think we should do it sooner rather than later. After the trip."

"What's the hurry?"

My half brother has escaped from jail, and we need all the security we can get, she thought but didn't say. "I really like having a dog around."

"Not all dogs are as well trained as Crackers. They've spent a lot of time and money on him. Unless you're willing to invest in classes and trainers..."

Devon's familiar diatribe floated into the air around her. She'd heard it before and stopped listening.

She would have to tell him about the prison break before he heard it on the news, but as soon as he knew, he'd come running home. Home wasn't safe for Caleb. If she could keep them up there until—

"Fi? Are you listening to me?"

"Um, yeah. You were saying dogs are a lot of work."

"No. I mean I did say that, but I'd moved on. I was telling you about the sled run I'm taking Caleb to tomorrow."

"Sorry, I got distracted. Tell me again."

He did, and she listened this time, asked all the right questions, and laughed at his dad-jokes. They made plans to touch base the next day when Caleb was awake so she could talk to him, said goodnight, then hung up. She didn't tell Devon about the jail break.

Maybe tomorrow.

5

I couldn't sleep with all the noise in the back seat. Chuck sounded like he was hacking up a lung. It was disgusting.

I pulled myself out of the car, walked to a nearby tree, took a pee, and shivered. The night air was clean and free, but it was cold, too. I leaned against the Honda and stared up at the sky. Next stop, I was getting some cigarettes.

The stars danced and popped like tiny firecrackers. Lots of guys probably forgot about them when they were inside. Forgot to even miss them. Shoot, I was sure there were things had I forgotten about. Things I wouldn't remember until I saw them again.

We talked about the stuff we missed all the time, but it was big stuff —food, sex. The alkies talked about booze. The druggies about their drug of choice. Some couldn't talk about anything but home. Other dudes got tight-lipped when home got brought up. But I didn't remember anybody talking about stars, or the smell of pine trees, or the scream of an owl. I didn't remember that at all.

Chuck's coughing broke my reverie. I swear, the whole car shook. This wasn't going to work. We couldn't go anywhere with him like this. He'd get too much attention. He had the virus. Which meant I was going to get the virus if I didn't have it already.

I opened the back door and stared at him. He was curled up like a baby, eyes tight shut, face glinting with sweat in the moonlight. He didn't look good, not good at all.

I closed the door, went back to my place by the front fender, and pondered my position. I could take him to a hospital, toss him out, and run, but then the cops would know where I was and what I was driving.

No good.

I could dump him under this tree, but he'd most likely die before he was found. Seemed an unkind thing to do. I mean, Chuck was his own kind of bad. I knew he'd done things but wasn't sure he deserved a long, slow death.

No, there was only one way. I didn't like it though. There was something dark living inside Chuck. I wasn't convinced it would die with him.

A big star, the North Star, or maybe it was a planet—the only constellation I knew for sure was Orion. Anyway, it winked at me as if to say, "You got it, bro. You can do this." I winked back and opened the trunk.

The gym bag was still there. I grabbed a large towel, folded it into quarters and carried it to where Chuck lay sleeping.

I didn't look at him this time. Didn't want to see his eyes. Didn't want to see the look he'd give me. He'd know what I was up to because it was exactly what he'd do if our positions were switched.

I slapped the towel over his face and threw my weight into it. He didn't struggle much. I think he was too weak from the sickness. I looked up at the stars until he stopped kicking and tried not to think about cats stealing the breath out of babies.

When he was still, I pulled him out of the car and dragged him under the tree. I was careful not to lay him where I'd taken a leak. I might not be able to bury him, but that didn't mean I was going to disrespect him.

I folded his hands over his chest like I'd seen them do with dead folks in movies and looked up at the stars again. I felt like I ought to say a few words, but for the life of me, I couldn't think of anything.

I cleared my throat. "Chuck wasn't a bad man." I shook my head. It didn't do to lie. Orion would know the truth. The stars saw it all. "Okay," I said. "He was a bad man, but I've known worse, much worse."

I bowed my head for a quiet moment, got in the car, and backed out of the clearing.

THE SUN WAS PEEKING out over the rim of the world when I got to Twin Peaks. I was almost out of gas. Leave it to a computer geek to drive around with a mostly empty tank.

Now I had a dilemma. Did I get gas with the last of the money Chuck had found in the jeans, or did I take another car? Grabbing a car seemed best, especially because the black-haired chick I'd taken the computer from may have seen what we were driving. There were risks involved with that, however. First, I had to find the right car; then, I'd have to dump the Honda somewhere. I decided to fill the gas can I'd found in the back while I made up my mind.

An idea dropped into my head while I was pumping petrol. Arrowhead. A bunch of rich people had extra homes in Arrowhead. People who can afford extra homes can afford extra cars. They might leave vehicles up here for snow driving or for guests. "Thank you, thank you, thank you," I said under my breath, paid for the gas, and headed for Arrowhead.

A half hour later, I found a gated community with a wide-open gate. I drove through and circled the neighborhood. These weren't the mansions I'd pictured, but they were nice, upscale condos.

As I toured the tight streets, I found three snow-covered vehicles sitting in three snow-filled driveways. I revisited each, one after the other. Since the cars were all relatively new, it came down to the one that had a hide-a-key in a magnetic box on the undercarriage.

Turns out it was a six-year-old Subaru. Fewer bells and whistles than the other two models, but less attention getting on the road. Besides I liked the color—khaki green. Seemed like luck was still with me.

I left the Honda in its place in the driveway—a nice touch if I do say so myself. The two cars were about the same size, and it was supposed to snow again in a few hours, which would cover the oxidized blue paint of the Honda. Nobody would notice a thing until the owners got there. Should buy me a day or two at worst, a month or two at best. Next stop, Big Bear.

6

DEVON

Devon's heart seemed to take up half his chest cavity. It had been beating hard, begging for attention all morning. Now, as he dragged Caleb on his sled up the long, low hill, it felt as if it were banging a cowbell. As much as he wanted to, he couldn't blame the altitude alone. Fiona lost weight when she was stressed; he gained it. He was definitely going to start working out again. Soon.

When they reached the top, he pointed the sled down the hill. "You ready?"

Caleb pivoted in his seat. "You come too."

"Daddy's bottom hurts from the last time," Devon said.

"I scared."

This would be Caleb's solo flight. Devon had ridden it three times with his son. It was a gentle slope with no rocks or trees to hit. "You'll be fine." Before Caleb could protest again, Devon gave him a shove and he was off.

The red plastic slid over the snow, bouncing lightly over ruts and bumps. Caleb caught air on one particularly big mound, his butt leaving the sled and thudding down again. Devon bit his bottom lip. He hadn't considered the weight difference without him. He strode downhill.

On each previous ride, the sled had come to a halt in the flat space before the trees. Would it do the same this time? Without Devon's weight to slow it? He began to jog.

Caleb's tiny form careened forward, hit level ground, and kept sliding. Devon watched in dismay as the sled headed straight for a large pine tree only yards away. He ran, but it was too late. The right front edge of the sled hit the tree, turning it on its side and dumping his son into the snow.

Caleb lay on his back, mouth open in a silent scream. Devon knew that face, the one that came before an ear-shattering howl. It meant his son was hurt, or very scared, or both. He dropped to his knees and lifted one of Caleb's arms. It was still attached—a good start.

He hesitated. Should he pick him up? What if his spine was injured? Devon was sure he'd read you should never move an accident victim. He wished Fiona were there. She'd know exactly what to do.

He fished his phone from his pocket, ready to call 911, but before he opened the screen, Caleb sat up and let loose a yowl of pain. Relief rushed through Devon. He stroked his child's head, feeling for bumps or blood but didn't find either, then stood him on his feet and ran his hands over his limbs, his back, his ribs. Caleb stamped an angry foot, and Devon smiled. He was fine. Gradually the tears slowed, the screams became sobs and finally hiccoughs.

"Want to do it again?" Devon asked.

Caleb's eyes widened in unbelief. "No."

"Just checking."

"Want to go home." Caleb sniffed.

Devon stood and slapped the snow from his knees. It was almost lunchtime, but he would bring his son here again before they left the mountain. Get back on the horse and all that. He didn't want this to be Caleb's final sledding memory. Next time, Devon would be waiting at the bottom of the hill to grab him.

As they reached the clearing where the car was parked, Caleb ran ahead and disappeared behind the trees.

"Wait for me," Devon called after him.

Caleb didn't, and Devon had a momentary flush of last night's panic, but saw his son hopping up and down next to the Audi when he entered the open area. "Have to go potty?" He asked.

Caleb scrunched up his face and nodded.

"Here's a good tree." Devon drew him away from the car.

"No tree," Caleb protested.

"This is one of the great things about being a guy." Devon flashed him a smile but felt a stab of guilt. Maybe he'd handed over too much of the parenting to Fiona. Apparently, there were some things a dad should teach.

Caleb frowned at him as if considering the statement.

"Daddy has to go, too." Devon unzipped.

Caleb watched for a long moment, then pulled his pants down and joined the party.

That done, they climbed into the car, and Devon navigated up the bumpy dirt road to the main highway. "What do you want for lunch?"

"Grilled cheese," Caleb sang out. He seemed completely recovered from his accident.

"We have to stop at the store, then. I didn't bring any American cheese."

"Can we get Oreos?"

"Yeah, if you don't tell Mom."

Caleb giggled. Fiona was very disciplined in her eating habits. No sweets ever entered the house if they weren't made with honey or agave nectar, except maybe a spot of ice cream now and again.

Devon put no such limitations on his appetite. He ate pretty much whatever he pleased, which had worked fine until he'd turned forty. How did his body know he'd officially become middle-aged? Where did it get the signal to expand his girth in proportion to his timeline? Fiona could explain it, he was sure, but he'd never asked.

The highway left the trees and entered the small city of Big Bear. The lake shimmered like a topaz in the noon sun, and the once pristine snow bordering the road became dirt encrusted.

Devon pulled into the Von's grocery store lot and parked next to a khaki green Subaru. "Maybe we should pick up some healthy stuff too, like apples and yogurt. What do you think?"

There was no answer. He craned his neck and gazed at his son. His head had fallen to one side, and he breathed softly. Must be nice to be able to fall asleep on a dime, anywhere, at any time. Devon hadn't slept well since he'd taken Emily's case.

But that was over, he reminded himself. In the past. Myron had done him a favor. Myron was the reason Devon was up here in the mountains bonding with his son.

Devon had turned off the computer when he'd left home and didn't plan to reboot it until he drove down the mountain next week. This was a reset. He'd go back rested, rejuvenated, and ready to start fresh. At least, that was the plan. He hadn't quite counted on the amount of attention a three-and-a-half-year-old demanded. "Hey, Caleb." He wiggled his son's leg.

Caleb's eyes shot open, he blinked twice, and said, "Can we get Cap'n Crunch, too?"

"Cap'n Crunch or Oreos, you decide," Devon said.

"Both," Caleb said.

Devon unhooked his son and lifted him from the car. "Nope. One treat."

As they walked up and down the aisles of the store, Caleb changed his mind five or six times about what that one treat would be.

"Maybe M&Ms," Caleb said. A dark-haired man in black sweats glanced at him as they passed a shelf full of candy.

"Sounds good," he said, his voice raspy and thick.

"Everything with sugar sounds good to him," Devon joked, but the man only lifted one side of his mouth and dropped it into place again —a ghost of a smile. They pushed past him.

Caleb, after much hemming and hawing, clutched a box of Double Stuf Oreos in his tiny arms, the word "double" on the label making him feel as if he were getting more bang for his buck. And they headed to the checkout.

The parking lot had emptied while they were shopping. The Audi sat alone in the first line of spaces. Only a handful of other cars were parked in the far corners of the lot. A wind had whipped up and a sky full of leaden clouds had blown into town while they were inside the store. "Looks like more snow is on its way."

"Yay!" Caleb shouted. "Can we make a snowman? Please?"

"After nap time," Devon said a little uneasily. More snow could mean impassable roads. He'd been looking forward to seeing Fiona in the next day or two.

Caleb kicked his feet as Devon buckled him into his car seat. "I not sleepy."

"Well, I am."

After a lunch of grilled cheese sandwiches and tomato soup, the phone rang. Devon checked the screen even though he knew it would be Fiona. He'd left strict instructions with his legal assistant not to call unless there was an attack on the offices. "It's your mom," he said to Caleb, who looked like the victim of said attack. Red soup stained his shirt, coated his hands and arms, and painted his mouth.

"Me, me." He grabbed at the phone.

"Oh, no. You're not touching my phone like that." Devon answered the call, tucked it under his chin and yanked several paper towels off the roll. "Hey, babe."

"Hey, yourself," Fiona said. "Miss me?"

"Always. How was your night of peace and quiet?" At 1:30, 3:25, 5:10, and at again at 6:40 when he'd finally gotten out of the lumpy, twin-sized bed and moved to the lumpy, living room couch, Devon had imagined her stretched out on their very expensive California King mattress with a cross between envy and longing.

"Great," she said, but her voice was lacking the enthusiasm he'd expected. Maybe she slept as poorly without him as he did without her? The thought made him stupidly happy. "Did Caleb do okay?" she asked.

"Out like a light," Devon said.

"Can I talk to him?"

He covered Caleb's face with a damp towel, scrubbed until his son squealed, then inspected his work. "Here he is." He handed the phone to his child.

Caleb held the cell to his face with both hands. "Mommy."

Devon could hear the warmth in his wife's voice but not her words as she spoke to their son.

Caleb grinned. "Angels. Lots of them."

Devon plucked the soup bowls and sandwich plates from the table and carried them to the sink as the two most important people in his world chatted. He loved his parents. They were good parents. They'd cared for him, provided for his needs, but he'd never had the relationship with them that Caleb had with Fiona. She was intuitive with their son, seeming to know the right thing to say on every occasion.

Devon, on the other hand, planned his conversations with Caleb. He'd store up factoids during the day as he went about his work, things he hoped his son would find interesting. *Did you know that Labrador Retrievers can swim? Or Chow Chow's were bred to herd cattle?*

Unfortunately, the conversations rarely ran according to plan. Caleb would be deeply involved in building a track for his cars when Devon got home and only grunt responses. Or he'd be in the middle of a cartoon, and Devon wouldn't even get a grunt.

At those times, Fiona would remind him that Caleb was not even four, that he didn't know how to be polite yet, and that his little mind could only focus on one thing at a time. Devon had read one or two parenting blogs. He understood where she was coming from, but he didn't fully embrace it. Which was why this trip was so important. He needed to prove to Fiona that he was a capable parent. Different, but every bit as capable as she was.

"It was dark." The wobble in Caleb's voice brought Devon back to the present. "I was lo—" Devon covered the phone and shook his head.

"Don't tell Mommy," he mouthed.

Caleb frowned. "I was lo—"

Devon took the phone and Caleb howled. "Hey there." He said into the receiver sounding out of breath.

"What's happening?" Fiona said.

"He dropped the phone," Devon said over his son's loud protests. "I think he's getting tired."

"No, no, no!" Caleb yelled.

"What was he trying to say? Let me talk to him. I think he's just frustrated."

"Give me a second." Devon held the cell against his thigh and gazed at his son. "Please don't tell Mommy you got lost in the woods. She'll get really worried, then she'll want us to come home."

Caleb narrowed his eyes. "Don't want to go home."

"Me, either." Devon held his son's gaze as he handed him the phone again.

"Hi, Mommy." Caleb's voice was subdued this time. He listened to her for a long minute, then said. "I just missed you."

Devon exhaled.

After they hung up, he led Caleb into his bedroom for a nap. "We'll tell Mommy when she gets here, promise," he said. "I just don't want to worry her now."

"I was scared in the woods." Caleb's face clouded with the memory.

"I know you were. I was scared, too, because I couldn't find you."

His son's eyes cleared and a smile tugged at the corner of his mouth. "But now we're buddies."

Devon held up his fist. "Buddies."

Caleb fist-bumped him.

"Time for a nap?" Devon said.

"Not sleepy." Caleb yawned. "Read me *Thomas*." He handed the book to his father. He was out by the third page.

Devon padded into the living room in stocking feet and peered out one of the front windows. A flurry of snow hid the world outside the cabin. Claustrophobia gripped him for a moment, but he pushed it away. This—seclusion, disconnection, quiet—this was why he'd come here. The snowstorms were a gift. He couldn't leave if he wanted to. He was sure Highway 18 wouldn't see a plow for at least twenty-four hours, but what did he care? He wasn't planning to go anywhere anyway.

He'd seen a pile of old newspapers in the mud room the night before. He went and got some now, balled up several sheets, tossed them under a half-burned log in the fireplace and looked around for a lighter. He didn't see one, but remembered he'd used a wooden match from the box on the kitchen stove the night before.

He jogged into the kitchen, grabbed a match, brought it back and lit it against the brick surround of the fireplace. In a few minutes, he had a warm blaze crackling in the grate. That was better.

He picked up the TV remote from the rustic pine coffee table, threw himself onto the couch and flipped the set on. He would like to know how long the storm was expected to last, but there was more snow on the TV screen than outside the window. He flipped the set off.

A book. He should have brought a book. There was a small bookcase in the master bedroom filled with paperbacks. He'd noticed it when he was looking for Caleb the night before.

Devon walked down the hall, popped his head in on his sleeping son, and was about to keep going toward the larger room, when he noticed something strange outside the window.

He crossed the room in two strides. There, in what should have been a pristine carpet of new snow, were footprints. For a moment he thought they might have been his. He'd walked that way the night before searching for his son.

But if they were his, where were Caleb's? And why were they only going, not coming? In fact, where had they come from?

Devon flattened himself against the bedroom wall and peered at the ground beneath the window. The snow was beaten down there, a jumble of quickly-filling footsteps. When he cast his gaze to the right, he saw they came from the road just beyond the house.

It could have been a neighbor, come to check on the place. Perhaps he'd been here while Devon and Caleb were out sledding, got no answer to his knock, and decided to look in a window.

It was a likely explanation, but it didn't erase his concern. His gaze slid across the expanse of white to the forbidding trees. *Anything could hide in there.* The thought he'd had the night before came galloping back, but it was as illogical and unbelievable as the Headless Horseman. Why would anyone want to hide in the dark trees outside the cabin, in the snow, in the freezing temperatures? For what purpose?

He turned away from the window and walked to the living room, books forgotten. He pulled his phone from his pants pocket, sat on the couch and began perusing news sites. The storm was supposed to last through the night and into the next day. Fiona may not be able to join them on Monday. That bothered him.

He began checking headlines. There'd been a five-car pileup on the 405. The governor had reopened movie theaters and sports arenas. If the owners hadn't already gone bankrupt, they'd be glad. It was pouring down the hill, which was good for the water tables if not for areas prone to mudslides.

He was about to drop the phone on the couch next to him, when he noticed another headline, "The Manhunt Continues." He clicked open the story.

THE SEARCH for the two inmates who escaped last Wednesday night from San Bernardino County Jail has yet to turn up any leads. "It's like they dropped off the face of the earth," says Police Chief Gonzales. It's believed the men used a cellphone video of a 2017 escape from a Santa Ana jail to plan their own escape.

DEVON DROPPED the phone into his lap and stared at the fire. It was a terrible time of the year to plan a prison break. Even down the hill where it rarely snowed, the temperatures were in the low 40s at night. Most criminals weren't known for their IQs, though. He yawned.

If he were going to break out of jail, he'd do it in the spring when the nights were more pleasant. It could rain, of course, but rain… He nodded off and dreamed about Mexican beaches.

7

The cabin had seen better days, but it looked good to me. I was hungry, tired, and I couldn't stop shivering. Smoke curled from the chimney, which meant there was a fire inside. I knew the kitchen was stocked full of food. I'd seen the man fill his cart at the market. And there were sure to be spare jackets and boots. I glanced down at my prison-issued tennis shoes that offered no protection from the wet and the cold. Yeah, the cabin looked good to me.

I walked around the side of the house and found the kid sleeping in a bedroom. I watched him through the window for a while and let my thoughts flow like the ocean. I was only a little older than the kid lying there the first time I saw the Pacific. My mom took me. I thought it was the best place in the world.

I lay in the wet sand and let the water cover me with its soft foam, then rush away like it had someplace important to go. A minute later, it would be back tickling my toes again. I liked it. Unlike my life, it was steady and predictable.

So what was steady and predictable here? That's what I needed to know. Patterns were power. The problem is, the man and the kid had only just gotten here, no time to get in a rut.

Kids did like their routines, though. I had no personal experience with them, but I'd heard they got hungry at the same times, sleepy at the same times. This one probably ate lunch an hour ago then dropped off. I thought it would be best to introduce myself while the kid was sleeping and the dad was relaxed, but it would be a while before he was sleepy again.

My body gave a convulsive shudder. Too long for me to stand here.

I'd found a hoodie in the gym bag, put extra socks on my feet and used another pair for mittens, but I was cold to my bones. Either I walked onto the porch and knocked on the door right now, or I went back to the car and bided my time.

I'd been warm most all day. It might have been adrenaline, but I was afraid it was the fever. When the sun hid behind the clouds and the snow began falling, the frozen ache in my bones started up again.

I gave the bedroom one more long look. What would it be like to be that kid? To be warm and full and sleeping in a bed with other people looking out for me. I shook my head. No point in thinking that way. Besides, I wouldn't want to be that kid tonight. Nope. Not tonight. Tonight, I'd rather be me.

The kid was the best bargaining chip I had. I knew his parents would do anything, give anything for him. Who knows why? Little kids put me in mind of little dogs—useless. The owners do it all, and for what?

Big kids—especially boys, sons—I could see wanting them around, but in order to get the big ones, you had to put up with the little ones. Not hardly worth it when you could find yourself a fully grown man and strike a deal. Like me and Chuck.

A cough wracked my body, and I thought about his last moments. Okay, maybe that wasn't the best example. I wiped the spittle from my face before it froze. Didn't matter what I thought anyway. What mattered was this kid's parents would cut off their hands and feet to save him. Not that it would come to that. At least, I dearly hoped it wouldn't.

I turned around and trudged across the snow to the woods. I had work to do. I'd seen a helicopter or two circling the mountain. Just in case anybody was looking for that Subaru, I intended to camouflage it.

The car was parked under the trees in a clearing. It was a pretty fair distance off the road, but better safe than sorry, as my grandma always said. I began pulling branches from nearby pines and laying them on top of it.

Once the car was covered, I crawled inside to wait for night, for the kid to go to bed, and for the stars to come out. I had a plan. I thought it was a good one, but I wanted to check with the boys upstairs. I pulled the towels out of the gym bag, huddled under them, closed my eyes and let my mind drift away to the beach and those soft, predictable waves.

8

FIONA

Fiona aimed the remote at the television. She'd stayed away from the news all day on Saturday, not wanting to feed her imagination. It hadn't been difficult at the studio, where she'd been distracted and busy. Her only tense moments until now were on the trail that morning. Not because she saw or heard anything, but because she hadn't. She'd been more alone than she'd expected, with only the occasional mountain biker for company.

She knew she had nothing to fear, not on the trail anyway. Crackers would have noticed if someone were hiding in the bushes, but fear wasn't logical. False expectations appearing real—she'd heard that acronym somewhere. It was clever. Too bad cleverness didn't calm her nerves.

Now she debated whether she should watch the news or not. If you're scared of the dark, should you leave the lights on or turn them off and face your demons? She flipped on the set. Face them. She had to know if the police had learned anything about her half brother's whereabouts.

The top story had to do with a wayward congressperson who'd upset his constituents in some way. Fiona left the sound on and walked into the kitchen to start her dinner. Crackers followed close behind.

"You hungry, boy?"

The dog smiled and wagged his whip-like tail so hard he almost lost his footing on the tile floor.

"I guess you are." She took the can of food she'd opened that morning out of the fridge, put a few spoonfuls into a bowl, topped it with the dry food Olivia had left for her, and set the whole thing on the floor. Crackers attacked it.

Fiona stared into the fridge for a long moment, but nothing looked appealing. *A body was found on the side of a fire trail off Highway 28,* a man's voice intoned from the living room.

Local news. That's what she'd been waiting for. She grabbed the end of last night's bottle of wine from the counter and a glass and returned to the television. A good-looking Hispanic man in a warm jacket stood against a backdrop of leafless scrub oaks. There were patches of white on the ground.

"At this point, authorities are looking at this as a suspicious death, although it is possible that the man hiked onto the fire road and was overcome by natural causes."

The camera shifted to a lovely blond in the studio. "Could this have anything to do with the two men who escaped from San Bernardino County Jail yesterday, Miguel?"

Miguel shrugged. "The police aren't talking, Bethany. All I can tell you is that an investigation is underway."

"Who found the body?"

"A police helicopter pilot noticed something suspicious while he was on patrol this morning and called it in."

"Thank God he did." Bethany inclined her head solemnly. "Someone out there will be thankful for closure." She paused for a moment, then smiled at the camera and said, "Local firefighters rescued a cat from a tree today, a very large cat." A close-up of a mountain lion lolling over a branch filled the screen. "That story after these messages."

Fiona turned off the set, and silence wrapped around her. No news. Why weren't the police talking about the prison break? Didn't they usually sound the alarm long and loud, show pictures of the cons, ask for help from the public? For some reason, they were keeping this escape very close to the vest. Could it be embarrassment? The Orange County Sheriff's department had lost two other inmates in the exact same way only a handful of years before. You'd think they would've learned from their mistake.

The tap of claws on wood brought her out of her dark thoughts. She set her glass down and squatted until she was eye-level with the dog. "I'll be sorry to send you home on Monday."

Crackers aimed a lick at her nose. She laughed and stood to get her face out of reach, but that moment of happiness quickly faded. What now? The evening stretched in front of her like the last ten miles of a marathon.

She might not be hungry, but she needed to eat. She wandered back into the kitchen, stared into the refrigerator again, and decided on a veggie omelette. She pulled odds and ends from her vegetable drawer and began chopping.

As onion sizzled in the pan, a thought struck her. She should call Gwen. Gwen Bishop had been her agent when the real estate murderer was active. She was the one who'd found the first body. Sylla might have told her about the escape, but she might not have. Gwen should know he was loose.

Fiona turned the heat down on the frying pan and picked up her cell. The phone rang three times before Gwen answered. "Fiona? Gosh, long time. How are you?"

She sounded so cheerful, Fiona hated to give her the bad news. "I've been better." She inhaled, exhaled, then said what she'd called to say.

The phone was silent for a long minute. "They don't know where he is?" Gwen finally said, the cheer in her voice gone.

"No. Somewhere between San Bernardino and here, I assume. But if they have any leads, they're not telling me."

"What are they doing to protect you?"

"They scheduled extra security checks on my house, but I don't know how they'd know if something was happening inside."

"At least you have Devon. That should be some deterrent."

"I don't, actually. He and Caleb are in Big Bear."

"Fiona." Gwen's voice rose. "You shouldn't be alone."

"I'm not. I have Olivia and Davy's dog with me."

"A dog is not enough. He's dangerous, Fi."

"I know, which is why I called you. I don't think he would have any reason to go after you, but..." She didn't want to finish that thought.

There was another long silence, then Gwen said. "No, I don't think he does. He wasn't after me to begin with."

"You have a house full?" Fiona said in a lighter tone.

"I do."

"But I think you should be aware. Keep your eyes open."

"Definitely. Thanks for letting me know."

Her duty done, Fiona was anxious to get off the phone before Gwen turned the conversation to her safety again. "Well, I'll let you go—"

Gwen interrupted her. "Why don't you stay here? I can move Emily out of her room for a couple of days, at least until Devon and Caleb get home. I know it's not pandemic sanctioned, but this seems like a valid exception."

"No. Really. I have Crackers. The police are keeping an eye on me, and I'm heading to Big Bear on Monday, late afternoon. I'll be okay." She didn't mention the gun. Guns made most people nervous. They used to make her nervous. Gwen said a reluctant goodbye, and they promised to meet for an outdoor coffee when all this was over.

The quiet rang around Fiona when she disconnected. There was too much space for thinking when Caleb was gone. His constant chatter chased away her worries. There didn't seem to be anything she could do to shut them up now.

Was she being foolish? Should she go to Gwen's? But how was that fair? Gwen had suffered at his hands once, and it had been no fault of her own. What if Fiona drew him to her home?

Perhaps she should cancel all the client appointments for the next two days and head to Big Bear early? But if he were watching her, she'd lead him to Caleb and Devon. She wouldn't put her family in danger.

She moved to the frying pan, turned the heat up, and began cutting mushrooms. The clack of the knife on the cutting board was rhythmic and comforting.

She didn't see any way to keep both herself and others safe. Her half brother was dangerous. He'd killed and would have kept killing if he hadn't been stopped. During that time, she'd been terrorized. She hadn't known who was committing the crimes, hadn't understood why they seemed to revolve around the house she was trying to sell. Once she discovered the truth, her terror turned to anger.

She tossed the mushrooms into the pan and grabbed a couple of eggs from the fridge. She'd been angry at her father for never telling her she had a sibling. Angry at the way that sibling had been treated. Angry because her father's mistake had ultimately impacted her life. She beat the eggs faster with every memory. Her rage had abated when he'd been incarcerated, when she thought she could put the whole thing behind her, but now it flared hot and bright.

She wasn't going to run from her problems like her father had. She wouldn't allow other people to pay the price for her family's sins. If her father had stood up and faced the consequences of his actions…

She scooped the vegetables from the pan and poured the eggs into it with abrupt movements. But he was gone. There was no point in going over and over the should-haves and shouldn't-haves of the past. What mattered was now. Fiona was the only one left to right her family's wrongs.

If that means shooting my half brother, so be it.

That last thought was so startling, she stopped moving, spatula in hand. Was that why she refused to leave her home? Did she *want* to confront him?

No. No, that wasn't it. She flipped the eggs. She remembered the relief she'd felt as she watched him being led from the courtroom in handcuffs on the last day of his trial, knowing she'd never see him again.

The sins of the fathers…

No. She stopped that thought cold. The sins of her father would not ruin her life or her child's life. She slammed a plate onto the counter so hard, it cracked. She breathed deeply, attempting to calm herself. She was not her father, not her sibling. She was a decent person. A good person.

She threw the plate into the trash and wiped the counter with a wet rag. She wouldn't run and hide, wouldn't set that example for her child. She would meet the problems of her family head on and deal with them. Whatever that meant.

She sat at the kitchen table and ate without tasting her food. Then she cleaned up the kitchen, went into her bedroom, washed her face, and changed into a pair of black leggings and a baggy T-shirt. On her way to the living room, she turned off all the lights in the house except for the one on the end table in the living room and the nightlight in the hallway.

Fiona surveyed the room with her hands on her hips. There were windows on the wall to the left of the front door and windows on the fireplace wall. She closed the blinds, then pushed the couch against the far wall where she had a clear view of the shuttered windows.

Crackers watched the entire proceeding with a puzzled expression on his doggy face. "Come on." She patted the couch. "You can sleep here, just for tonight."

He approached slowly, apparently not sure he'd understood her correctly. Sleeping on furniture was expressly forbidden at his house. She sat and patted the cushion next to her again. He jumped up, turned three tight circles, curled up against her thigh, and sighed. Fiona trained her gaze at the front door, resting one hand on Crackers' back and the other on her gun.

9

DEVON

Caleb didn't sleep very long. A half hour at most. He came barreling into the living room and jumped into Devon's lap. "Can we make a snowman?" His eyes were bright with excitement.

Devon yawned and ruffled his hair. "Let's see if it's still snowing."

Caleb leaped off his father's lap and grabbed his hand. "It's not. Come look."

Devon allowed himself to be tugged along to the front door. Caleb had to stand on tiptoes to get enough leverage to turn the knob, but he managed. A moment later, he threw the door open.

A flurry of wet snow fluttered moth-like into the cabin, disappearing almost immediately as it hit the wood floor. "See?" Caleb threw an arm into the outside world like a game show host. He was right. The sky was so white it was difficult to find the horizon. However, there were no flakes falling at the moment.

"Let's do it," Devon said.

Caleb charged toward the door, but Devon grabbed the back of his shirt. "Not so fast, buckaroo. You don't have any shoes on." His son glanced at his stocking feet in surprise, then gave his father a sheepish grin.

The bundling up process was long and arduous. Caleb lost interest about halfway through and began rolling a wooden truck up the walls and down Devon's back, making it that much more difficult to stuff his chubby limbs into his snowsuit.

How did parents with small children and real winters have time for anything? He couldn't imagine wrapping and unwrapping his child like a Christmas present every time he wanted to walk outside. Southern California had its drawbacks, but lack of sunshine wasn't one of them.

When Caleb was dressed, he immediately ran for the great outdoors. "Hang on there, mate." Devon hadn't put his own boots and jacket on yet, but it didn't appear that Caleb heard him. He ran out, down the steps, and disappeared from view.

A moment later, Devon followed, zipping up his jacket, his heart thudding a little harder than usual. Maybe from exertion or altitude, but more likely from the memory of the night before. "Buddy system," he yelled.

"I here." Caleb lay in the snow at the foot of the porch stairs creating a snow angel. "The angels were gone."

Devon pulled him to his feet. "If we're going to make a snowman before the storm starts up again, we'd better get moving."

"Snowman," Caleb sang.

An hour later, three misshapen snowballs, one mounted on top of the other, stood in the front yard. With hands on hips, Devon and Caleb surveyed their work.

"He doesn't got eyes," Caleb finally said.

"Or a nose or mouth, but we can fix that. Wait here." Devon had planned ahead. He jogged into the house, the warmth from the heater hugging him as soon as he stepped inside. A moment later he reemerged with a carrot, a handful of grapes, and a kitchen towel.

He placed two grapes where the eyes should go, then helped Caleb arrange the others into a smile. He wrapped the kitchen towel around the snowman's neck like a scarf and picked up his boy so he could place the carrot a little crookedly in the middle of the snowman's face.

"Now we need a couple of branches," Devon said.

"What for?"

"Arms."

He trudged up the hill and around the side of the house toward the pines. Caleb scrambled along behind him. As they crossed the snow field, he noticed indents about every three feet, remembered the footsteps he'd seen during nap time and felt disquieted.

He'd come up with a perfectly logical explanation for the prints at the time. If pressed, he could come up with four or five more. There was nothing intrinsically sinister about footsteps in the snow. It didn't prove anything other than that someone had been by the house and stopped to look in a window. His internal arguments didn't erase the unease, however.

Devon stopped at the closest tree, having no desire to go any farther into the woods than necessary. He found a branch of about the correct length, pulled a pocket knife from his jacket pocket, and cut it off. "How does this look?"

Caleb gazed at it with a serious expression for a long moment then held up two fingers. "Don't he need two?"

"Yes, he does. Why don't you find another one?"

Caleb circled the tree three times, pulling at all the low branches and studying them. He finally settled on one and held out his hand. "Knife, please."

"Oh, I don't think so." Devon cut the limb for his son, and the two tromped to the front of the cabin where their snowman waited for his prosthetics.

By the time they were done attaching limbs, admiring their work, and making a half-dozen more snow angels, flakes began to fall from the darkening sky.

"Hungry?" Devon said.

"Yeah, two more angels first, though."

"Two more."

Caleb made three, and they went inside.

After a dinner of hotdogs and beans, they sat by the fire. Caleb did the puzzles Fiona had packed for him, and Devon read a chapter of *Winter Kill,* a C.J. Box book he'd found in the bedroom. The setting of the story was cold and snowy and perfect reading for a stormy night in the mountains.

Caleb yawned and wiped his eyes.

"Getting sleepy?" Devon said.

"Nope." Caleb pulled another puzzle from the bag of toys and yawned again.

"Want to read a story?"

"In a minute," Caleb said. "I busy."

Devon flinched. Wonder where he'd heard that? All the times he'd brought work home with him and had repeated the same line to Caleb rushed into his mind. He'd been too busy for his son too many times.

The day he stood on the courthouse steps and Myron screamed his threats, a realization had struck Devon. Even this abusive husband, this terrible father, seemed to understand the importance of family better than Devon. He was grieving and angry over his loss. Devon took Fiona and Caleb for granted. How did the song go? You don't know what you've got 'til it's gone?

Devon had been the apple of his parents' eyes. Instead of imitating them, he'd gotten as wrapped up in himself as they were. Thankfully, a crazy man who'd suddenly lost everything brought Devon to his senses. In that moment, he'd decided things were going to change. This trip was just the beginning.

"I done." Caleb put his puzzles into the bag. Fiona must have taught him to clean up after himself because Devon certainly hadn't.

"Let's get jammies on first."

Caleb wailed in protest, but Devon picked him up under one arm, ran him like a football to the bedroom, tossed him on the bed, and tickled him into submission. Once PJs were on, they read two books, and Caleb was out.

Devon buried his nose in his son's hair and closed his eyes. He wanted to imprint this moment on his memory forever. The closeness, the scent of baby shampoo, the faint sweetness of baked beans from dinner.

Caleb murmured, rolled over, and ended the moment. Devon turned off the light, walked into the living room, and settled himself in front of the fire again. He sighed. This was exactly what the doctor ordered. He hadn't realized how much he'd needed this break from the chaos of his life.

When he drove off this mountain, he would be a different man. He couldn't promise never to work crazy hours. It went with the job. But he could promise to take time off between cases to make it up to Fi and Caleb and the other children that may come along. Fi was making noises about having a sibling to keep Caleb company.

Devon had been noncommittal. After all, they'd both been onlys and they'd turned out okay. Fiona didn't feel the same. She'd always wished for a sibling, then when she got one… Well, best not dwell on that.

The point was, he'd changed his mind. The more family, the better. A yawn started behind his ears and drew his mouth open as wide as it could stretch. It was only 8:30, but he was fading fast. He leaned his head against the back of the couch and closed his eyes. It must be the altitude. As he dozed off, a knock sounded at the cabin door.

10

DEVON

Devon yawned, stretched, and made his way to the door, shouting, "Hang on." He unlocked it, flung it open, and started. An apparition stood in the dim illumination from the porch light. The face was pale and made all the more pale by the black hair peeking out from a black hood. The man was so covered in snow, Devon had a fleeting thought that this was Caleb's snowman come to life. The apparition smiled and broke the illusion with a mouth full of yellow teeth. "My car broke down. I was wondering if I could use your phone?"

Devon hesitated. There was something familiar about the man, but he couldn't place it. There was also something unsettling about him, but Devon couldn't place that, either. "Yeah. Yeah, sure." He moved out of the doorway, so he could enter.

"I must have dropped my cell while I was checking under the hood. Couldn't find the damn thing anywhere." He had a smoker's raspy voice.

"It's a bad night to be out," Devon said.

The man nodded. "I was headed home."

Devon walked to the couch, grabbed his phone and brought it back to the man who stood dripping on the front mat. He ought to offer him a cup of coffee, something warm on a night like this, but he hoped he wouldn't be there long enough to drink it.

The stranger took the phone and punched in a set of numbers. Devon could hear a voice on the other end, then a long beep. That didn't bode well. Whoever he'd called hadn't answered. The man dropped the phone to his side. "I was afraid of that."

"What?" Devon said.

"The tow companies are busy pulling cars out of snowbanks and ditches on a night like tonight."

They stood, staring at each other for a long minute, then Devon sighed. "Want a cup of coffee?"

"I'd be obliged."

Devon turned and headed into the kitchen. The man followed. He lowered himself into a chair by the table as Devon filled the automatic coffee machine.

"You live up here full time?" Devon said, more to make conversation than anything else.

"No, just visiting the area."

"Me too. My son and I came up to do some sledding. He's only three. Well," Devon corrected himself, "almost four. This is the first time he's seen snow."

"How does he like it?"

Devon pressed the brew button and turned. "Loves it." The man had pushed the hood from his head, and the sense of familiarity returned. Devon furrowed his brow in concentration. Where had he seen him before?

"That's nice," the man said. "Father and son spending time together."

It wasn't a comment that required a response, so Devon didn't offer one. For several minutes, the only sound in the kitchen was the gurgle of the coffee pot.

Devon had run out of small talk. "Maybe you should try another tow company?" he finally said. He didn't want to sound rude, but the man must be as uncomfortable as he was, sitting there not talking, although he showed no signs of it.

The stranger leaned into the chair and stretched out his legs in front of him. "I will, after that cup of coffee, but I fear it's a useless gesture."

The pot sputtered out its final drops. Devon filled two mugs, set one on the table in front of the stranger, then sat across from him cradling the other. "My name is Devon, by the way." He didn't offer a hand. Under the bright kitchen lights, the man looked pasty, his lips almost blue. He could be ill. Besides, nobody shook hands anymore.

The stranger lifted the cup to his lips. "Rico," he said and sipped.

"I can try a couple of places for you," Devon glanced at his phone still clutched in Rico's left hand. He wanted it back. "I have triple A."

"Don't want to put you out." The man shot him a yellow grin but didn't offer over the phone. He took another sip of coffee, threw his arm over his mouth and erupted into a deep cough.

Devon stood, moved toward the coffee pot, and grabbed it. He carried it to Rico, topped off his mug, then leaned against the counter. Rico hadn't needed more coffee, but Devon had wanted to step away. He'd been vaccinated, but after the last year and a half, it had become instinctual to distance himself from strangers, especially strangers who seemed under the weather. He'd sanitize his phone when he got it back.

"Daddy?" A sleepy voice broke into his thoughts. Caleb, looking impossibly small, stood in the doorway.

"Hey, buddy." Protectiveness stole over Devon, and he opened his arms to his son.

Caleb shifted his gaze to the man at the table, gave him a shy smile, and ran to his father. Devon lifted him onto his hip.

Caleb fingered a button on Devon's flannel shirt. "Who's that?"

"His name is Mr. Rico. His car broke down."

"Why?"

Rico answered. "I think it's the alternator."

Devon's heart sank. A faulty alternator wasn't an easy fix. He could possibly jump the car, if he had cables and could navigate the roads to get to it, but ultimately it would require a mechanic. He wondered how much time this whole Good Samaritan thing was going to cost him.

"What's an alternator?" Caleb said.

Devon ignored the question. "Now that Caleb is up, how about we drive you home? It might be a while before you get a tow, as you said." That seemed the most efficient thing to do, from Devon's perspective anyway.

The man breathed deeply which triggered a few small coughs. Devon took another step back. He didn't love the idea of putting this man in the Audi with Caleb, who hadn't had the vaccine, but he couldn't think of another solution.

"We won't make it. The snow is too deep."

"But you were on your way home." Devon heard the irritation in his voice.

"Yes, but I have a Jeep."

"My Audi is all-wheel drive."

"It's gonna take 4-wheel."

They stared at each other for several beats, then Devon dropped his forehead to the top of Caleb's head.

"I hate to put you out, but I think I'm gonna have to bunk here tonight. I'll sleep on the couch." He gestured toward the living room.

Devon's head shot up. That was a terrible idea. "We could call the sheriff's department." The words blurted out of him. Inviting a stranger in to use the phone was one thing. Allowing that stranger, who was obviously unwell, to camp out for the night was another thing entirely.

Rico barked a laugh that transformed itself into a cough. "They've got their work cut out for them already. They're not coming out for me, not when I'm all tucked up all safe and sound."

"Is Rico gonna sleep over?" Caleb asked.

Devon felt a muscle in his jaw tighten. How could he throw him out on a night like tonight? "I guess so." He gazed at the man. "I'll put this guy back to bed and find a blanket and pillow for you."

Devon marched out of the kitchen and down the hall to the room he and Caleb were sharing.

He dropped Caleb onto his bed and lifted the covers. "Did he get lost on his way home from the grocery store?" Caleb said.

Devon paused, blankets in his hands. The grocery store. That's right. That's where they'd seen him. He tucked the covers around his son.

This knowledge made him feel a little better about allowing Rico to sleep on the couch. The familiarity he'd felt hadn't been because he'd seen the man in the newspaper, or on the computer or television. He'd seen him in the grocery store. Shopping. A normal, everyday activity.

"I don't think so, buddy. You go back to sleep. We're going to have a busy day tomorrow."

"Busy?" Caleb echoed.

"We're probably going to have to help Rico get home."

Caleb snuggled under his covers. Devon kissed his head and put a hand on the bear lamp to turn it off. "Light on," Caleb murmured.

Devon pulled his hand away. Caleb must have picked up on his apprehension. If he felt it, Rico would as well. He needed to relax, or he'd come across as rude.

He took one more glance at his sleeping son before he pulled the bedroom door shut. Love overwhelmed him like a tidal wave. Despite the snowstorm, despite his child getting lost in the woods and taking a spill while sledding, despite the stranger on the couch, it was good he'd gotten away with his son. They were making memories. Hopefully Caleb would always remember this trip.

11

I slept hard. Woke up twice to cough, but I knocked out again as soon as I was done. It was the best night's sleep I'd had in a long, long time. Prison is loud. Men snore, talk in their sleep, and make other even more unfortunate noises. You hear it all night long. The cabin was silent under its blanket of snow.

I lay on my side now, staring at the cold fireplace. I should get a fire going, but I felt too lazy to do it. Devon wasn't happy about putting me up, but what was he going to do? Throw me out in the cold? That's the thing about civilized people. They want to be polite. Generally, you can push them pretty far before they crack, and by then, it's usually too late. You'd already got the upper hand.

Speaking of upper hands, or winning hands, before he woke up was the time to stack the deck. I rolled onto my back and stared at the ceiling. Question number one: What did I want?

Chuck had a dream, a big dream with lots of zeros in it. I'd been willing to go along with it for a while, but that was no longer necessary. My needs were more modest: a car and enough cash to make a fresh start.

Question two: what cards did I hold? I took inventory and decided

I didn't have enough. The element of surprise and freedom from the constraints of polite society weren't enough.

I pushed myself off the couch and wandered into the kitchen. In ten minutes or less, I'd armed myself with a very nice butcher knife and removed the rest of the sharp implements. I also rounded up glass bottles and anything that could be fashioned into a shiv without a ton of filing—which I'd notice.

Next, I hit the bathroom and grabbed the aspirin and a bottle of peroxide. I didn't know if either of those could be used to poison somebody, but why take a chance?

The master bedroom hadn't been slept in yet. I rummaged around through Devon's suitcase and a backpack that sat next to it on the floor, but the most dangerous thing in either of those was a stupidly mongo flashlight. I took that and headed toward the living room. My gaze fell on the fireplace poker sitting next to the hearth. Now that was a weapon. I added it to my collection in the kitchen.

The mudroom contained some useful things—an old pair of boots, a brown jacket hanging on a peg, and a box of plastic zip ties. I left the zip ties in the cupboard where I'd found them, put on the boots and jacket, took my stash outside, and glanced around. Where to hide it all?

My gaze fell on an old kettle barbecue half buried in snow. It would do just fine. I opened it without knocking all the snow off its top, tossed the potential weapons inside, and closed the lid.

Now for question number three: how to present my dilemma to Devon and help him understand why it would be in his own best interest to aid me?

I walked inside, took off the jacket and boots, and lay down on the couch to ponder when the boy came peeking into the living room.

"Hi," he said.

"Hello yourself," I said. The kid slipped around the couch and stood by the fireplace. He didn't talk. Just looked at me. "You hungry?" I said.

He nodded.

I stood and stretched like it was my first time off the couch that morning. "Let's get some grub."

Caleb stared at me through serious eyes while I got the coffee going and pulled eggs and bread out of the fridge. He made me nervous. I wasn't used to kids.

Then I had a brainstorm. I found a quarter in my pocket and pretended to pull it out of his ear. That did it. He grinned like a Halloween pumpkin. He was still grinning when his daddy came into the kitchen looking like his hair was on fire. He must have slept later than he'd intended.

"He got a quarter out of my ear," Caleb told his dad.

"A little magic trick I picked up as a kid," I said.

Devon seemed to relax a little but started up on finding a tow truck and driving me to town a second later. When we sat down to eat, he pushed his phone across the table. I think he wanted me to start making calls. Instead, I checked the news. I almost got sick.

They found Chuck. I'd thought it would take them longer. I didn't think about helicopters. Stupid mistake. I could've covered him with brush like I did the car. Now they'd know which way I was headed, and they'd be all over this mountain like ticks on a mutt. My dream had just become a bit more complicated.

12

DEVON

Devon's eyes sprang open, and he sat up all in one motion. He had figured, somewhere around three in the morning, he wasn't going to sleep. The stranger on the couch had been like a sliver in his finger. He'd worried it and worried it but couldn't shake the throbbing discomfort. Apparently, he'd slept anyway.

He glanced at the other bed, expecting to see Caleb, but his son was gone. A shot of anxiety hit his bloodstream like the first cup of coffee in the morning. He threw back the blankets and hurried into the living room.

A child's gasp sounded from the kitchen. Devon bolted through the doorway. Instead of seeing a fearful Caleb as he'd expected, his son's eyes were bright, and a smile spread across his face.

Caleb turned those eyes on Devon. "He got a quarter out of my ear." He held up a coin.

"A little magic trick I picked up as a kid," Rico said.

"That's, that's amazing." Devon's heartbeat slowed, and he glanced around the kitchen. Eggs bubbled in a frying pan on the stove, coffee filled the pot, and the scent of toast was in the air.

"Hope you don't mind." Rico waved around the room with a spatula. "But your little guy woke up looking for breakfast."

Devon ran a hand over his short-cropped hair. "No, no. That's great. Thanks." He walked to the cupboard, took a cup and filled it with coffee. "Sorry I stayed in bed so late."

Devon sat at the table in a patch of sunlight streaming through the kitchen window. "Did you sleep okay?" The question was directed at Rico. "That couch—"

Rico cut him off with another wave of the spatula. "I was dead to the world."

Caleb's nose wrinkled. "Like Grandpa Hank?" Grandpa Hank was Fiona's deceased father. Rico cough-laughed.

Devon put a hand over Caleb's. "No. It's just an expression. It means you slept really good." He turned his attention to Rico as Caleb puzzled over that. "So, what's the plan?"

The toaster popped, and Rico busied himself with buttering toast and filling plates with eggs. Once they were all seated with food in front of them, Devon tried again. "Were you able to reach a tow company this morning?"

Rico glanced at him from under his lashes. "I don't have a phone."

"Oh, right." Devon snorted a laugh. "I forgot." He fished his cell from his sweatpants pocket and placed it on the table.

Rico grabbed the phone, but tucked into his food like a starving man, head bowed low over his plate to create the shortest distance for the fork to shovel. He slowed down a long minute later to type something into the phone and read the results. His appetite seemed to leave him then. He set his fork down before finishing his food.

Devon's nighttime worries returned. He pushed his food around on his plate, appetite gone. "Thanks for breakfast."

Rico only grunted an answer. He was upset, and that made Devon upset. First order of the day, get rid of Rico.

When he was done eating, Devon stood, picked up the empty plates, and carried them to the sink. "Want to make some calls while I clean up? I can drive you to your car, or home, or wherever you need to go after that."

Rico pushed his chair onto its rear legs, pulled a toothpick from his pocket and stuck it in his mouth. "About that. We need to talk."

A chill whispered over Devon's skin. He froze for a long moment, then in the most casual voice he could muster said, "Don't worry about putting me out. I'm on vacation. No agenda."

"I'm not worried, but unlike you, I do have an agenda."

Devon filled the frying pan with water, put it on the stove to warm and dried his hands on a towel before speaking. "Caleb, you done?"

Caleb kicked his feet and nodded his head. Eggs and breadcrumbs dotted his face and pajama top. Devon wiped him down with a damp paper towel, lifted him from his seat and set him on his feet. "Why don't you play with your puzzles. I'll be there in a minute, and we can get dressed."

He waited until he heard Caleb's footsteps disappear, then turned to Rico. "What's your agenda?" His voice was cold.

Rico moved the toothpick to the corner of his mouth with his tongue. "I wasn't entirely forthright last night."

Devon waited.

"I came here to see you."

Do you know what it's like to lose a child? Myron's words filled Devon's head. "Why?" The word stumbled across his lips like a drunken man. He held up a hand. "No, don't tell me." Years of working in law had taught him it was better not to know some things.

He left the kitchen in search of his wallet. This was about money. Rico was probably an old client, or new client of Myron's. He'd hit hard times—a constant condition for most of these guys—and Myron offered him free services or cash to shake Devon up. He didn't believe Myron would order a kidnapping, or worse. Probably just wanted to scare Devon.

Either way, this wasn't personal for Rico. Why go to all the trouble of committing a crime when you could make money for doing nothing? Whatever Myron was paying this man, he would pay more.

He entered the bedroom where Caleb sat on his bed busily building something from b bricks, took his wallet from the bedside table and returned to the kitchen. He gazed into Rico's bloodshot eyes. "I'd like to pay for your car repairs. What do you think it'll take to fix it?"

Rico blinked several times. "That's mighty generous of you."

Devon opened his wallet and took out a hundred and two twenties. "I know this isn't enough, but it's a start." He threw it on the table.

The stranger shifted the toothpick again but made no move to take the bills. "You're right. It's going to take a lot more than that to fix things."

Anger bubbled in Devon's gut, mixing with the coffee and the eggs. "Instead of paying you, I could go to the cops."

Three things happened in such quick succession, they seemed simultaneous. Rico's chair hit the floor. Devon's arms were pinned to his sides. A knife—long, sharp, and deadly—was pressed to his throat.

"No cops," Rico said.

Sweat broke out on Devon's forehead. "All right. Calm down. No cops."

"I don't want to hurt your boy." Rico's breath was hot and fetid against Devon's face.

"That makes two of us."

"Can we work together, then?"

"Yeah, yeah. We can work together."

Rico's grip loosened and the knife dropped. "Let's go to town, then."

Devon rubbed his arms. "It's Sunday. All I have access to is the ATM until tomorrow."

Rico seemed to ponder this for a long moment. "As long as you're doing the best you can," he said and headed for the door.

DEVON PARKED in front of the bank, exited the car, and opened the rear door where Caleb was buckled into his car seat.

"No," Rico said.

"What do you mean, no?" Devon said.

Rico gazed at the roof of the car showing the yellow of his eyes. "What does *no* usually mean?"

"I'm not leaving Caleb here."

The stranger trained his eyes on Devon. "I think you are." His voice was as cold as the day.

Devon glanced at the ATM in the niche of the building, back at the car, then reached into the front seat and snagged the keys. Rico couldn't go anywhere without the keys.

The ground was frozen. Devon slid across the lot in his new hiking boots and almost went down but caught himself. The last thing he needed was an injury. He didn't think it would come to it, but just in case, he needed to be fit enough to grab Caleb and make a run for it.

He pulled his debit card from his wallet and stuck it in the machine. He walked through the prompts: *Savings or checking?* Checking. *Deposit or withdrawal?* Withdrawal. *Amount?* He paused.

How much should he ask for? He didn't want to set off any alarms by requesting too much, but he also wanted Rico to go away. If he got a couple of thousand, maybe he'd take it and leave.

Devon punched in 5,000. *Amount exceeds your maximum withdrawal.*

Damn it. He placed a hand on his head and rubbed his hair. How many tries would he get before they shut him out? Okay, okay. He'd try for a grand from this account and a grand from the savings account.

He changed the withdrawal amount to $1,000 and held his breath. It worked. A pile of hundred-dollar bills appeared in the plastic window.

Would you like another transaction?

Yes, yes he would. He hit savings, withdrawal, and put in $1,000 again.

You have reached your daily withdrawal limit.

"What?" He tried again but got the same message. His massaged his forehead. "Think, think."

He could get cash at the grocery store, but how much would they give him? A hundred? Two hundred? Not enough to make a difference. He had the money to make this problem go away, if only he could get to it. He shoved the bills into his jacket pocket and felt something solid.

An image of cutting tree branches the day before with Caleb emerged in his mind. His pocket knife. Comfort warmed him like whiskey. He had a knife. It wasn't big, but he kept it sharp.

He slid behind the wheel and handed the wad of bills to Rico, being careful not pull the knife out along with the money. "It's all I could get."

The stranger counted the cash, and a dark cloud covered his face. "A thousand? You only got a thousand? I thought you were a big money man."

"It's all the machine would give me."

Rico raised his voice. "Man if you're—" He broke into a coughing fit.

Devon rolled the windows down. "Can't you take that outside?"

His answer was a deeper, painful sounding paroxysm.

"Stick your head out the window, Caleb," Devon ordered, but Caleb had nodded off. Cars were like sleeping pills to his son.

"What's the matter with you?" Devon asked.

Rico breathed heavily for a moment before answering. "Cigarettes."

"Doesn't sound like a smoker's cough to me."

"What are you, a doctor?"

Devon didn't bother answering. He sat listening to the labored breathing of the man beside him, and a prickle of nerves ran up his arms. The situation struck fear into him.

What could he do? He took in shallow breaths, illogically fearing deeper ones, and tried to slow his racing heart. Caleb should be okay. He'd read children rarely got the virus, and Devon had been vaccinated. They'd be fine.

"Where can I drop you?" he asked.

Rico raised an eyebrow. "I guess I'll be staying with you until I can afford to…" He paused. "Fix my car."

Devon closed his eyes. This was untenable. He couldn't bear having this man in the cabin for another night. "I can send you the money."

Rico coughed, or laughed, Devon couldn't tell which, but he didn't bother responding.

Devon's phone rang as he started the ignition. It was Fiona. "I'd better get this. It's my wife. She'll worry if I don't."

"Best you don't mention me to Fiona," Rico said. "She'll want to leave your cozy house in Dana Point and come up here. That would be a mistake."

Devon stared at him. He'd uttered his wife's name and the location of their home as threats. Even if Devon was able to escape, to take Caleb and run, Rico knew where Fiona was. He knew where they lived. The horror of that permeated his mind as he reached for his phone.

13

FIONA

Fiona was awakened by a thunder clap on Sunday morning. Her eyes opened, and she had a moment of disorientation. Why was she on the couch? Why was Crackers coiled into a tight black ball next to her?

She rolled her head from side to side and groaned. A sharp pain jabbed her in the neck, and the night before came rushing back. She'd tried to stand guard, or sit guard, but had nodded off.

Crackers lifted his head without effort and gazed at her. There was hope in his eyes.

"Want to go out?" she asked.

His tail thumped against the cushions, and he leaped from his spot with a grace and ease she envied. Fiona pushed herself up with more effort. "You're going to have to go out back. I'm not dressed for walking."

He followed her to the dining room. She slid aside the wide door that opened onto the backyard, and he stuck his head out. It was pouring. He hesitated, then ran for the shelter of a bougainvillea and did his business in record time.

While he was outside, Fiona grabbed an old towel from the hall cupboard. She dried him when he came in again, and he wagged his gratitude. The two padded to the kitchen, and she set about making coffee.

Why would you think the dog is grateful? The question came to her in Devon's voice. The next thing he'd say was that she was anthropomorphizing. He'd find a book or a blog or a nature video that delved into the science of dog body-language, pack mentality, and canine instincts. He'd then explain—in that patient voice that made her itch—gratitude was a human construct, like love, or greed, or pride.

Fiona set a bowl of food in front of Crackers. He dug in. "You are grateful, aren't you, boy?" He wagged again.

That was the difference—one of the differences—between her and Devon. Fiona was a big believer in intuition and instinct. She thought Crackers was grateful because he seemed grateful. She could shell out a meal of Porterhouse steak to some dogs and never feel a second of thankfulness from them. Crackers was a special animal.

This, in her opinion, was the problem with all the research Devon was doing about dog breeds. Oh, it was fine to decide you wanted a shepherd mix, or a lab mix, or a chihuahua, or whatever you had a hankering for. And it was true that different breeds had tendencies toward different behaviors, but she had met all kinds of dogs in all kinds of dog bodies. She'd met sweet and submissive pit bulls and golden retrievers that would tear your face off. She was sure she'd know the right dog for their family when she met it.

She glanced at the clock. The first appointment at the studio wasn't until 10:00. She had time to call Dev and Caleb before she got ready. She walked into the living room, plucked her phone from the coffee table, and called.

The phone rang and rang, then went to voicemail. She disconnected and stared at the screen. Maybe they were out tromping in the snow. It had dumped on them during the night. She'd checked the weather in Big Bear while she'd had her first cup of coffee.

She opened her text messages and typed, *Call me when you can.* Then headed to the shower. After she was dressed, she tried calling again. Again, it went to voice mail. She chewed her lower lip. Maybe they'd gone sledding? She'd try at lunchtime.

The studio was dark and cold when she arrived. The Fishbowl

sparkled on sunny days, but on days like today, it felt oppressive. She shelved some of the packages that had come the day before and put the rest into the storeroom. When she was done, she stood and watched the churning gray waves outside the window until she heard the front door chimes, then turned to face her first round of students.

WHEN THE LAST of the morning clients disappeared into the rain, Fiona fished her phone from her bag and tried Devon again. They must be home by now. It was noon. Caleb got hangry if he wasn't fed on time.

The phone rang so many times she was about to hang up, but Devon's breathless voice stopped her. "Hello."

"Hello to you. Where've you been all morning? This is my third call."

"We, ah, we were out playing in the snow. I guess I didn't hear the phone." Devon sounded distracted.

"Everything okay?"

"Yeah, sure. Why do you ask?" He spoke quickly, defensively. Fiona was used to his distracted voice, but defensiveness was unusual.

"I don't know. You don't sound like yourself." Her son's face appeared in her mind. She'd been concerned about sending the two of them off together. Devon was often preoccupied with work, maybe too preoccupied to care for a three-year-old. "Is Caleb okay?"

"Caleb is great. He misses his mom, but he's great."

"Can I talk to him?"

There was a long silence on the other end. "He went down for a nap. Maybe later," he finally said.

Fiona's gaze strayed to the clock on the wall, 12:12. "It's awfully early."

"We were up at six, and all this outdoor exercise is knocking him out."

It was Fiona's turn to remain silent. Devon's explanation was logical, but something about it didn't feel right. "You sure he's okay? Maybe he's coming down with something. Did you feel his forehead?"

"He's fine, Fi, really." Now Devon sounded irritated. Maybe having

Caleb all to himself was more stressful than he'd realized? He'd probably been relishing his few quiet minutes of nap time, and she'd interrupted it.

"Okay, then. Sounds like you have things under control."

"I do."

That was abrupt. Based on his mood swings during the conversation, she wondered how he'd react to what she was about to say. "By the way, I may not be able to make it up there on Monday evening." If the police hadn't caught her half brother by then, she couldn't take the chance of leading him to her family.

She heard an intake of breath and braced herself for an argument.

"That's probably for the best. It's been snowing like crazy here. I doubt they'll have the roads plowed by Monday. I hate to think about you driving the ridge in this weather."

"It almost sounds like you'd rather I stayed home." She added a playful note to her voice.

"Don't be ridiculous, Fi. Of course, we want to see you." He didn't respond in kind. He still sounded irritated, distracted, and defensive. "We miss you, both of us do. But the most important thing is that you're safe."

A flash of lightning out on the ocean put an exclamation point on his comment. "You stay safe, too," she said.

"We will. Don't worry about us, babe. I love you." She thought she heard a hitch in his voice when he said he loved her and didn't know whether to be relieved or more concerned.

"Love you, too." And they hung up.

Fiona sat staring at the rain. It was coming down in sheets, billowing like a sail in the wind and creating pockmarks on the sea below. Everything Devon had said made perfect sense. Neither one of them should be driving in this weather, but she couldn't shake the uneasiness she felt. Something was wrong. She heard it in his voice and felt it in her bones.

Thunder boomed. Crackers slunk from his bed in the corner and tried to shove his whole body under her stool. He wasn't happy either.

14

DEVON

When they returned from the bank, Rico posted up on the living room couch and began trolling the internet on Devon's phone. Devon went directly into the kitchen, poured himself the end of the morning coffee, and put it into the microwave to warm.

He didn't need more caffeine. There was enough adrenaline pumping through his veins to keep him awake for a week, but he wanted the sound of the microwave to mask his real chore.

As it whirred, he slid open drawers looking for a weapon that could compete with the knife Rico had pressed against his throat earlier. There were butter knives in the top drawer, and every kind of utensil you could think of in the second, but no sharp knives. He yanked open the drawers next to the refrigerator, nothing. Then the cupboards. No knives, not even a cast iron frying pan. Rico must have hidden them while Devon slept.

The microwave dinged. Agitation flushed Devon's face and heated his body. He loosened his collar, struggling to breathe. Air. He needed air.

He strode into the living room. "Want to make snow angels?" he asked Caleb, who was sitting on the living room floor running a toy truck across the brick hearth.

"Yes." Caleb leaped up and headed toward the door.

"Snow suit," Devon said.

His son pivoted and raced to the bedroom. Devon caught Rico's eye as he followed. Rico gave him a curt nod. He looked away. He wasn't asking for permission. Rico wasn't his warden.

Ten minutes later, they were packed like sausages into their snow clothes and heading out the door. "Stay where I can see you," Rico said.

Rage mixed with the agitation coursing through Devon. He didn't trust himself to answer. He slammed outside.

Caleb dropped to the ground in the front yard and began swiping his arms and legs frantically, but there was no smile on his face. The joy his son had exhibited in the snow their first day in the mountains was gone. Devon had to fix this, but he couldn't see any way to do it before Monday. He paced between the house and road thinking while his son created angels.

Five or six angels later, Caleb said, "Can we go sledding, Daddy?"

Devon stopped pacing. He was surprised by his son's request. He thought he'd have to drag Caleb to the hill after his accident. "Sure, but not today. When Rico leaves."

Caleb stood. "When is Rico leaving?"

"Tomorrow," Devon said with more confidence than he felt.

Caleb moved three feet to the left and dropped to the earth again.

"How many of those angels are you going to make?" Devon said.

"All the way around the house."

"That's a lot of angels."

"They're safe."

Caleb's words were like a punch in the gut. Devon couldn't protect him from the tension in the cabin. He might not understand the danger. Might not understand what was happening, but he knew something was wrong, and he was doing the only thing he knew to do —make angels.

Devon wished he could shield Caleb emotionally as well as physically. He'd have to try harder to act as if Rico weren't a threat.

"Hello, there." A voice startled Devon from his thoughts. He glanced up to see a tall man, gray hair sticking out from under a hunter's hat with earflaps.

Devon smiled, but felt his shoulders tense. He shot a glance at the house. "Hello."

The man waved behind him. "I'm your neighbor, from down the road. The green A-frame."

Devon hadn't noticed the house, but it must have been at least a quarter of a mile away. He'd watched the odometer from the last house to the cabin on the way back from the bank. He'd wanted to know how far he'd have to run if he got the chance.

"Name's Bob," the man continued.

Devon stuck out a gloved hand. "Devon."

"I'm friends with Roger and Gayle," Bob said as he shook hands. Devon must have looked blank. "The owners of your cabin."

"Oh, right," Devon said. "I forgot their names."

"I told them I'd pop by since I was in town this weekend. They had a little trouble with the hot water heater last month. Wanted me to check everything was working right."

"Seems to be," Devon said. "We've got plenty of hot water."

Bob's eyes shifted toward the cabin. "Maybe I should take a look at the pilot."

Devon stiffened. "It's fine."

Bob chewed the inside of his cheek, obviously torn between his promise to Roger and Gayle and being pushy.

What if Devon let him in? What would Rico do? Nothing most likely, but Devon didn't want to anger the man. On the other hand, if he could get it through to Bob that there was a problem, that he should send the police…

"I making angels." Caleb interrupted their conversation.

Bob pointed to the pile of snow and branches they'd erected yesterday. Had it only been yesterday? Seemed like so much longer. "I like your snowman," he said.

Caleb popped up, his back as covered with white powder as a sugar doughnut and ran to the dilapidated edifice. "He lost his face."

"We can fix that." Bob walked over and began wiping at the snow.

"Here's your eyes." More digging. "And mouth. A raccoon must have eaten the nose. I've got a carrot at my place you could use."

Bob turned to Devon again. "Want to stop by later for a hot drink and a visit? It can get lonesome up here in the winter."

"And a carrot." Caleb pumped his fists.

Rico wouldn't allow that. Devon pulled his son into a hug. "Maybe. We'll see."

"It'd be nice to have company." Bob grinned.

Devon gazed at him for a long moment trying to think of what to say and how to say it in front of Caleb, but Bob spoke first.

"Well, I'd best be heading back before the snow starts again." The man put a finger to his hat and shot it forward in a kind of salute.

"Thanks for stopping," Devon said, then hesitated. He needed to say something before he let him wander away. This could be his only chance to get help. A creak and a slam sounded behind him.

"Hello there," Rico said.

Caleb wilted in Devon's arms. The smile on Bob's friendly face wilted as well. Rico's poison infected everybody, apparently. Devon had sensed it as soon as he'd seen him in the doorway, but he hadn't trusted his instincts. He'd relied on logic, and logic had failed him.

"Hi." Bob's eyes shifted to Devon. "I thought you and the boy were the only ones here until your wife came up?"

"Rico's car—" Devon started to say, but Rico interrupted.

"My car broke down last night, and Devon was nice enough to let me sleep on the couch."

"Do you need a ride to town? I have my truck back at the A frame," the ever-helpful Bob said.

Rico shook his head. "Nope. Tow truck is on the way. Devon, here, offered to give me a ride home. We're good."

"All right, then. Let me know if you need anything. I'm just down the road." And with that, he trudged off in the direction he'd come.

Devon watched his retreating form with a sense of loss completely out of proportion to the event. Even if he'd gotten a message to Bob, and the cops came and arrested Rico, what was to stop Myron from sending another thug?

No, the best plan was to pay off Rico, suggest he tell Myron he'd roughed Devon up, then he could collect whatever Myron was going to pay him, as well. It was a win-win for Rico, and Devon could be rid of both of them.

Bob stopped and turned back. An illogical hope leaped into Devon's chest. "I'd double check the pilot light on that heater if I were you," Bob called.

The hope burst like an over full water balloon. What had Devon expected him to say? *I'll let the Sheriff's Department know what's going on up here.* Or, *I'll be back with my shotgun.* "Will do," Devon said and steered Caleb into the house.

15

FIONA

The afternoon appointments ended at 3:30. Fiona spent the next two hours vacuuming, dusting counters, and sterilizing equipment. At 5:25, the rain slowed to a drizzle, and she decided to make a run for the car. She drove home slowly on the slippery roads, listening to the music of the windshield wipers.

As she pulled up to her house, she searched the street. She'd seen police cars patrolling last night and wished there was one around now. She'd feel better if an officer checked under the beds and in the closets before she entered the house.

Fiona jogged to the porch with her purse over her head and unlocked the front door. Crackers entered at her prompting. He didn't need much encouragement. He was happy to get out of the rain.

She waited outside for several minutes, feeling like a traitor. Sending the dog into a potentially dangerous situation alone seemed disloyal, but his nose would protect him. He could smell a hidden intruder from the foyer.

The nose poked through the doorway and nudged her in the knee. "Looking for me?" she said. He gave her a happy bark, turned, and ran toward the kitchen. Apparently, all was well. Crackers wanted dinner. Fiona followed him inside.

The sun never actually set that evening. Milky daylight faded slowly into wet blackness, and any positive feelings she'd drummed up during the day faded with it. She walked into the living room and stared at the couch still pushed against the far wall. Dread dropped heavy on her.

Crackers seemed to feel her unease. He padded behind her when she went into the bedroom to change, into the bathroom when she washed her face, and back to the living room again. She almost tripped over him three or four times, but she didn't reprimand him, only patted his head. Olivia was supposed to pick him up tomorrow, then Fiona would be alone. Really alone.

At 7:00, she curled up on the couch to watch the news. Ten minutes into the show, the doorbell rang. Crackers launched himself at the front door, barking hysterically. Fiona paused the TV and went after him.

She peered through the sidelights, hoping it was Inspector Sylla with good news. It wasn't. Gwen stood on the front porch, an overnight bag over her shoulder and a bottle of wine in her hand. Fiona threw open the door. "Gwen?"

"I come bringing gifts." She held up the wine. Crackers stepped outside to sniff her leg. "Who's your friend?"

"This is Olivia's dog, Crackers. But why are you here?"

"I came to spend the night. I didn't think you should be alone." She offered a hand to Crackers. He approved it and darted back inside out of the drizzle. "Can I come in?"

"Yes, of course." Fiona stepped out of the doorway. "This is so nice of you, but honestly I'm okay."

Gwen entered, dropped her bag, and gazed around her. "I like what you've done with the living room."

"I was… Last night, I…"

"I get it. I'd have done the same thing. Can we open this?" She held up the wine again.

Fiona led the way into the kitchen. "Are you hungry?"

"No, I ate with the kids." Gwen gave her an appraising look. "How about you? Are you eating?"

"Always." Fiona laughed, but it sounded disingenuous, even to her own ears. The truth was, she'd hardly eaten since Sylla had stopped by with the news. Her stomach was so tangled there didn't seem to be any room inside it.

Gwen leaned on the doorframe and crossed her arms over her chest. "Have you heard anything?"

Fiona shook her head. "No."

"What about the body they found off Highway 28?"

Fiona's gaze snapped toward her friend. "You think that has something to do with the jail break? They didn't say that on the news."

Gwen lifted one shoulder. "I just assumed. I mean, same county, only a few miles away from the jail."

"But San Bernardino County has one of the highest per capita murder rates in the country. Why would you assume?" Fiona realized she sounded shrill and shut her mouth.

Gwen dropped her arms to her sides and stepped toward her friend. "Hey. I'm sorry. I didn't mean to upset you."

"No. No, it's okay. I'm just on edge." Fiona grabbed the corkscrew and attacked the wine bottle. It was Red Ravish. She wished it wasn't. She wished it was any other wine, a five-dollar grocery store wine, anything but the wine that had been introduced to her during that terrible time.

She poured two glasses, and they took them into the living room. Gwen settled herself into an overstuffed chair that normally cozied up to the couch. Fiona sat on the couch, and Crackers hopped up beside her. "I think I've ruined him for furniture sitting."

"How long do you have him?"

"They're supposed to get him tomorrow afternoon."

Gwen pulled her long legs into the chair and sipped her wine. "I can stay over tomorrow night, too."

Fiona gazed at the woman who everyone said looked so like her. They had the same auburn hair, although Fiona had cut hers short when she was pregnant with Caleb. Gwen's was shoulder length. They were both tall, ectomorphic body types, and their eyes were the same —hazel green in some lights, gray-brown in others.

Superficially, they were very alike, but beyond that she didn't think they were the same at all. Gwen had an elegance and confidence Fiona had never acquired. There were wells of wisdom in her eyes that hadn't been there when they'd first met.

They were only an inch apart in height, but their shared past had seemed to make Gwen taller and stronger, whereas it had shrunken Fiona. She'd learned to shoot. She'd kept the business going, but she felt brittle, like if she fell, she'd break. Gwen seemed indestructible.

"They'll get him," Gwen said.

Fiona gave her a curt nod. "Right. I'm sure. But what kind of damage will he do first?"

"He's on the run. He's hiding."

"But that body…"

Gwen set her glass on the coffee table and pulled a throw over her lap. "I shouldn't have said anything about that. You're absolutely right. That could be anyone."

"I hate it that he's out there, hurting people."

"You don't know that he's hurting people."

"I know he will if he gets the chance."

Silence descended on them, during which Gwen searched Fiona's face with a penetrating gaze. Finally, she said, "You can't blame yourself for his actions."

Fiona fiddled with her wine glass. "But he's my brother."

"Half brother."

Fiona huffed at the irony. She'd corrected Sylla only two nights ago for using the same term, then used it herself. "There are shared genetics."

"What does that mean?"

"Exactly what I said. We share common genes."

"And that makes you responsible for the things he does? Makes you like him? What?"

Fiona sipped her wine. The taste, the scent, they slammed into her memories. A vision of a body, a woman, dead and bloody in her parents' old bedroom, shot into her mind. She set the glass on the floor. "My family started the problem, and I'm the only one left. So, yes, I guess I'm responsible."

Gwen shook her head slowly from side to side. "We had this conversation three years ago. I've moved on, moved ahead, sucked the good out of that experience, spit out the bones. You need to do the same."

"It's not over for me." Fiona almost yelled the words. She stood, knocking Crackers to the floor.

Neither woman said anything for a long moment. Fiona's phone broke the silence. She strode to the side table where she'd left it. It was Olivia. "Hey, Liv." The name came out strident, angry. She modulated her tone. "Everything okay?"

"Actually, that's why I'm calling. I don't think we'll be able to get home tomorrow, at least not by afternoon. We've been watching the weather. Apparently, they don't plow the roads until it stops snowing, and it's not supposed to let up until tomorrow late afternoon or evening at the earliest. I'm so sorry."

"No, don't be. I'm not going to Big Bear tomorrow anyway. Same reason."

"You don't mind keeping Crackers?"

"I love having him here," Fiona said with genuine emotion.

"Really?"

"Yes, really."

Olivia filled her in on their adventures, Fiona updated her on the state of the studio, and they hung up. Fiona turned to Gwen again. "I'm sorry. I shouldn't have gotten so emotional."

"Stop apologizing." She gestured to the couch. "Come, sit, I have something to say."

Fiona made her way to the couch and dropped into it. She would take whatever wisdom her friend had to give.

Gwen knit her fingers together in her lap as if getting ready to recite a poem. "I believe every person has their own special brand of BS, in other words, their besetting sin. It's the negative personality trait we struggle with most in life. Mine was, or is, lust."

She glanced up and grinned. "Not sexual. I mean, Art is amazing, but that's not my problem. No, above all I wanted to be important. I lusted for success and acclaim."

Fiona waved a hand in the air, dismissing Gwen's confession. "We all want success."

"Want is different than lust. Lust is never satisfied. There's always something more to achieve, something more to gain. If you get what you thought you wanted, it doesn't scratch the itch. At least not for more than a nano-second."

"I never saw that in you."

Gwen tilted her head. "I think you're being nice. I think you did see it, but either way, you know where that drive took me."

"I know where you were taken," Fiona mumbled.

Gwen leaned forward, dropping the throw to the floor. "I'm grateful to your half brother."

"What?" Fiona couldn't believe what she was hearing. "How could you be?"

"It was terrible, horrible, the most frightening thing I've ever been through. But it changed me for the better. I'm so grateful for my life now. I can't tell you what a relief it is not to be controlled by that desire for self-importance anymore."

Disbelief dropped like a wall between the women. Fiona couldn't wrap her head around what her friend was saying. Fears were things to be avoided, not trotted toward in the hopes you'd learn an esoteric lesson. She was saved from having to respond by a ding on her phone.

She glanced at the screen. It was a bank alert. Someone had taken a thousand dollars from the checking account that day. There was a number to call if she wanted to report it to the fraud department. Her thumb hovered over the text app on her phone. Should she ask Devon if he'd withdrawn the money?

Why would he? He was in the mountains. There was nothing to spend that much on up there. Could it have been her half brother? Could he have figured out how to hack into her account? She glanced at Gwen. "Give me a minute."

She stepped into the kitchen, called the number on the screen, and put a hold on her checking account. She'd let Devon know about it tomorrow.

The bottle of wine sat on the kitchen counter. She snatched it up, brought it to the living room, filled Gwen's glass, and set it on the coffee table. Her own glass was still full. She wasn't sure she could bring herself to drink it.

"You're obsessing over him," Gwen said as if their conversation had never been interrupted. "Don't give him that kind of power."

Fiona sank onto the couch again. "He escaped from prison." She enunciated each word because it seemed Gwen had forgotten.

"I know." Gwen was unfazed by her sarcasm. "That's why I'm here, and that's not what I mean."

The two women stared at each other for a long moment. Fiona had the eerie sensation she was watching her doppelgänger sitting there on her chair in her living room, drinking from one of the wine glasses she got from Devon's Aunt Ida as a wedding present. The woman may look like her, but she was from another dimension.

"What do you mean?" she finally said.

"He's dangerous, and he's free. That's a rational fear." Gwen waved her glass. "That you are somehow responsible for his actions and must right the universe for his wrongs, that's irrational."

Fiona's jaw tightened. What did Gwen know? She didn't have a murderer in her family. She didn't know the oppressive weight of guilt that Fiona lived with.

"My father killed my mother," Gwen said casually, as if announcing a sale at Nordstrom. "Not outright, but ultimately. His actions drove her to drink, and the bottle killed her. I felt like that was my fault for a long time."

Fiona thought she knew where Gwen was going with this, and it wasn't the same thing at all. "How could that be your fault? You were a child when your father left."

"You were a child when your father committed his misdeeds." Again, silence permeated the room. "Thinking that all this is your fault is the height of pride."

Fiona's spine went ramrod straight. "Pride?"

Gwen took a sip of wine, then set her glass down again before speaking. "You don't control the universe, Fiona. Somebody else already has that job."

Was Gwen right? Was she being presumptuous? Prideful?

"Most people don't have to go hunting down their demons. They'll come to you, and when they do, I have faith that you'll be up for the challenge."

Would she be? Fiona wasn't sure, but she sipped her wine and allowed the memories it brought to wash over her.

16

DEVON

The rest of Sunday afternoon and evening were so taxing Devon actually slept that night. He'd been exhausted from having to paste on a happy-daddy face and pretend Rico was a regular guy for Caleb's sake. Exhausted from running his dilemma over and over in his mind with no new input to interrupt the cycle.

The only plan of action he'd been able to come up with was the original one, wait until Monday and take everything he could out of the bank to buy Rico off. He just hoped it would be enough.

He woke early Monday morning, and tried to keep himself busy until the bank opened at nine. He made breakfast for Caleb and Rico but couldn't eat any himself. He did the dishes. When the clock hit 8:30, he put on his boots.

"You headed to town?" Rico asked from his perch on the couch.

You. Why, you? Why not us? "Aren't you coming?" Devon tried to keep his tone casual.

Rico shook his head. "Nah. I'm tired. I think you can handle it on your own."

A tiny flicker of hope lit in Devon's chest. Alone. He and Caleb could go to the sheriff's station. "Caleb," he called. "Come on, let's get your snow clothes on."

Caleb had been in his bedroom all morning doing puzzles and looking at his books. He knew things weren't right, despite Devon's attempts at cheerfulness. He also seemed to avoid Rico whenever possible.

"He's not going." Rico let loose a string of wracking coughs.

Devon stood completely still until the attack passed. "He'll be upset if I leave him."

Rico wiped his mouth with the back of his hand. "Be that as it may, that's what we're going to do."

Devon stared at the man on the couch. There was no way he was going to leave his child with a thug. A sick thug. A sick thug who didn't look nearly as menacing this morning as he had the day before. Devon turned on his heel and walked into the kitchen.

He wasn't a violent man. He'd never been in a fist fight, not even in grammar school. He'd put up with Rico because he'd believed he could buy him off with a few thousand and be done with it. He was beginning to wonder what would happen when the money was delivered. Would he leave them in peace? Or would he decide to carry out Myron's orders anyway?

All the knives were gone, but maybe there was something else he could use as a weapon? He picked up the frying pan from the stove top. It was light, coated aluminum. He set it down again, and pulled out the drawer under the oven where more pots and pans were kept, hoping there was a cast iron pan he'd missed the during his earlier search. There wasn't.

He stood and began to tear through cabinets. An alcohol, vinegar, or olive oil bottle could be broken and used to stab, but there were no glass containers other than small spice bottles.

He ripped open the silverware drawer and saw a large serving fork he'd missed before. It was wedged into the corner between the plastic tray and the edge of the drawer. He pulled it out. Whatever he used had to do enough damage to stop Rico from grabbing his much more lethal knife. Devon shifted the fork from hand to hand. It didn't have much heft to it. He stabbed at the air. The prongs were only a few inches long. Maybe he—

"What're you doing?" Rico stood in the doorway leaning against the frame.

"Um, just..." So much for thinking on his feet, the courtroom trait he was so proud of. "Thought we'd have steak for dinner," he finally said.

"You afraid the cow is going to make a run for it?" Rico adopted a comical expression and mimicked the stabbing motion Devon had made. "Got to hunt it down before we can eat it?"

Devon didn't answer. He couldn't think of a thing to say.

Rico stepped away from the wall and took the fork from Devon's hand. "I don't want to, but I will hurt Caleb if I have to. Don't put me in that position."

"I'm not leaving him here."

Rico sank into a kitchen chair and expelled a weary sigh. "Let me run down your options for you." He tapped a finger on the table. "First, and best, you run to the bank, get the cash, and I stay here and keep an eye on Caleb. No trauma for anyone."

He coughed twice, then continued. "Next option, you try to fight me. If you win, that's good. If not, it's very, very bad for you and for Caleb."

A rock landed in Devon's gut. He couldn't bear it if anything happened to his son.

Rico shrugged. "You might beat me. I'm not feeling well. But you might not. I'm more experienced, and I have a knife."

"What guarantee do I have that you'll leave us alone when you get the money?"

"The only guarantee you have is what I'll do if you don't cooperate."

His logic was impeccable. Case closed. Devon couldn't risk his son. He had no choice but to rely on this man's compassion for a three-year-old. "If anything happens to Caleb, I will hunt you down."

Rico rested his forehead in a hand. "Already told you, I don't want to hurt the kid."

Devon strode out of the kitchen, down the hall, and into his son's bedroom. Caleb lay under the covers, a Bob the Builder book in his chubby hands. He turned his head when Devon entered, but the grin that usually came when he saw his daddy never arrived.

"I've got to run to the bank," Devon said.

Caleb hopped off his bed. "I come, too."

Devon squatted until he was eye-level with his child. "No, buddy. I need to you stay here with Rico. I'll be back as quick as I can."

The left side of Caleb's mouth drooped—the precursor to tears. Devon pulled him to his chest. "Someone has to take care of Rico. He's pretty sick."

"Don't like Rico." Caleb's voice quivered.

Devon hugged him tighter. "I know, bud. I don't much like him either. If I go to the bank and bring him back some money, I think he'll go away. You want him to go away." Caleb's head nodded against Devon's shoulder. "Then I need you to be brave."

He pushed Caleb away so he could look into his gray-brown eyes. They were brimming with tears. "We gotta do this together, buddy. Daddy can't do it alone." The words weren't easy to say. Devon had been depending on himself, his own intelligence, for so long. Whether he wanted to admit it or not, the truth was, he did need his little boy to be on his side, to cooperate with the plan right now.

"You can lock yourself in your room and keep it locked until I return. Does that work?"

Caleb nodded again.

"Okay." Devon stood. "Lock the door when I leave." He marched from the room without looking back and shut the door behind him. He heard the lock click. He tried the handle. It wouldn't budge.

A little voice came through the wood. "I did it."

"Good job, Caleb." Devon swiped his hand across the top of the door. No key. He walked the hallway, feeling above each of the doors, found the key on the bathroom doorframe, and pocketed it. It was only a psychological help. He knew that if Rico really wanted to get into Caleb's room, he could do it. The tip of a knife, a screwdriver, a boot, all would break the flimsy lock, but it was the best he could do.

"I'll be back with the cash, then you'll be leaving?" He said with his hand on the front door.

"That's the plan," Rico said.

Devon opened the door, and Rico cleared his throat. "You understand that if the police show up, I'll have to use Caleb as a hostage?"

Devon walked out into the cold, gray morning without answering.

THE DRIVE to town was like a dream. A nightmare, really. Devon drove as quickly as he dared on the icy roads, the image of his son's bereft face clouding the windshield. He parked in the same space they'd parked in the day before, but this time, instead of going to the ATM, he walked inside the building.

The bank was almost empty. Two people stood in the teller line. One banker sat at her desk. He strode over to her. The woman, middle-aged, plump, and pretty, looked up from her computer screen. "Can I help you?"

Devon sat in a chair opposite her. "I need to close out an account." He slapped his debit card and driver's license onto the desk.

She took them, and her fingers began tapping. She stopped, read something on her screen and the pleasant smile she'd been wearing slid from her face. "I'm sorry, but there's a hold on this account."

"What do you mean, a hold? Why would there be a hold?"

"Apparently someone withdrew one thousand dollars yesterday."

"Right, that was me."

"Your account is set to send an alert for any withdrawal over fifty dollars. We sent an alert, and someone reported the withdrawal to the fraud department."

Devon's chest tightened. "I didn't see an alert?"

"It was sent at"—she ran an eye over her screen—"8:15 last night."

"I never got it."

"Did you check your text messages today?"

Devon's hand moved toward his pocket, then he realized Rico had his phone, which was why he'd never seen the notice. "It doesn't matter." He returned his hand to the desktop. "I'd like to close the account either way."

"We'll have to get the hold lifted before we can do that." She gave him a small, tight smile.

"Okay. Lift the hold."

"There are two signers on this account. You and Fiona—"

Caleb's sad face emerged on the screen of his mind. He cut the woman off. "My wife, right. She'll be okay with this. Just call her."

The banker tapped her keyboard again, and said, "The number we have on file is 949-248-3385."

"That's her number."

She picked up the phone on her desk, punched in the numbers, then waited. Devon chewed on the side of his thumb. *Pick up, pick up, Fi.*

"Hello, Mrs. Washington, this is Marsha Thompson from City Wide Bank up here in Big Bear."

Devon dropped his hand.

"Your husband would like to close your joint checking account, but I need you to withdraw the hold before I can do that."

Come on, Fi. Do it without asking questions.

"Please give me a call back at this number."

His heart thudded to his stomach. She wasn't there. He glanced at his watch—9:25. She must be teaching.

The woman shone her tight-lipped smile at him again. "As soon as we hear from Mrs. Washington, we can lift the hold, but there's nothing I can do for you until then."

Anger gripped him. This was his money. His account. This, this, woman, had no right… His right eyebrow twitched. Caleb's lip drooped in his mind. *Think, think.* Their other accounts, an IRA and a savings, were with a small bank with no branches in Big Bear.

Savings. They did have one savings account at this bank. He reached for his wallet and searched for a second card. He didn't have one. "We have another account, a savings account."

"Yes, I see it here."

"There's no hold on that, is there?"

"No." She said the word slowly, making two syllables of it.

"I'll close that one, then." There wasn't much in it. It was Fiona's Christmas fund which had been all but depleted a couple of months ago, but he didn't want to show up at the house empty handed.

"That account appears to be in your wife's name alone." The banker said.

"Yes, but..." Damn it. He dropped his head into his hand. What was he going to do? What would Rico do if he turned up without the cash?

"Is there a number where I can reach you? I'll call as soon as we hear from your wife, and this is all straightened out." Her voice was cold.

Devon gazed at the face that had been so open and friendly when he sat down. It was now shuttered and hard. She thought he was trying to steal his wife's money, that they were in the middle of a nasty divorce. It happened all the time. He knew better than anyone what people did to those they'd vowed to love and protect.

This was useless. He gave the banker his number and walked to the car. A sheriff's department vehicle was at the end of the lot, fog flowing from the tailpipe. He paused.

Should he? He could walk right over to that cop, explain what was happening, and call in reinforcements. That's what he'd tell his client to do if their spouse had kidnapped their child.

But what if they handled things poorly? What if they provoked Rico to violence? A vision of a SWAT team stationed outside the cabin, Rico in the window holding a knife to his son's throat played across his mind. He pivoted, walked to his car, and drove out of the lot.

17

FIONA

"Great job today, ladies," Fiona called after her 9:00 class as they left by the front door. Crackers popped up from his bed in the corner and wandered over, head down, tail wagging. She rubbed the fur on the top of his head. "You're a good watch dog, aren't you?"

He apparently thought so because he trotted to the cupboard where his treats were stowed. Fiona gave him one, poured herself a cup of coffee from the break room, and wandered to the front desk again. She glanced at the schedule and saw she had a private client at 10:30, which gave her twenty minutes or so to relax. That was enough time to call Devon and Caleb. She hadn't spoken to her son in over twenty-four hours—too long.

Before she got to her phone, she heard it ring from her purse under the counter, and she retrieved it. It was Devon. "Hey. I was just going to call you."

"Did you put a hold on our checking account?" He didn't bother with a greeting, just shot the question at her like a bullet.

"Yes." She couldn't keep the hurt from her voice. "The bank contacted me and said someone withdrew a thousand dollars yesterday. I thought we'd been hacked."

"That was me. I withdrew the money."

Fiona didn't speak for a long minute. He sounded so angry. She chose her words carefully. "Why?" It was the only thing she could think of.

"I wanted to have cash on hand. The weather is rotten. The roads are rotten. I thought I might need it if power went down and the ATMs weren't working."

That sounded rehearsed. Fiona knew her husband. She'd been sensing something was wrong for several weeks, which was why she'd agreed to let him take Caleb away without her. She figured he needed down time. But she hadn't felt he'd been lying to her. Withholding information, yes. Lying, no. This sounded like a lie.

"That's a lot of cash, Dev."

"Who knows how long we'll be stranded?" He paused then spoke in a softer voice. "I guess I overreacted."

"Okay," she said.

"Anyway, the bank called you. Could you ring them back and lift the hold? I think they thought I was trying to wipe you out or something." He gave a half-hearted chuckle.

"Sure." Fiona chewed her lower lip. Why did he need the hold lifted if he already had a thousand in cash? She'd do it. She needed to go to the store later, and although she could use her business fund, she liked to keep home and work separate.

"Thanks. Love you, Fi."

Was he saying goodbye, getting ready to hang up? "Can I talk to Caleb?" she blurted out the words before he could.

"Ah, he's in the middle of a puzzle. I don't think we should bug him."

"Devon," her voice was sharp. "What's going on?"

"Nothing. Everything's fine."

She chewed on his words for a moment, then a thought struck her so hard, she jumped from her stool. "Did Caleb get hurt sledding? Did you need the money for Arrowhead Hospital?"

"No." He sounded alarmed. "Why would you think that?"

"It's the only thing that makes sense. You didn't want me to see the bill, so you paid in cash." She hugged herself with her free arm. "Dev, talk to me. You have to tell me the truth, or I'm getting in the car and coming up there."

A pause. "Okay, okay. You're right. Caleb fell off the sled, but he's okay. Just got the wind knocked out of him. I took him in just to be on the safe side, but he's okay."

"Let me talk to him."

"Honey, he's—"

"Let me talk to him." She'd yelled that time. She and Devon never yelled at each other, but he'd never kept her son from her before.

"Calm down. I'll get him."

The phone went dead for a very, very long time. She thought she heard muffled voices in the background—Devon's, Caleb's, but there was another one. A quiet rasp of a voice. It could've been Dev speaking quietly, but it could've been a third person. She couldn't be sure.

Finally, she heard what she'd been waiting to hear. "Mommy?"

Relief weakened her knees, and she sank onto the stool again. "Hi, baby. How are you?"

"I okay." He sounded so small.

"Are you having a good time with Daddy?" Her heart thudded as she waited for the answer. It never came.

"I miss you, Mommy." There was a crack in his voice. He was near tears.

"I miss you too, baby. Daddy says you got hurt sledding."

"I fell."

"Are you all right? You're not hurt, are you?"

"No. I not hurt."

Again, relief cascaded over her. It was short-lived. A sound, like something being scraped against the phone came, then a muffle of voices she couldn't interpret.

"I gotta go now." Caleb's voice was clear.

"So soon? I wanted to talk more."

"Yeah. Rico—"

His words were cut off and Devon came on the line. "We're getting ready to go out and play in the snow."

"What was he talking about? Who's Rico?"

"Oh, he made a Lego man. He's calling him Rico for some reason."

"Like Uncle Rico, the Napoleon Dynamite character?"

"Yeah. Funny, huh?"

"Has he even seen that movie? I hope you haven't watched that with him. It's too mature for a four-year-old."

A pause. "No, we didn't watch it. Must have heard someone talking about it, maybe a kid in preschool. Anyway, he's all bundled up and sweating. I better get him outside. Don't forget to call the bank."

"Right."

When they hung up, Fiona had more concerns than she'd had before she called, but she didn't have time to ponder them. Her 10:30 client was walking in the door.

About halfway through Fiona's 11:30 appointment, she made a decision. She was going to call Sylla to see if she could get someone to drop in on Devon. Things weren't right up there. It was unlikely, but it was possible that her half brother had discovered where Devon and Caleb were and had decided the best way to punish her was to punish them.

She ended the appointment exactly at 12:30, then her client, a young woman attempting to get her pre-pregnancy body back postpartum, wanted to chat about her diet. Frustration surged through Fiona's veins, but she contained it, smiled, sold the woman a package of five more appointments, and shooed her out the door as gracefully as possible.

At 12:47, she called Sylla. The detective had given Fiona her cell number, which probably wasn't something she normally did, and Fiona was grateful. It was lunchtime, but Sylla answered on the third ring.

"Fiona?" It sounded as if her mouth was full.

"Hi, Inspector Sylla, I'm sorry to bother you at lunch."

"No, no worries. Just grabbing a bit of grub. What's up?" The cheerful tone in her voice disappeared. "Something wrong?"

"No. Well, maybe. But not with me." She said hurriedly. "It's Devon."

"He still in Big Bear, yeah?"

"Yes. He and Caleb, but something's not right up there." Fiona filled her in on the last three phone calls, the bank withdrawal, and the voice she may or may not have heard through the phone.

Sylla didn't respond immediately. When she did, she seemed to choose her words carefully. "Your marriage—everything okay?"

"Yes. I mean we have our ups and downs like every couple, but Devon is a great husband and father."

"So it couldn't be that he's—"

Fiona cut her off, "Planning to leave me and take Caleb with him? No. It couldn't be that. I'm afraid…"

"You're afraid he found them." Sylla finished her sentence for her.

"Yeah."

"How could he? Could he have called Devon's office? Did you post the trip on social media?"

A rock dropped into Fiona's gut, and she closed her eyes. *Stupid, stupid, stupid.* "I did. I didn't give an address, but I posted that Dev was taking Caleb to Big Bear, and I bragged about having a weekend to myself."

Sylla's answer was thoughtful, not condemning. "How would he have found them? Big Bear isn't a big town, but there are hundreds of vacation rentals. You didn't put anything on the internet other than what you told me?"

"Just a picture, that's it."

Fiona heard the crush of paper through the phone, then Sylla spoke again. "Is your Instagram account private?"

"No. I keep it public for the business."

"What's the name?" Fiona told her, and the phone was silent for a long moment.

"Ah. Okay, then. Look in the background."

Fiona quickly opened the Instagram app on her phone. "Oh, no." Her heart sank. There, in the corner of photograph, was a street sign.

"I'm not going to lecture you," Sylla said, and Fiona braced herself.

"But this is why we should never post about vacations until we are safely locked into our homes again. Criminals love social media."

Fiona didn't answer, didn't defend herself. Sylla was right. Guilt wrapped scaled arms around her and squeezed. "So, what do we do?" It was almost a wail.

"Well, we don't panic. Honestly, your worry that your son was injured while sledding and hubby doesn't want you to know is the most likely scenario. However, I can ask somebody to go by and check on them."

"Would you?" Relief cascaded over her. "I'll give you the address."

Fiona read the address off to Sylla, and they disconnected. Then she returned the call from the bank in Big Bear and lifted the hold on the checking account. That done, she walked to the wall of windows and gazed at the roiling waves below. A patch of sunlight created a blue section in the gray tableau, and inside the sunlit space, she saw the tailend of a rainbow.

She hoped it was a sign. Fiona wasn't usually superstitious, but she wasn't usually terrified out of her mind, either. Hope was a thing with wings, wasn't that how the poem went? It had flown out of her world, but just knowing that Sylla was in her camp, that the police would send someone to check on the people she loved most in the world, beckoned it back.

A cold, wet nose thrust itself into her hand. She glanced down at Crackers. "You missing your family, too?" He gave her one wag, sighed, and leaned his shoulder against her leg.

It hadn't rained since the night before, which meant the snowfall was probably slowing in Mammoth and Big Bear. "The roads should be clear by tonight," she told the dog. If they were, she was going to head up the mountain, whether she had to take Crackers with her or not.

18

DEVON

"How did it go?" Rico's voice was a rasp. He sounded worse than ever.

Devon walked to the fireplace and warmed his back. "Apparently Fiona put a hold on the account last night when she saw the withdrawal."

Rico's rheumy eyes narrowed to slits. "You fooling me?"

"No." Devon heard the weariness in his voice. "I'm as frustrated as you are about this."

"What are you going to do?"

"The bank said they'd call as soon as they hear from Fiona." Devon held out his hand. "If you give me my phone back, I can try to reach her as well."

Rico closed his eyes, and his chin fell to his chest. He stayed that way for so long, Devon thought he may have fallen asleep. Just when he was about to walk away, head to the kitchen to start lunch, Rico's eyes opened. "I'll wait."

A realization dropped onto Devon in that moment. He was a prisoner of this man. He'd been pushing that truth away, telling himself he, Devon, had chosen to pay Rico off. Telling himself that this was a tight situation—no one could deny that—but he had options, autonomy. That was a lie. He was a prisoner.

The room felt stifling, the air stale.

Devon had never given much thought to what it would be like to be locked up. He didn't send people to prison in his field of law. He conducted interviews there from time to time. Occasionally, an abusive spouse would end up in jail after he counseled a client to press charges. But Devon didn't defend or prosecute criminal cases.

Prison. A sudden certainty made his skin prickle. "I'm going make Caleb some macaroni and cheese. Want something?" he said abruptly.

Rico coughed into his blankets. "I don't care what I eat. I can't taste anything anyway."

Devon entered the kitchen and began assembling the lunch things. Rico had been in jail recently. The pale skin, the lean, ropey muscles, the speed at which he'd pulled a knife on Devon. Even his shoes. Devon was almost certain they were prison-issued sneakers. How had he not noticed this right away?

This changed things. What did a newly released con value more than anything? Freedom. It had to be. Myron had probably preyed on that desire, offering Rico enough money to get away, start over.

The feeling of claustrophobia that had come over Devon when he stood by the fire was intense. He couldn't imagine being locked up in a cell for months, let alone years. Trapped animals chewed their legs off.

When the water on the stove came to a boil, he poured the noodles in and set the timer without thinking. A long ray of sun shone through the kitchen window and crept toward him. There was warmth in its touch.

He walked to the window and looked out at the blinding fields of snow, the road, and the woods beyond. Freedom. It was a beautiful word. He whispered it and savored the feel of it in his mouth. Freedom.

He'd heard the phrase from desperate criminal many times. It was bandied about in TV shows and movies, by news reporters and even law enforcement, but he'd never really thought about what it meant. He did now.

Could he use it? That was the question. Was Rico's desire for freedom a weakness? Or a threat?

The timer startled Devon. He moved quickly to the stove, picked up the pot, and poured the hot liquid through a colander. If Rico was desperate to remain free, he'd be dangerous if he felt a net closing on him. Devon needed to help Rico get away. Give him money, a car, whatever he needed. If he couldn't help him, he was afraid he'd have to kill him.

That idea thudded like a brick in his chest. Its reverberations echoed within him. *I might have to kill Rico. Kill Rico.*

Devon had been taught since he was a child that violence was never the way to resolve an issue. He'd been taught that thoughtful persuasion, understanding, cooperation, and compromise were the way forward. He'd pretended he was fine with Fiona's gun, but he wasn't. Not really. The only reason he agreed to have it in their home was because he didn't think she'd ever have to use it.

Now he wished he had it with him, because sometimes violence *was* the way forward. It was the only language some people spoke. Devon woke up today in a foreign land. He needed to become fluent in its language.

He scooped food into two bowls. Placed one on the table and carried the other to the living room. "Caleb, lunch is ready," he called as he set a bowl in front of Rico.

The stranger's eyes were closed but shot open as soon as Devon spoke. "Thanks," he said.

Thanks. Politeness, human niceties, they seemed as out of place in this new world as guns were in his old life. The life before. The life that would never be the same again.

Caleb walked into the room, paused, then ran past the couch toward the kitchen. Whatever Devon did, he would have to do it soon. He didn't want this experience to change his son the same way he was being changed. He didn't want Caleb to know captivity and violence and desperation.

He turned to follow Caleb into the kitchen, and the doorbell rang. He froze. Rico froze, fork halfway to his mouth. They looked at each other and something unspoken passed between them. Devon shivered.

He was becoming more like his captor every passing hour. Yes, he had to do something soon.

Rico rose from the couch, yanked his blankets around himself, and headed into the kitchen. Devon watched him pull a chair next to Caleb's and place an arm on its back. "Get it," Rico said.

Devon walked to the door, heart hammering. It was probably Bob. He'd get rid of him.

As he put his hand on the doorknob, he glanced into the kitchen. Rico leaned toward Caleb and whispered something to him. Caleb shrank away. Devon pasted on a smile and threw the door open.

The smile dropped with a thud. It wasn't Bob. It was a sheriff's deputy.

"Afternoon." The deputy was a large man with a wide-open face, friendly in a practiced way. He reminded Devon of a Newfoundland or a St. Bernard. "I'm Deputy Connolly from the Big Bear Station. How're you doing today?"

"Fine." Devon's voice sounded strained. He cleared his throat and spoke again. "What can I do for you? Am I parked in a no-parking zone or something?" He laughed lightly to show he wasn't concerned about the officer's visit, that he had nothing to hide.

The sheriff lifted the corners of his mouth and dropped them again —a polite acknowledgement of Devon's attempt at humor. "Nope. Car's fine. I'm actually here to check up on you."

Devon didn't have to pretend surprise. "Me? Why's that? If it's that snafu at the bank—"

The sheriff shook his head. "No, no. Nothing to do with a bank. We got a call from the Orange County Sheriff's department asking us to give you a visit in connection with the prison break."

Devon had read something about a manhunt but couldn't think what it had to do with him. He must have remained silent too long. A frown furrowed the sheriff's brow. "You have heard about the breakout?"

"Yes, yes." Devon said. "But I don't see how I can be of any help."

Connolly turned his massive head and gazed into the stand of trees behind the house as if his next statement might be found there. "Your wife didn't tell you?"

"Tell me what?" Confusion wound around Devon's head like cotton batting. This conversation made no sense.

"I'm sorry to inform you, but one of the prisoners was your wife's brother."

Devon stared. "That's impossible. Her *half brother,*" he accentuated the word, "is in San Quentin. The escape was from San Bernardino County Jail."

"A number of state prisoners were moved to county jails over the past three months due to virus outbreaks. Your wife's brother was one of them."

"Does she know this?"

"Yes, she was informed the morning after the breakout."

"She could be in danger." Devon's voice rose in outrage. He glanced behind himself toward the kitchen and lowered it not wanting Caleb to hear. "You moved a murderer who was serving life from a maximum-security prison to a county jail, and he escaped?"

The officer cocked his head to one side. "Well, actually, I didn't move the prisoner. You can thank the California Supreme Court for that. I'm only here to make sure you haven't heard from him."

Devon stared at his stocking feet. Rico. Could he have been all wrong about Rico? He'd never actually said Myron had sent him; Devon had assumed it.

Panic, cold and raw, blew through him. Had he mistaken a rattler for a garden snake? "I haven't," he said.

The idea that the man holding his son in the kitchen could be a murderer who'd been sentenced to life—a murderer with a vendetta against the child's mother—made him unsteady on his feet. He swayed and put a hand on the doorframe.

"You okay?" Connelly asked.

"Fine. Still adjusting to the altitude." Devon glanced nervously over his shoulder but couldn't see Caleb from where he stood. *Desperate*. The word rang in his mind. He had to get rid of the deputy.

When he returned his gaze to the doorway, he saw Connelly trying to look around him into the house.

Nerves short-circuited, popping up and down Devon's spine like faulty lightbulbs. What if Connelly asked to come in? If Devon said no, he'd be suspicious. If Devon said yes… He didn't want to think about the repercussions. "But I will check every door and window after you leave."

Sheriff Connelly didn't respond immediately. After a long pause, he said, "I'll take a look around the perimeter."

Devon relaxed his shoulders just an inch. "I'd appreciate that, but is someone keeping an eye on my wife? She's the one he'll go after if he goes after anyone."

"Yes, they have security checks going by your house every few hours. However, we have reason to believe that the cons headed up here after they got out."

"Both of them?" The cotton batting made it hard to think straight. Could the man in the kitchen be the other con? The one who escaped with Fiona's brother? That thought was only marginally less terrifying.

"Yes," Connelly said.

"How do you know they're on the mountain?"

"I'm afraid I can't talk about an open investigation."

Thoughts raced through Devon's mind like a car chase in LA, knocking out innocent spectators as they went. If only he'd gone to the trial with Fiona, he'd know who the man in the kitchen was, or at least who he wasn't. Devon had wanted to go, but she'd said no. She'd been ashamed.

He'd told her how wrong that was, that she had nothing to be ashamed of, but it had done no good. For all her modern feminism claims, she still carried the notion of family guilt. Her mother was a first-generation American, raised by Eastern European parents who'd had more of the old country in them than the new.

CONSEQUENTLY, Devon had never seen the man other than in grainy newspaper photos and a few terrible shots on the Internet. Could he and the man in the kitchen be one and the same? Was he here to hurt Devon and Caleb in order to punish Fiona? Suddenly, a thug sent by Myron to rough him up seemed a small problem.

"Well, keep us informed," Devon said, signaling the end of the conversation.

"Will do." Connolly turned and made his way off the porch and into the snow. He looked at home in the landscape, and the impression of a St. Bernard grew stronger. Devon's heart dropped into his churning gut as he watched him walk away. It seemed foolish to let him leave. He wanted to call out to him, to point to the kitchen and yell, "In there!"

But he couldn't. Caleb was there, sitting with a rattlesnake. Devon couldn't give it any reason to strike.

19

Chuck came to me in my dreams last night. He was standing strong and tall—well, as tall as Chuck could stand—under the stars, out by that tree where I left him. He was talking, per usual, about going south, "getting his," how life had short-changed him. That was the difference between us.

I believe we are all dealt a hand when we come into this world, and we have to make the best of it. Some get excellent cards, some poor, but good poker players can win even with crap hands. I wanted to be a good poker player. Chuck wanted everybody else's cards.

He asked me why in my dream last night. *Why'd you kill me?* The answer I gave him surprised me, but in the light of day, I guess it was the truth. I didn't say, *'Cause you were going to die anyway*. Which was what I'd been telling myself.

I told him, *Because you're a loser, and I can't partner with a loser*. Losers drag people down. Turn others into losers. I had to win this hand.

The door slammed shut. I shoved myself away from the kitchen table, limped to the couch, and sank into its lumpy softness. Devon stood by the fire staring at his hands. Something had changed in him, and it wasn't positive. I'd seen this kind of thing before. Guys in prison, docile guys, guys who didn't want trouble. But when they got backed into a corner, they went feral.

We all have a wild man inside. In most it's dormant, but if it wakes up... Well, that's a problem. That wild streak ran me around for most of my life, but I leashed it a good part of the time now.

The kid padded into the living room and sat on the hearth. He looked small. The sight of him made me hope Devon could leash his demon. I'd hate to have to leave the boy without a father, although I was beginning to think that was inevitable.

"You did good, getting rid of the sheriff," I said. Praise was a weapon I didn't use often. It was dangerous game. There was a guard at San Quentin who used to make guys cooperative, make them think he was their friend. It didn't work for long.

Eventually, the guys started expecting things from him, things he was never going to give. He must have realized his error, because he changed his MO. Started acting like the rest of the guards. Well, you know those guys felt betrayed. One sunny morning, they killed him in the yard.

I was running out of things I could give Devon. Letting him go was no longer a possibility. Not now that the sheriff's department knew where I was.

You see, I knew something about lawmen Devon didn't. I could tell by the hard look on his face that he believed he'd pulled the wool over that deputy's eyes. He hadn't. Police, like cons, are trained to read a person, not just listen to them. Devon was a headline.

"Has the bank called or texted?" Devon said, ignoring my comment.

"Yes, they have. You can withdraw the money now." He made a move toward the door. I raised a hand to stop him. "I think we should wait until tomorrow."

His eyes narrowed. "Why?"

"It wouldn't look good, going into town right after the sheriff stopped by."

"I don't see what difference it makes. I was there yesterday. I told them I'd be back again today." His tone was belligerent. He was getting harder to manage.

"What if he's watching you?"

Devon rotated his palms to the ceiling as if demanding an answer from heaven. "What if he is?" In my experience, mail from the heavenlies was always slow.

I yawned. Lunch had hit my stomach hard. "Don't you think he'd find it strange if you left your three-year-old home alone."

He worked his jaw as he chewed over a response. Finally, he said, "I could take him with me."

I shook my head and smiled. It wasn't worth wasting my breath on. He had to know that wasn't going to happen. We stared at each other for a long time, then Devon dropped his gaze. "Let's take a nap, Caleb."

Caleb, happy to get away from me, scooted into the hallway and out of sight. Devon followed.

I lay down and closed my eyes, but I didn't sleep. Different scenarios played across the screen of my mind. In the first, we waited until morning and all three of us went to town together, hit the bank, then headed down the hill. We'd take Highway 38 this time.

Problem—if we hit a roadblock, which we most certainly would, what would Devon say to the cops that stopped us? Could he point to Caleb in the backseat and say it was just him and his son in the car? Could he ignore me hiding on the floor with a blanket over me? I didn't think so. His wild man was tugging at the leash.

Scenario number two: We all go to the bank. Devon gets the cash. We head back here, and I get rid of him and the boy and take off by myself. Two problems with that. How do I kill Devon? He's not a small man, and knowing death is imminent can turn even the most passive guy into a bull. And how do I get through the roadblock? I'm sure my picture is all over the place.

The last scenario is the only one that works. I rest for a bit, kill Devon while he's napping, grab the kid, and go. They'll have to let me through the roadblocks if I have the kid. He's my insurance. I can get the money later, in the form of a ransom.

Having made my decision, I let my mind drift to that star that winked at me the night I put Chuck out of his misery. Stars are there during the day. You can't see them because of the sun, but I see that star now. It's in my head, and it's winking at me again.

20

FIONA

After exchanging her work clothes for sweats, Fiona walked into her kitchen. She'd been on edge all afternoon. She'd picked up her phone a thousand times to call Devon or Sylla. She wanted reassurance everything was as it should be up in Big Bear.

Crackers seemed to pick up on her restlessness. He'd only eaten half his dinner, then he followed her from room to room, never allowing her out of his sight. He was collapsed in the kitchen now, gaze trained on her as she fished around in the refrigerator, trying to find something appealing for dinner.

Her phone danced across the counter. She pulled her head out of the vegetable bin and looked at the screen. Finally. It was Sylla.

"Fiona. Good news here. Well, can't really call it good news, but relieving news anyway."

"Devon and Caleb?"

"They're fine. A deputy dropped by and spoke with Devon. Seemed everything was in order."

"Thank God," Fiona said.

"That wasn't the good news I was referring too, however."

"You caught him?" Fiona's pulse quickened.

"In a manner of speaking." Sylla paused. "We found his body."

Emotions slid across Fiona like skaters on an ice rink. Relief, followed by happiness, followed by joy, followed by shame. Her half brother was dead. That wasn't something she should rejoice about, but she couldn't help herself. "You're sure it's him?"

"Absolutely. We found him on a fire road off the Rim of the World. The autopsy hasn't been done as yet, but the ME's first guess is asphyxiation."

"Asphyxiation?" Fiona repeated dumbly.

"Yes, as I said, we can't be sure, but it appears someone smothered him. We don't know with what. There was nothing nearby."

She digested that information. "He was murdered, then."

"Looks like it."

"Have you found his partner? The man he escaped with?"

Another pause, then Sylla said, "No. The manhunt continues. But you're safe, anyway. I wanted you to know."

"Thanks for calling."

Sylla promised to keep her posted on future developments, and they hung up. The fizz of happiness she'd felt when she'd first heard the news returned. She punched in Devon's number, wanting to share it with someone, but disconnected before the call went through. How could she share the good news when she'd never told him the bad news? She couldn't, at least not on the phone. That kind of conversation should happen in person.

She glanced at Crackers, then dialed Olivia's number. It rang five times and went to voicemail. Fiona googled Mammoth weather conditions. It was still snowing there. Then she looked up Big Bear road conditions. The Rim of the World Highway was clear, but chains were required. She had chains in the garage. She'd never put them on herself, but she'd figure it out.

"Want to go on a road trip?" she said to the dog. He wagged his tail. "Let's do it."

A half hour later, Fiona had rescheduled the next day's clients, and she and Crackers were packed into the car with snow clothes, groceries, dog food and a bottle of wine. She needed liquid courage to tell Dev all the things she'd been keeping from him. Besides she was celebrating.

She understood Sylla's hesitation at calling her half brother's death good news, but it was. He'd been a very confused, very sad man who'd become an evil man. Fiona was sorry for him, for his tragic childhood, for the rejection he'd felt by their father, but many people had gone through the same and hadn't done the things he'd done. The world was a safer place without him in it.

She stopped at a red light, found an upbeat playlist on her phone, and played it through the car speakers. It was time to drive away the ghosts of the past. Her family's shame had been dealt with, and she was relieved she hadn't been the one to do it. It seemed strange to be grateful to the man who murdered her murdering brother, but there it was.

The freeways were clear. She ran into light traffic in LA, but that was to be expected. She hit Highway 18, Rim of the World, in record time and began to climb. Caleb would be asleep when she arrived, but that was okay. She needed some time with Dev alone, and it would be fun to surprise her son in the morning with pancakes. She'd packed the ingredients at the last minute.

Twenty minutes up the mountain, the fog rolled in. Fiona slowed. On her right was a sheer drop, hence the name of the road. She could see the twinkle of lights from the city of San Bernardino below, but the highway in front of her was obscured by a wall of white.

The turnoff to Lake Arrowhead should be coming up in fifteen minutes or so, but she had no place to stay in Arrowhead. The desire to see her family had become an ache in her gut. She crept forward, training her eyes on the center line, or what she could see of it.

She rounded a wide bend and glanced in her rearview mirror. A string of headlights trailed behind her. She was leading the pack. Great. Talk about the blind leading the blind. Her palms began to sweat.

Five minutes later, she rounded another bend and skidded on black ice. For a few terrifying seconds, her car slid toward the edge of the cliff, but she righted herself. She should have put the chains on at the bottom of the hill, but she'd been in too big a hurry.

Stop. Stop. Stop. Everything within her screamed the word, but she couldn't. The drivers behind her wouldn't know she had. They wouldn't see her. They didn't know about the patch of black ice. She could cause a pile-up, a pile-up that could push her off the mountain.

Fiona gripped the steering wheel and continued on, heart dancing in time with a Taylor Swift song about not caring anymore. She reached out a hand and turned it off. It required all her concentration to navigate through this strange world of swirling shades of gray and white where time seemed to stand still. There was no before, no after, only the few feet of asphalt with its center line revolving beneath her like the pad of a treadmill.

A sob escaped her lips, and Crackers whined in response. She'd forgotten he was there, and a new panic struck her. She was responsible for more than herself and the string of unknown drivers behind her. She was responsible for him as well. Why was it always her? Why was she always the one shouldering everyone else's burdens?

A thought whispered in the recesses of her mind. Could it be this was her own doing? Not this particular foggy-highway moment, but did she take things upon herself she didn't need to? That's what Dev said. Olivia and Gwen agreed with him. Even Sylla had said as much.

But how? How would she change? Because she had to. The weight of the world was beginning to break her. She choked back another sob. "Please," she said, unsure of who she was talking to. She gripped the wheel and drove on.

21

DEVON

Banging woke Devon. For a long moment he didn't know where he was. The room around him was dim and cold. He glanced around and saw Caleb cuddled under a bedspread, his arms wrapped around a teddy bear.

It came back to him in a rush of dread. He was in the Big Bear cabin where he was being held by Rico—a waking nightmare.

The door banged again, this time a voice accompanying the pounding. "Devon, Devon. It's Bob. I need to talk to you."

Devon got up and entered the living room. His eyes flashed toward the couch. The stranger lay there, his eyes glittering.

"I'll get it," Devon mumbled, but Rico held up a hand.

Devon watched as he moved to the entryway, pressed himself against the wall, and pulled the door open, hiding himself in the process.

"Hey, Devon, hate to bother you, but I heard some disturbing news. I thought you needed to know." Bob hesitated on the threshold for a moment. "I wanted to make sure you and the boy were okay."

"We're fine," Devon said.

Bob's gaze rested on Devon for a moment. His brow furrowed with confusion, but he crossed the room with faltering steps. "A deputy stopped by my house a few hours ago. He said—"

His words cut off with a choke and a gurgle, and a ribbon of red slid across his neck. Devon's mouth opened, but no sound emerged. He was too horrified to scream.

Bob dropped to his knees, revealing Rico, a knife hanging from his hand.

"Daddy." Caleb said from somewhere behind Devon.

Devon choked, then found his voice. "No! Don't come in here." He couldn't let his child witness this. He turned to look at Caleb and gentled his voice. "Go into your room. Lock the door behind you, and don't come out."

"Daddy."

The name, the special name that only Caleb used, was a sob. An ache opened up in Devon's chest. "Do as I say."

Caleb disappeared from view, and a moment later, a door slammed. Devon spun and fell to the floor next to Bob. The man's eyes were wide with surprise, but their light was already fading. Devon grabbed the afghan, thinking he could staunch the flow of blood, but it was hopeless. The gash was too wide. He hugged the blanket and rocked back and forth instead.

Rico had gone into the kitchen, leaving them alone together. Devon heard water running in the sink, then a door open and shut.

"Bob, I'm so sorry," Devon whispered, but he wasn't sure the man could hear him any longer. A pool of blood had spread around them more quickly than Devon had believed possible. A door thumped again, footsteps sounded on the kitchen linoleum, and a moment later, Rico was standing over them.

"I'm going to need your help." He said the words matter-of-factly, as if he were discussing stuffing a turkey or jumpstarting a car. Maybe murder was matter-of-fact for him.

Devon didn't know if this was Fiona's half brother or if he was the man who'd escaped with him. He hadn't wanted to know. Hadn't wanted to know what manner of man he was dealing with. That had been a mistake. Every decision he'd made since Rico had come to the door had been a mistake.

"Stand up." Rico's voice was as cold and sharp as the icicles hanging from the cabin's roofline. "We got to get rid of him." He pushed Bob's body with his toe. It rocked then fell into place again. Bob was gone.

"Why? Why not just leave?" Devon heard hysteria in his voice. He tried to modulate his tone. "You heard what he said. That sheriff's deputy went by his place. They're looking for you."

"I plan to, but I don't plan to leave a trail behind me."

What did that mean? Was Devon part of that trail? Was Caleb? "I'll help you, but I want to talk to Caleb first."

Rico's eyes became slits. He pondered the request for so long, Devon began to wonder if he'd heard him at all. "All right," he finally said. "Three minutes. Leave the door open."

Devon rose stiffly. He hurried to his son's room. The door handle wouldn't budge. Good. Caleb had obeyed him. "Caleb, honey." He whispered through the wood. "Can you let me in?"

A scrambling sound was followed by the click of the lock. The door swung open, and a moment later Devon's arms were filled. His son was shaking. He lifted him, carried him to the bed, and sat hugging the boy to his chest. "It's going to be okay." He repeated the phrase again and again, hoping one of them would believe it.

When the shivering slowed, Devon lifted Caleb's face and smoothed his hair. "Daddy is going to take care of you. I'm going to make sure you're safe, you hear me?"

Caleb's head bobbed up and down.

"But you're going to have to do exactly what I say, when I say it. Can you do that?"

Another head bob.

"Even if you're scared?"

One more bob.

"Good." Devon hugged him again. He had no plan other than to look for an opportunity to kill Rico. When he found one, he'd have to act fast. Caleb would have to act quickly, too.

Devon stood and set Caleb on the bed. "Lock the door after me. Don't open it for anyone but me, got it?" He left and heard the lock settle into place behind him.

When he reached the living room, Rico was dressed in a jacket and boots. He looked stronger than he had in days. Maybe it was adrenaline, maybe purpose, but he seemed more alert, more dangerous than he had before. He nodded at Bob. "Let's roll him."

Together, they wound the body into the shag carpet that had lain in front of the fireplace. When they were done, Rico stood and gestured toward the front of the house. Devon began to pull the rug toward the door, but when they reached the kitchen doorway, Rico grabbed it and tugged in that direction. "This way."

It took both of them to get Bob over the threshold, through the kitchen and into the mudroom. They laid their burden down, and Rico threw open the mudroom door. Frigid air rushed in.

The evening was clear, all its moisture frozen. Devon stepped outside and saw Caleb's red plastic sled in the snow at the bottom of the steps. Rico reached past him, pulled the rug, and Bob thudded down the stairs, bouncing off each tread.

It was obscene. A toy that brought so much pleasure just two days ago—something caught in Devon's throat. He couldn't think about that now. He had to focus on the task at hand, had to find a way to kill Rico. *Kill Rico.* He repeated that in his mind like a mantra as they tied Bob to the sled. *Kill Rico.* It was Caleb's only hope.

Devon dragged the sled, and Rico came behind, knife in one hand, shovel in the other. The sled was so much heavier now than when he'd dragged Caleb up the hill the other day. Pulling his son hadn't been a burden, regardless of what he'd imagined at the time. This was a burden.

The snow field behind the house was bright in the fading light. They made their way across it, but before they entered the shadow of the woods, Rico paused and looked up at the sky. Two early stars glowed in sky. A moment later, he nodded as if interpreting a silent message, then plunged into the trees.

They walked for about five minutes before Rico said, "Here." Devon dropped the sled's rope and looked around. They stood in an open space between five pine trees. It was large enough for a man to lie down in. Rico handed him the shovel. "Dig."

Devon stared at the instrument. Its blade shone in a shaft of light that beamed through the branches of the pines. It was as if heaven was pointing the way. This was his opportunity. He took the shovel without haste, so as not to alarm his captor. A tremor rocked his hand—the only tell. He glanced at Rico to see if he'd noticed, but he stared through the opening in the trees above them.

Devon placed his boot on the end of the blade and shoved it into the snow. It wasn't a heavy shovel, but it was heavy enough. He would dig awhile, get used to its heft, and wait for Rico to be lulled into the rhythm of the job. His heart pounded with anticipation. He tried to channel the anxiety to prepare him for what he was about to do the way he did before a trial.

Several long minutes later, Rico still stared at the night sky. A constellation peeked through the trees. Maybe a piece of Orion? Devon wasn't sure, but it seemed to have captured the stranger.

He slowed the pace of his digging gradually, as if fatigue was catching up with him, which it was. The goal was to create enough time between shovelfuls to raise the tool above his head and down onto Rico's without the man noticing until it was too late.

He shoved into the dirt, then tossed the dirt behind him, counting beats between each effort—ten seconds, then twelve, then fifteen. At fifteen, Rico glanced at him. Devon paused and wiped the sweat from his brow. Rico's gaze returned to the stars. This was it. This was the moment.

Devon lifted the shovel as if to thrust it into the dirt but flipped it high into the air and brought it crashing down. Rico must have felt the wind whistling around him, because he ducked at the last moment and the shovel bounced off his shoulder.

Still, he was injured. Devon had heard the crack. But one second later, Rico righted himself, brandished the knife, and sprang forward. The blade, cold and sharp, ripped through Devon's jacket but he felt no pain. He raised the shovel again, but Rico was too close to strike.

Devon danced backward, holding the shovel like a baseball bat and swinging. It made contact, but not with Rico's head as he'd hoped. This time, it glanced off his other shoulder. Devon took another step back, rocked on a tree root, and fell. Rico was on him in a moment, holding the knife to his throat. "Don't move."

Devon stilled. Not for himself. His heart raced; anger flared hot within him. He would have gladly fought to the death at this moment, even if it meant they both died. But Caleb. He couldn't abandon Caleb to this monster.

Rico lifted his face to the sky. "I want to end this." He spoke as if he were asking permission. Several white breaths later, he took the knife from Devon's throat, stood, picked up the shovel, and pointed it at Bob's body. "Get him in the hole."

22

FIONA

The fog surrounding Fiona made everything surreal. Each passing minute could have been an hour or a year. Time was meaningless. She felt as if she'd been on the edge of the world forever and would be here forever.

She'd searched for signs for the Arrowhead turnoff for miles, but at some point, she'd given up. She was terrified to remove her gaze from the road and its disappearing and reappearing center line. Cold sweat trickled between her shoulder blades.

Something red flashed through the car. A split second later, it flashed again. As if waking from a dream, Fiona chanced a glance in her rearview mirror and saw an emergency vehicle light circling round and round, coming closer.

The relief she felt was akin to joy. She laughed out loud. "Help is coming, Crackers." She heard the thud of his tail on leather in the back seat.

A moment later, a San Bernardino County sheriff's black and white SUV pulled in front of her. The vehicle, with its high beams shining into the mist, took the lead. Within twenty minutes the white cloud turned gray then the red of a dying sun. The outside world returned in a blaze of sunset color. The sheriff's car had led her into Big Bear City.

Fiona pulled into a grocery store parking lot and plugged the cabin's address into her GPS. It was only minutes away. She was limp with exhaustion from the drive. A fire, food, wine, and her husband's arms sounded like heaven.

She navigated through the town and found the road to the cabin. Soon, it became dirt and narrowed to one lane. Devon had really wanted to get away from it all. This place was more secluded than she'd have chosen, but at this point, it was okay with her.

She almost drove past the house and would have if she hadn't noticed Devon's car parked in the driveway. There were no lights on. She pulled in behind him and turned off her engine. Uneasiness settled on her like ashes from a distant fire.

Why weren't the lights on? Where was the curl of smoke she'd expected to see floating from the chimney? The cabin appeared empty, but Dev's car was here.

Fiona opened the door, let Crackers out, then walked across the snowy yard to the porch steps. Crackers immediately ran into a stand of trees at the property's edge to take care of business. She needed to do the same, desperately.

As she climbed onto the porch, she saw a faint glow came from the back of the cabin as if a bedroom light was on. Maybe Devon was putting Caleb to bed? But why leave all the other lights off?

She tried the door handle. It turned. She pushed open the door and stepped inside. A moment later, Crackers bolted in past her. "Dev," she called into the darkened space, but there was no answer.

Crackers ran into the small living room and began sniffing an area of the floor near the cold fireplace. He whined. She couldn't tell if it was with excitement or dismay. Fiona toed off her wet boots, picked them up, and moved across the space silently in stocking feet toward the glow she'd seen from outside.

She'd been correct. It came from under a closed bedroom door, at least she assumed it was a bedroom. There were only three doors on the hallway—one closed, two opened. Thankfully, one of the open doors was an empty bathroom. She couldn't think straight until she used the toilet.

That done, she walked across the hall into the other open room.

Inside was a queen-sized bed flanked by rustic bedside tables that were topped with lamps carved into the shape of bears. Devon's suitcase was on a chair, his backpack leaning against the wall. She dropped her boots on the floor next to the bed and walked into the hallway again.

She turned the knob of the remaining door. It was locked. Her uneasiness grew. This entire night was so strange. Nothing had been as she'd imagined it. It was as if she'd passed through the fog and entered a parallel universe.

Fiona knocked softly on the door and spoke through the crack. "Dev?" Crackers joined her. He sniffed at the bottom of the door and began wagging his tail enthusiastically. Encouraged, she knocked and called louder. "Devon, are you in there?"

A thump, the patter of feet, a fumble at the door and her arms were suddenly full of sobbing boy. "Caleb, sweetie, what's wrong?"

"Daddy left." Was all she could get out of him.

She lifted Caleb into her arms, held him against her and rocked him until he quieted. "Talk to me, baby. Where did Daddy go?" she said as she deposited him on the bed.

Caleb wiped his eyes with the back of his hand. "Don't know."

Devon might not be Mr. Rogers, but she couldn't believe he'd leave Caleb alone unless there'd been an emergency. "Did he go with someone?"

Her son nodded. "Rico."

Rico, wasn't that what Dev had said Caleb called his Lego man? "Who's that, sweetheart? Who's Rico?"

Caleb's lip drooped, and a tear slid from his eye. "I don't like him."

A pinprick of fear trailed up Fiona's spine. Had *he* found them? She gave her head a small shake. No. He was dead. Sylla said he was dead. "Is he a neighbor, honey?"

Now Caleb's eyes filled with tears, and his mouth opened in a silent wail. She hugged him, and he screamed into her chest. What had happened here? Her son had been traumatized, that much was clear.

Something was very wrong here. All of her spider senses told her to get out. She'd take Caleb to town, then call 911 or go straight to the sheriff's station. She didn't like running when she had no idea where Devon was, but her first priority was her child.

"Come on," she said and took Caleb's hand. "Let's go."

"Daddy," he said.

"Daddy will be okay." She didn't know if this was true. "The policemen can come find Daddy," she added, more for herself than for Caleb.

They held hands and ran down the hallway toward the open front door, Crackers clicking beside them. As they drew closer to the kitchen, the dog stopped. Fiona stopped with him. A low growl rumbled in his chest.

She could feel a cold breeze through the halfway open door. She wanted to rush through it, but she trusted the dog's instincts. There was something dangerous ahead.

The low rumble grew in volume until it became a chain saw of sound. A shadow appeared on the wood floor between her and the exit. Caleb whimpered and pressed his face into her hip. "Who's there?" she said.

"Fiona." It was an anguished cry, but she recognized Devon's voice. "Fiona, run."

She snatched up her child and took a step toward the door, but something slid in front of it, blocking the light. A moment later, it shut with a thud.

The something took shape, a man's shape. A blade gleamed in his hand. Confusion fogged her thinking. For a moment, she believed it was Devon, that he had lost his mind or been possessed like Jack Nicholson in *The Shining*. Crackers' growl became a snarl, then a warning bark, his teeth white in the dim light, and the man laughed. It wasn't Devon's laugh.

"You must be Fiona," he said. "I've heard a lot about you." His hand moved toward the wall and flipped a switch.

Light flooded the room, blinding her for a minute. She blinked. When her vision adjusted, she saw the man before her clearly for the first time. He was tall, but gaunt, with a tangle of dark hair surrounding a very pale face. The beginnings of a beard hid his chin. "Who are you?"

"Name's Rico."

Devon stumbled into the foyer, and Fiona winced. His face was wild with fear, and blood stained his jacket. "Dev, you're hurt," she said.

"It's nothing. You need to leave. Take Caleb and leave." His voice was a rasp.

Rico waved the knife like a teacher's pointer. "Oh, I don't think so. I think you're both going to sit." He pointed toward the couch.

Fiona hesitated.

Rico moved so fast she hardly registered the motion. A second, less, and he had Devon, the knife to his throat. Crackers lunged, snapped, then backed into Fiona's legs, his ruff standing on end.

"Put your dog in the mud room first." The man jutted his chin toward the kitchen.

Fiona grabbed Crackers' collar and waited for the man to move out of her way.

"And don't think about leaving. Your husband is a dead man if you do."

Fiona hiked Caleb higher on her hip and tugged Crackers into the kitchen. Her gaze traversed the dirty linoleum floor, the laminate countertop and the outdated appliances, and came to rest on the door at the end of the room. She hurried to it. She set Caleb down, then squatted to hug Crackers. "I'll get you. Don't worry." She whispered the words to the dog, knowing he couldn't understand them. The promise was for herself.

After closing him in, she lifted Caleb and returned to the living room. Devon was on the floor near the fireplace. The man was bent over him. At first, she thought he was tending Devon's wounds, but when he stood, she realized he'd been placing plastic ties around her husband's wrists and ankles.

"He needs medical attention," she said.

"Be my guest."

She bolted to Devon's side, dropped Caleb next to him, and stared into his eyes. "What happened?" His answer was a shake of his head.

She unzipped his jacket, unbuttoned the green flannel shirt she'd thought so comical only days ago, and lifted the thermal shirt beneath that. The gash was an angry red, but it wasn't deep. Not nearly as bad as she'd imagined.

"I need my first aid kit," she said.

"Fine," the man said. He'd sunk onto the couch and was watching her. She moved to lift Caleb again, but he stopped her. "Leave him."

Caleb whimpered. She smoothed his hair from his forehead and gazed into his eyes. "You watch Daddy for me. Okay?" His lower lip quivered, but he cuddled next to his father.

Fiona jogged out into the night, into the freedom of the navy-blue sky and stinging air. It would be so easy to run if she weren't tethered to those she loved in the house. They anchored her to this place.

She popped the hatch of her car and rummaged around until she found the first aid kit Devon had bought for her when they'd purchased the Lexus. She'd laughed at him and said the bandages inside would be yellow before she used them. He'd spouted statistics about injuries and accidents.

The kit was still in its plastic wrap. She ripped at that as she walked to the house, dropping pieces of cellophane as she went. The man was blowing on a pile of kindling in the fireplace as she entered. Caleb had backed away from his father and pressed himself against the far wall. He gazed at Rico through terrified eyes. What had he seen with those gray-brown eyes?

Fiona dropped next to her husband and opened the kit. She swabbed the wound with peroxide first, and Devon gasped. His face blanched, and a sheen of sweat erupted on his forehead and upper lip. He needed stitches, but that was something she didn't know how to do.

After squeezing half a tube of antibiotic salve on the gap, she did her best to pull the skin together with butterfly bandages, then covered the whole thing with gauze and tape. When she was done, she pulled an afghan from a nearby chair over him and scooted next to her son.

"What is happening here? What do you want?" She kept her voice calm despite the racing emotions inside her.

"Just looking for a place to rest," the man said.

"We have money."

"I know you do. Your husband has very generously given me some of it."

"We have more. I can go to the bank in town tomorrow, make a big withdrawal. You can take one of our cars and leave."

Rico sighed. "I'd like nothing more, but I'm sure there are roadblocks on the 18 and the 38."

She hadn't seen one, but she hadn't seen much. There were only two roads in and out of the mountain communities. Two roads that were easy to watch. Since her half brother's body had been found on a fire road off the 18, she assumed he was correct. "Why did you kill him?"

The man's eyebrows rose. "Who? Chuck?"

Fiona frowned. She didn't know a Chuck. "My brother, why did you kill him?"

Rico gazed at the ceiling for a long moment. "It was a mercy killing," he finally said. "Chuck had the virus."

"I don't know who Chuck is."

"That's right." He turned his gaze on her and smiled. "That wasn't his real name, but that's what we called him. It was short for Two-Buck Chuck, you know, like the wine."

Ah, it made sense. Trader Joe's famous cheap wine. "He must have hated that."

"He got used to it."

They sat in silence for a long moment. This man had nothing against them, no vendetta, no animosity. He was simply a trapped animal who wanted freedom. If she could provide that freedom, perhaps he'd leave them in peace. What she needed now was a plan.

23

"I brought stuff to make pancakes," Fiona said. She was a beautiful woman. I'd forgotten how beautiful real women could be. She didn't have the plastic looks of the women on TV or the shiny looks of the women in the magazines. They weren't people. They were bait put on hooks by men to trap other men. Fiona was real.

"Pancakes are good," I said.

Even the boy perked up. He sat up straighter and ran a hand under his nose. "I like pancakes."

"Want to help?" she asked.

He nodded.

"I'll get the bags." She stood, and the child stood with her. I could see the resemblance now. I'd thought he looked like a lighter version of his dark-skinned Daddy, but he had a lot of her in him—the eyes that changed from hazel to gray, the freckles that sprinkled his nose like stars in a night sky.

"You stay here," I said to the boy. He dropped to the floor again, his brightness dimmed.

"I'll be right back," she assured him and left.

I wasn't worried about her running. Her whole life was here, in my hands. She wouldn't leave them behind.

A moment later, she returned, two grocery bags in her arms. I heard her drop them on the counter in the kitchen. Caleb's eyes followed the sounds hungrily. He wanted his mother. I couldn't blame him. I gave him a nod, and he scurried after her.

The father was sleeping—at least his eyes were closed and his breathing even. The attack with the shovel had been stupid on his part, but even stupider on mine. I was off my game. I'd blamed the virus, but it wasn't a valid excuse. I should be more vigilant because I'm under the weather, not less. Devon almost got the better of me.

I shook my head at the memory. Devon, with the pot belly, the soft hands, and the inflated ego, almost got the better of me. If he hadn't been wearing a green shirt, he'd have wound up in the hole alongside Bob. When I saw the color, I thought it might be a signal. You know, that he would bring me luck in the future. That I might need him for something else. The stars confirmed it.

I'd been too sure of myself. I hadn't been taking my signals into consideration, not enough anyway. But I was listening now. Didn't want to make that mistake again. It wasn't the first time my ego had almost gotten me killed.

When I was a kid, they called me Slap Hands because I beat everybody in this slapping game we used to play. One guy holds his hands out and the other rests his ever-so-lightly on top. The guy on the bottom has to flip his hands over and slap the top guy's hands. If the top guy pulls away before the bottom guy can whack him, they switch positions.

I was the champion of my neighborhood. They'd line up, and I'd take them out one by one, playing until my skin was red and bloody. I had the fastest hands around, and I was proud of it.

When we lived in Vegas, I used to watch the magic guys do their tricks on the street corners for spare change. I started thinking I'd be good at that because of my fast hands.

I saved up and got a magic kit. I learned to pull quarters out of kids' ears, hide marbles up one sleeve and have them come out the other, make playing cards disappear. My mother made a big fuss over me. I guess she liked it that I was doing something with my time besides getting into trouble. One day she pretended to pull two tickets out of my ear. They were for a big magic show at the MGM Casino.

I swear that show was a revelation. I'd thought I'd found my calling. I wanted to be a magician in a black tux, with beautiful girls prancing around me on stage. But Hal found out my mother spent money taking me to the show.

He tossed the house, slapped Mom around and threatened to smash my fingers if I didn't knock off the tricks. I learned right then and there not to attract attention, not to think more of myself than I ought to. My magic had to be the quiet kind. The only skill I focused on after that was making things disappear from the local liquor store.

I closed my eyes and listened to the chatter of the boy and his mother in the kitchen. She was putting on a brave face for him, and he was so happy to be with her he'd forgotten all about me. I understood now why Chuck hated her so much. She was everything he wasn't.

Her arrival had gotten me all confused. On the way back to the cabin from the shovel mishap, I'd pretty much decided I was going to kill Devon just as soon as I figured out what the green shirt meant.

After I got rid of him, I figured I could get the kid some cough medicine to make him sleep and take him with me down the hill. The cops might not recognize me with a kid in the back seat, but if they did, he was my wild card.

Now Fiona was here, and I didn't know what to think. Was she sent to be a help or a hinderance? Was she sent at all? She'd have been uncooperative if I'd dispatched her husband, and maybe that was why the green shirt stopped me. She was fierce, and she was loyal. He didn't deserve her.

I heard the sizzle of batter in the frying pan and opened my eyes. Devon was awake. He stared at me with a look that made me decidedly uncomfortable. He was like one of those zombies on the TV. One minute they're shuffling and pathetic, the next they're trying to rip your head off. Whatever I did, I'd have to do it soon. He was unpredictable.

"What do you want?" Devon's voice was a growl. "I gave you money. I can get you more, but I don't think that's going to satisfy you, is it?"

"I'm thinking it through," I said. "After that trick you played out in the woods, you're lucky to be alive."

"Why didn't you kill me?" He sounded defiant.

I grunted, but I didn't answer him. I wasn't going to tell him about my talismans, about the things the stars and colors and numbers spoke to me. That was my magic, and it was private. "Your wife is making pancakes."

"I asked you a question," Devon said. "What do you want?"

I gazed into his eyes for a long moment. They were black and dead in the dim light—zombie eyes. "Freedom," I said and pushed myself off the couch. "I'm going to check on the status of the pancakes."

24

DEVON

Devon watched Rico disappear into the kitchen and despair filled him like black sludge. Danger had just entered a small space with his wife and child, and he was helpless. He struggled against his bonds, a violent, useless gesture that did nothing but tear the skin around his wrists and cause a sharp pain where he'd been wounded. A moment later he felt wet warmth dampen his bandages.

He lay still, panting. This wasn't doing anyone any good. He had to think. His gaze skittered around the living room, seeking something to cut the ties at his wrists and ankles.

"Haven't had pancakes in years." Devon heard Rico talking from the kitchen. His voice was pleasant. "My mom used to make them for me, too." Devon assumed that was addressed to Caleb.

What was he doing? Trying to create a bond with his family? Caleb didn't answer, or if he did, it was so low Devon couldn't hear him. Caleb was terrified of Rico, and that comforted Devon somehow. Rico couldn't lull his child into believing there was no danger. Caleb knew Rico was a rattler, but Fiona didn't.

What if she didn't appreciate how dangerous Rico was? What if she didn't take the situation as seriously as she should? Devon hadn't. He'd been a fool.

That thought drove him to search the room for solutions again. The brick hearth caught his eye. It was low enough for him to reach with his shackled hands, and it was rough.

Devon lifted himself onto his elbows and paused, breathing deeply until the pain in his side passed. When it dulled, he scooted himself along the floor the few feet to the fireplace and fell against the bricks. He paused again waiting for the pain and nausea to pass. When they did, he lifted his wrists behind him, found the brick ledge and began to saw at the bonds.

"Why don't you sit and eat with me," Rico said. Devon heard the lust in his voice. He was attracted to Fiona. He wanted her.

A pipe burst in the basement of Devon's soul and panic flooded in. He wanted to scream, to rage, to beat his chest, race into the kitchen and put a fist into Rico's ugly face. He ground his teeth and sawed at the plastic tie with renewed strength.

"I'm still cooking." Fiona's tone was bland, as if she didn't hear his desire, but she did. Of that Devon was sure. They'd had conversations about this.

Fiona had both male and female clients and had learned to create hard and firm boundaries with certain ones. *Why do they think women who provide a service are available to service all their needs?* she'd said. They'd laughed, and Devon had offered to punch out the offender. She'd assured him she could handle things.

But could she handle Rico? He wasn't a stressed-out accountant looking for release, or a smarmy dentist craving a quick thrill with his Pilates instructor.

Devon began to sweat. The fire was hot on his back. He yanked at his ties again. The brick ledge wasn't sharp enough. It would take all night to saw through the plastic.

He looked over his shoulder into the flames. Could he melt it? A log crackled and spit behind the screen. If he could stand the heat, maybe. There was no way to put the ties into the fire without putting his wrists in with them.

A low laugh echoed across the kitchen tiles and into the living room. "I'll have another one of those pancakes," Rico said.

"Can I untie Devon so he can eat?" Fiona's voice held a rebellious note.

Rico laughed again. He'd never laughed this much before. "I don't think that would be a good idea."

"How's he going to eat?" she demanded. *Don't demand, honey. Play it cool.* Devon threw his thoughts at her.

"You can feed him if you want to." Rico, the big man, was going to let her take care of Devon. He raged at Rico's arrogance and shoved the fireplace screen aside with his shoulder.

Devon pushed himself up until he sat on the hearth then shoved his hands toward the flames. The heat was bearable for a moment, then he felt the burn. The pain quickly became so great it overwhelmed the pain in his side. It roared up his arms. Devon shut his eyes and held on.

One second passed, two, three, and he couldn't take it any longer. He pulled his wrists from the fire, but the heat remained. He was blinded by it for a several seconds. When he could see again, he yanked at his ties. They stretched like cheese on a pizza for a split second then hardened to a stop.

He inhaled and exhaled readying himself for another round in the fire, but an idea formed in his mind. Rather than shove his hands into the flames again, perhaps he could wiggle them through the stretched opening. He began to twist his wrists and pull. Each time the zip tie rubbed against his burned skin, he wanted to scream, but he kept on.

"Devon?"

He stopped, eyes snapping toward the sound of his name. Fiona stood in the kitchen doorway, a plate in her hands. "I brought you some food."

He gave her a wan smile.

She hurried across the room, set the plate on the fireplace and examined his wrists. She gasped. "What did you do to yourself?"

"I have to get out of these ties. I don't know what he's going to do next," Devon said.

"Not like this." Her words were a whispered hiss. "You're a mass of blisters."

"He likes you, Fiona."

She stood and walked to the bookshelf where she'd left the first aid kit. "I know." She knelt next to him again and began smearing antibiotic salve on his burns. It hurt almost as much as the fire had, but he didn't complain. The grease might help him pull his hands through the tie.

"You don't know him," Devon said.

"Not him, but people like him." She recapped the tube of antibiotic salve and reached for the roll of gauze.

"No gauze." Devon jerked his head toward the kitchen. "He'll see it."

She gripped the white roll and glared at him as if deciding whether or not she'd acquiesce. "He'll see the burns."

"He might not notice them."

She dropped the roll into the kit again. "Why did you do that? I'll find a way to help you. You need to trust me."

"You don't know what he's capable of. He killed a man. Bob. A neighbor. Just slit his throat."

She didn't look shocked. She picked up the plate and thrust the fork into a big bite of pancake. "He and my brother were friends. I guess I know how evil he is."

Devon ate obediently. He wasn't hungry, but he'd need his strength if they were ever going to escape. When he was done, Fiona took the plate and headed toward the kitchen.

"Fi," he said.

She halted and turned toward him.

"Watch yourself." He mouthed the words.

She gave him a quick nod and disappeared through the kitchen doorway. Devon was too exhausted by pain to work on his ties. Instead, he scooted down to the floor and rested his head against the bricks. He'd try again that night, after Rico fell asleep.

Ten minutes later, he was roused from a doze by the bump of a little boy against his chest. Caleb cuddled against his father, and Devon wished he could wrap his arms around him. "How're you doing, buddy?"

"Okay." Caleb's voice was small.

"Where's your mother?"

"In the kitchen with Rico."

Devon could hear the distress in his son's voice. "What's she doing?"

"Cleaning."

The clatter of dishes was proof of Caleb's words.

25

FIONA

The kitchen window wasn't well insulated, and frigid air leaked into the room, encasing Fiona in its web. She wasn't sure which was worse, the cold or the conversation. She'd sat across from Rico to learn more about him so she could bargain for their lives. Instead, she found herself asking about her half brother.

"You said before that Chuck's murder was a mercy killing. How do you know he was going to die?" she asked.

He raised a shoulder and let it drop. "He was sick. Real sick."

"Must have been inconvenient." She didn't try to keep the sarcasm from her voice.

Rico's face hardened. "I didn't think you cared about him."

"I don't. I didn't." Then why was she asking all these questions? Gwen had suggested she was obsessed. Maybe she was. She couldn't seem to let it go. "How did you do it?"

Rico blinked. "Why do you care?"

It was her turn to shrug. "Curiosity."

"Want to be sure he's really dead?"

"The police called me. I know he's dead." Anger flared inside her, and she slammed a hand onto the tabletop. "He killed innocent people.

He made my life a misery for months. He brought shame on my family. I want to know if he suffered at the end."

A smile cracked the solid blankness of Rico's face. "Revenge. That's what you want." It wasn't a question.

"What I wanted was for him to rot in prison for the rest of his life."

The stranger pushed his chair onto two legs, the smile widening. "You are not what I expected."

Fiona felt her cheeks grow hot. She wiped one of them as if she could erase the blush. "How would you know anything about me?"

"We were cell mates, me and Chuck. At San Quentin first, then in San Bernardino. He talked about you all the time."

She wanted to ask what he said, but she didn't want Rico to know she cared. She didn't want to care.

A flash of memory invaded the kitchen. She was twelve, sitting in her beautiful room in her beautiful home in Laguna Beach, the sound of ocean waves crashing outside her windows.

She was reading *The Lion, the Witch, and the Wardrobe,* fully immersed in Peter, Susan, Lucy and Edmond's adventures when the loneliness hit her. She lay the book down and gazed at the crown molding surrounding the ceiling. She had so much, but at that moment she'd have traded everything for a sibling.

If Chuck—as Rico called him—had come to her after their father had died, had explained what had happened, she'd have given him half her inheritance. She'd have been his family, and he could have been hers.

"He hated you, but I guess you know that," Rico said.

"The feeling was mutual," she said.

The front legs of his chair came down with a thump. "I think he had you all wrong."

"How's that?" Fiona's cheeks blazed again. It was as if some childish imp from her past had taken control of her tongue. She, adult Fiona, couldn't care less if Two-Buck Chuck hated her, but the little girl inside wanted answers.

"He said you were entitled and stuck-up, that you wanted everything for yourself." Rico ran a finger across the back of her hand.

She snatched it away and scrubbed it with her other hand.

His voice lowered. "I think you're a giving person. A very giving person."

The suggestion behind his words made her nauseous, but it woke her up. She'd sat down at the table with a purpose but had allowed the past to derail it. The present was treacherous and needed all her attention.

She touched the spice grater she'd shoved into her pocket to give to Devon when she could. It was a cold, hard reminder of the task at hand. Her job was to free her family.

"You're in a precarious position, and I'm willing to help." She forced a business-like tone into her voice and sat up straighter in her chair. "The police are looking for you, and I'm sure you want to head to the border or someplace safe?" The last two words of her sentence rose in question.

He nodded.

"I think the best plan is to leave Devon and Caleb here, and I'll drive you to the border in San Diego. We could stop for money on the way."

He reached a hand toward hers again. She dropped them off the table into her lap and out of his reach. His face tightened. "What would stop Devon from calling for help?" he said.

"Me," she said. "He'd know I was with you, that it would be dangerous for me if the police came after you."

He seemed to think that over for a moment, then shook his head. "Doesn't work. He doesn't trust me. He'd call the cops."

"We could take the phones."

Rico lowered his chin and looked at her through his lashes like she was an idiot. "He could walk to a neighbor."

"But we could explain to him—"

"No." The word was a blast. "That's not going to happen, Fiona." He separated the syllables of her name so it sounded like three names. "This is what we're going to do. You, me, and Caleb are going to head down the hill together."

Rico reached for the salt and pepper shakers and the syrup bottle sitting on the table. He lined them up making the space between them even. "I need three people."

She didn't understand, but she knew Caleb must stay here with Devon where he'd be safe. Fiona spread her hands wide, beseeching. "Caleb is a child. He won't understand."

"I'll hold Caleb under a blanket in the back," he continued as if she hadn't spoken. "He's my insurance that you'll do the right thing at the roadblock. If you do, things will go well. If you don't..."

"He'll be so afraid."

Rico's gaze left the condiments and met hers. "You'll have to explain it to him, then."

"It would be so much easier for everybody to leave him here with his father." She kept her tone light as if she was discussing plans for a dinner out.

"I want him with me."

She tried a different tack. "We can't leave Devon tied up. He's wounded."

Rico ran a tongue under his upper lip. "There's always another option."

A chill ran over her. She didn't want to hear that option.

"In fact, that could be the best way."

"No. You're right." She stumbled over her words. "Devon will be fine for a day or two. Caleb can take care of him." She grabbed the syrup, stumbled to the refrigerator, and put it away.

Crackers whined through the mud room door. She'd forgotten all about him, poor dog. Fiona poured dry food into one bowl, water into another and took them into the mud room. He whimpered and wagged his tail furiously between his hunched hind legs.

"Hey there," Fiona cooed as she pet his head. He ignored the food she'd set down for him and pressed himself against her instead. This moment away from the man in the kitchen was a welcome relief, but she knew she couldn't stay long.

Crackers' gaze focused on something over her shoulder and the rumble started in his chest again. The hair follicles at the back of Fiona's neck prickled—the reaction the result of a primal sense carried over from an early time. Somehow, she knew Rico was watching her. She rose and wiped her hands on her jeans placing herself between the dog and the man. She was afraid Crackers would attack and didn't want to think about what would happen to him if he did.

Rico stood in the doorway. He moved closer to her, so close she could smell syrup and stale coffee on his breath. "I like you, Fiona. Things will go easier for your family if you and I work together."

Pots and pans banged inside her, raising an alarm no one heard. "I… I…"

Crackers lunged. The only sound was the clack of teeth snapping at the air near Rico's leg. Fiona grabbed the dog's collar and hauled him back.

Rico eyed the animal dispassionately. "Control him, or I'll have to take him out back." The words were quiet, and she was sure he meant them. He turned and walked into the kitchen.

Please. The word rang inside her like a bell, resounding again and again, its reverberations circling like birds around a church steeple. *Please.*

She would bankrupt herself or kill or leave everything she knew to save her family, but *friendship* with Rico… Whatever that meant, she wasn't sure she could do that.

One last pet, and she closed the mud room door on Crackers. Rico had resumed his place at the kitchen table. He was reading something on Devon's phone and ignored her as she passed to go into the living room. She mumbled something about checking on Devon.

Her husband lay on the floor by the fireplace with Caleb nestled into the curve of his body. The child sucked his thumb, a habit they'd broken him of last year. A wave of love washed over her, raising a sob from somewhere deep within. She would do anything for them.

She knelt beside them and ran a hand through Caleb's hair. Devon's eyes opened. He gazed into hers but didn't speak. His face was flushed and feverish. "I'll put him into bed," she said. Devon nodded, and she lifted their son into her arms. Caleb's head lolled for a moment then fell heavily onto her shoulder.

Before she stood, she glanced behind herself. Rico hadn't followed her into the living room. In a swift movement, she slipped the spice grater from her pocket into Devon's back pocket. His eyes widened for a brief instant, but no words passed between them.

Fiona carried Caleb into the bedroom, nestled him under the blankets, then sat on the side of the bed. The thought of her innocent child huddled against Rico in the back of the car the way he had been huddled against his father filled her with an acid bath of emotions: rage, grief, helplessness, despair. She tried to isolate the rage and allow it to seep into her veins. The other emotions wouldn't help her now. What Rico wanted must never happen.

Except, perhaps, friendship. Another image filled her mind. She and Rico in the master bedroom. His lanky body, sweaty and foul, pressed against hers—a weapon in her hand. Perhaps she could make use of the common DNA she and Chuck shared, channel her inner psychopath. She'd read somewhere that there was a genetic component to psychopathy.

She stood. First, she had to find a weapon.

Fiona left Caleb's room and shut the door softly behind her, hoping her little one would sleep through the night and remain innocent of what would transpire. She glanced toward the larger bedroom. The door was open and faint moonlight glowed through the doorway. She walked toward it, thinking she might find something she could plant under a pillow or on the floor by the bed.

Before she stepped inside, she heard a growl, a sickening thud, and a cry of pain. She turned and ran to the living room. Rico, his face contorted in anger, stood over her husband, a spice grater in his hand. He drew his foot back and shot it into Devon's stomach. Devon cried out again.

"Stop!" Fiona bolted toward them and threw herself on the floor in front of Devon. "Stop. It's my fault. I put it in his pocket. He couldn't have gotten it himself."

Rico was transformed. The bland, sardonic expression he'd worn was gone. White showed all the way around his blue irises. His lips were bared, exposing yellowed teeth. His skin, normally so pale, was mottled purple, red, and white.

They stared at each for what seemed an eternity. Finally, Rico ripped a zip tie from a pile on the bookshelf, grabbed Fiona's wrists, and tied them together, pulling the tail so tightly she gasped. She didn't fight him. There was no point. He grabbed her by the back of her sweater, yanked her away from Devon, threw her into the easy chair, and tied her ankles.

He turned, paused by Devon's crumpled body, and launched another kick into him. As Rico stomped toward the front door, Devon vomited onto the pitted wood floor. The door slammed, and Fiona and Devon were alone for the first time since she'd arrived. She had so many questions, but Devon was too sick to answer them. He panted on his side, heaving bile between breaths. Fiona closed her eyes and tried to locate the rage she'd felt earlier, but all she found was despair.

26

The sky was clear. I turned in circles until I found Orion's Belt. *One, two, three,* I counted the stars. *One, two, three. One, two, three.* I counted them over and over until the hot, white anger inside me dimmed to yellow and finally red.

They were working together against me. I should have known they would. The woman only pretended she wanted to help me. She didn't want to help—it was a ploy to save her family.

I understood why she wanted to save the kid. She was a mother. Mothers should protect their children. That made me like her more, not less. But why the husband? He was useless and weak.

I walked across the field behind the house, my boots crunching through the thin crust of ice that lay on top of the snow. I had to calm down and think, find direction.

Getting angry at Fiona wasn't productive. I needed her to get past the roadblocks. I could use the kid to force her to do it, but I didn't want to. I didn't want to be like Hal. He'd enjoyed torturing my mother by torturing me.

I walked faster to escape the memories that threatened to crash over my head like a tsunami. I came to the edge of the woods and paused. If I walked between the trees, I wouldn't be able to see Orion's belt. But I had to walk between the trees to get to the car.

Things weren't happening the way I'd planned. First the bank wouldn't cooperate, then that cop came by, then Bob. When Fiona showed up, I thought maybe my luck was changing. How could I have been so stupid? She wasn't luck. He must have sent her.

I gazed at the belt one more time. It would be there whether I could see it or not. That thought fortified me. I plunged into the woods.

The moon made a patchwork quilt of the ground, lighting up a pile of dirt here, and a patch of snow there, leaving the rest in darkness. Something black flitted behind a tree ahead of me. I stopped and listened. There weren't many left, but there were still bears in these woods. Mountain lions too.

No sound. I moved ahead cautiously, knife ready in my right hand, but the shadows were still. Just as I began to relax, it happened again. Something dodged from tree to tree. I trained my gaze ahead where I'd seen the movement and tripped over a root.

I caught myself before I fell, and that's when I saw the neat pile of new dirt. This was where we'd buried Bob. He was restless. I paused, seeking a solution from the night sky. When it came, I searched the area, found three good sized stones, and lined them up equidistant on the grave. That would hold him.

I walked on more quickly now, wanting to put this whole thing behind me. The exercise and the altitude forced my breathing to become deep and regular. By the time I got to the clearing, I was in control of myself.

The Subaru was barely visible under the branches I'd thrown over it. I walked to the driver side door, wiped snow from the handle, and pulled it open. I smelled stale sweat and cheap cologne, just as I'd feared.

I leaned in and saw him. He lay on the back seat, curled into a fetal position, white-lipped and coughing. He acted like he didn't see me, but he knew I was there. "You were going to die, dude," I said aloud.

Chuck didn't answer.

"It was a mercy killing."

There was no response. I tried again. "Come on, man, don't be like that. Don't ignore me. I'm talking to you."

Chuck rolled onto his back and fixed his cold, cat eyes on me. I licked my lips. They felt dry and cracked.

"I'm sorry. Okay? I thought you were going out anyway. I swear it."

An owl cried in the distance, just like that night. I shivered inside my thick jacket and looked away. The cat eyes were making me nervous.

A moonbeam landed on a pine bough that hung over the car, lighting it up. The green was brilliant, St. Paddy's Day green, luck of the Irish green, four leaf clover green. It was a good sign. I never met my father, but my mother told me he was Black Irish. I liked that. Black Irish. It sounded wild and dangerous.

I looked at Chuck again. He was sitting up now, still wearing that dragon T-shirt. "What do you want me to do with your sister?" I said.

He didn't move.

"You still pissed at me?"

No answer. I was starting to get frustrated.

"I'm trying to do the right thing here."

His head pivoted on his neck. It was an unnatural gesture. More owl than man. His eyes beamed in the black interior of the car like the light of a projector streaming through a dark movie theater.

We stared at each other for a long minute, images playing on the screen of my mind. When he was done, he closed his eyes and lay down again. I shut the car door and trudged to the house. I knew what I had to do.

27

DEVON

Devon's cheek was pressed into the floorboards, the smooth wood cooling his flaming face. He might be sick, or it could be an infection from the knife wound. Either way, the better Rico got, the worse Devon felt. The man was sucking the life from him.

Why not? He had everything else—Devon's money, his phone, the cabin. His family.

The smell of vomit rose like a noxious gas from the pool on the floor. He scooted as far away from it as he could get, wishing for a glass of water with every fiber of his being.

"Dev?" Fiona said from her place on the chair.

He dampened his dry mouth and said, "Yeah."

"How bad is it?"

"I think he broke a rib." He knew what that felt like. Devon had broken two ribs in a Frisbee football match when he was in college. He'd been proud of that injury. He left off the word "Frisbee" in the retelling. Football sounded better on its own. He grunted a laugh at the memory, and instantly regretted it.

"We have to get out of here," Fiona said.

He wanted to laugh again but knew it would hurt too much. "How do you plan to do that?"

She didn't say anything for a long time. "He's... He wants..." She couldn't make herself finish her sentence, but he knew what she was trying to say.

"No." He gave the word as much husbandly weight as he could manage.

"I might not have a choice—"

He cut her off. Suddenly he was in the court room, intoning his closing argument. "You always have a choice. You can run. You can fight."

"You didn't let me finish."

There was no sound but the crackle of the fire for a long moment. "Okay," he said.

"I could find something, a lamp, a doorstop, something heavy. When he's... you know... I could hit him."

The thought of that man, with his chipped, bitten, filthy fingernails, touching his wife almost made Devon throw up again. "That's a terrible plan," he said.

"You have a better one?"

"I'm gonna get these ties off. My hands were halfway out when he found that thing you put in my pocket."

"The spice grater?"

"Is that what that was?"

"Yeah." She paused. "Sorry."

"For what?"

"I shouldn't have put it in your pocket."

Devon rolled onto his back and a fire lit in his rib cage. He wasn't sure if it was the knife wound or the broken rib, but he guessed it didn't matter. White lights danced in front of his eyes for several seconds. He didn't try to speak until they dimmed. "Yes, you should have put it in my pocket. This doesn't matter. Injuries don't matter. Death and rape—those matter."

"I'm not going to let him hurt Caleb, even if it means death or rape." There was no indecision, no room for argument, in her statement.

Devon drank in oxygen as he mulled over the situation. He searched for a precedent. Something from his past he could use in the present, but he couldn't think of a thing. He'd never experienced anything like this.

He'd had clients who'd lived for years with abusive spouses, trapped and fearing for their lives. He'd always said the right things, been sympathetic, supportive, encouraging. Told them they were strong and brave, that they had what it took to stand up to their abusers. But inside, tucked into a place he didn't often look, he'd thought they were weak.

If they weren't weak, they'd leave, right?

By that standard, he should have told the sheriff about the man in the kitchen with his kid. He should have let Bob know what was going on. Why hadn't he?

Caleb. It was always Caleb.

The women he'd defended, the ones who didn't leave until a friend or neighbor reported what was happening, they had kids. They'd been willing to sleep with the enemy for their children's sakes. Now that he had an inkling of what they'd gone through, he couldn't imagine that kind of courage. He was the weak one. His wife was courageous, like those women.

He turned his head to look at Fiona. "I love you."

"I love you, too."

"And you're right. We have to think about Caleb first."

"Yes." The word slipped from her lips without thought.

"How do we save him?"

"I look for a weapon. You work on the zip tie."

"We both look for an opportunity."

"Yes."

Talking took more energy than Devon had. He lay down again and rested while Fiona laid out her plan. As he listened, he made a vow. He would get loose, even if he had to put the tie into the fire again. And once he got loose, he'd wrap his burned and bloody hands around Rico's neck and squeeze until the life was gone from his eyes.

28

FIONA

Rico slammed into the house, bouncing the front door against the wall. Fingers of cold snaked across the floor and wrapped around Fiona's legs. He strode into the room and looked from Fiona to Devon and grunted.

They were where he'd left them. Fiona had made sure of that. She wanted him to believe they were beaten, ready to compromise. "It's cold," she said making her voice as high and childlike as she could.

He glared at her for a long second, then walked to the door and shut it. "Where're your boots?" he said.

Fiona and Devon shared a confused glance. "Mine?" she asked. "Or Dev's?"

"Dev? Is that what you call him? That's very sweet, a little nickname." Sarcasm dripped from his words.

There was nothing to say to that, so Fiona didn't speak.

"Where are your boots, Fi-o-na?" He said her name in that way she hated. He was still angry. She could feel it coming off him in waves, but now it seemed to be directed at her rather than at Devon. "They're in the bedroom," she said.

She hated using the word 'bedroom' in his presence, but that's where she had to lead him.

Rico walked to her chair and pulled his knife from his pocket. Adrenaline shot into Fiona's bloodstream. She pushed away from him, trying to bury herself in the cushions.

He bent, sliced through the ties at her ankles and wrists, then stepped away. The relief was so great, she became light-headed. "I have to go to the bathroom." She didn't, but she wanted a moment to think, to plan her strategy.

He jerked his chin in the direction of the hallway. She stood on wobbly legs, feeling the blood rush to her feet.

She hurried to the bathroom and closed the door behind herself. She scanned the small room for a weapon. Nothing.

She flushed, turned on the tap and began opening and closing cupboards and doors. No razors. That would have been too good to be true. No alcohol or peroxide or anything she could toss in his face. No leftover prescription sleeping pills she could add to his coffee.

All she found was a bottle of hand soap, a couple of yellow bandages, and a flat tube of antibiotic salve. His years in prison must have given him an eye for anything that could be used to harm another person.

"You coming?" he bellowed through the door.

She rinsed her hands quickly and reemerged. He stood in the hallway gazing down at her. Something had shifted in him—she wasn't sure what it was. "I'll get my boots." She gave him a tentative smile. He didn't return it.

She turned toward the master bedroom, and he followed. As they passed Caleb's door, Fiona offered up a silent prayer. *Please.* She didn't think she needed to elaborate.

They entered the bedroom together. Rico leaned against the door frame, and she retrieved her snow boots from the floor and sat on the bed. Her gaze skated around the room and landed on the backpack. Bear spray. Devon had packed bear spray, but how could she get to it?

She glanced around her again, and her gaze fell on the bedside lamp. It was a rustic thing—a bear carved from a piece of wood and varnished a deep brown. It should be heavy enough to do damage if she could bring it down hard enough. The bear spray would be a more efficient weapon, but the lamp was out in the open.

She pushed a foot into her boot and made a show of fumbling with the laces. "I need help. My hands are still numb from being tied," she finally said. Rico grunted and crossed to her. He knelt and began lacing up the boot.

Fiona's heart crept into her throat. She swallowed hard. "Maybe we should wait until morning to leave." Rico didn't respond. Instead, he grabbed the other boot and held it for her.

"We could rest for a bit." She placed a hand on the plaid bedspread and smoothed it.

Rico tied the laces of the second boot. Why was he disinterested in her all of a sudden? Had she read him wrong? She was sure he'd been coming on to her in the kitchen earlier.

She reached down and grabbed his hand. "I want to help you," she lied.

Rico snatched his hand away and rose. His jaw worked for several seconds, as if he was chewing his words before spitting them at her. "It doesn't matter what you want. Doesn't matter what I want."

Confusion furrowed her brow. What did he mean? "What you want doesn't matter?"

"Not now. Not yet." She saw a flash of something hot in his eyes, but he hooded them before she could be sure if it was the lust she'd seen earlier. "Let's go," he said.

She tried one more time. "Sit with me for a minute." She'd intended the words to sound sultry, but her voice wavered too much for sultry. The effect was more pathetic than sexy.

He stood as still as the bear on the lamp base for a long moment, then his hand snaked out. He grabbed Fiona by her hair, yanked her to her feet, and shoved her into the hallway.

She lurched ahead of him into the living room. Devon watched her enter with wide, fearful eyes. She gave him a quick shake of her head. *No, the plan didn't work.* His jaw tightened in understanding.

"The kitchen," Rico said.

Fiona walked toward the doorway. "You want me to fix something for you?" she said in a small voice, but she didn't think that's what he wanted. He seemed to be on a mission.

He shoved her across the linoleum toward the mudroom. Crackers was in there. Had he forgotten about the dog? He must have, because he reached around her and threw open the door.

Crackers launched himself at Rico. The man yelled and jumped behind Fiona, but the dog ducked between her legs and latched onto his shin.

Rico cursed loudly and kicked the dog off. Crackers hit the doorframe but was up and at him again. The dog snapped and snarled and feinted every time Rico tried to grab him. Fiona saw something glint in the man's hand. The knife.

Rico lunged for the dog, knife held low. Fiona lifted a booted foot and kicked it across the room. It spun in circles and came to a stop under the table. Rico watched its path, then turned his rage on her. He lifted an arm and backhanded her across the face. Fiona hit the wall.

With a guttural growl, Crackers flew at the arm that had struck her and sank his teeth into it. Rico made a fist with his free hand and punched the dog's head. Fiona heard the crunch of bone on flesh, but she couldn't help Crackers, not now. This was the opportunity she and Devon had promised they'd look for.

"I'm sorry," she whispered, and began to crawl toward the living room. Caleb needed her, and she needed Devon. She would get his ties off, even if she had to chew through them. Together they could overcome Rico.

She heard a scream of pain and a slam, and a moment later rough hands lifted her to her feet. Rico's face was altered almost beyond recognition. Rage made him appear more monster than man.

She shrank away, but he yanked her arm and strode toward the door in wide strides. She stumbled after him. As they plowed through the kitchen, she caught a glimpse of a still, black bundle of fur lying near the stove. A sob rose in her throat.

Rico pulled her through the mudroom. She didn't resist. What was the point? Grief dropped like a weighted blanket onto her shoulders, and tears sprang into her eyes. She should never have brought the dog to Big Bear. He was her responsibility, and she'd failed him, just as she'd failed Devon and Caleb. This was all because of her, because of her family, her half brother.

When they stepped outside, the cold slapped her face. The sting was a reproof. She had no time for self-pity, or self-hatred. She could become an alcoholic or a prescription drug abuser later, if she lived that long. Now, today, her husband and her child needed her. Her job was inflict as much damage on this man as was humanly possible. To do her best to save them.

The moonlight reflected on the blanket of snow between the house and the woods. It was brilliant and frigid. As they trudged across it, she was thankful for her boots but wished Rico had also given her time to get her jacket. The air that had revived her now worked its way through her flesh and into her bones. She began to shiver. Where was he taking her?

When they reached the tree line, Rico paused and tipped his head toward the sky. Fiona followed his gaze. Pinpoints of light dotted the charcoal night. The stars told a story. Ursa Major, the big bear, was high in the sky. Below him, Orion, the hunter, wielded his sword. Their placement gave the impression that the bear was sneaking up on the unwary hunter.

An image of the bear-shaped bedside table lamp popped into her head. She would have laughed if she hadn't been so cold and so grieved. Her bear hadn't helped her at all. There'd been no surprise attack. The hunter had taken her captive. A second later, they plunged into the woods, and the stars were snuffed out by tree branches.

It was more difficult now to keep up with Rico. She fell against him and righted herself more times than she could count as they struggled across roots and rocks. At one point, they passed a mound of dirt that looked like a freshly dug grave. She stared at it as long as she could, trying to decide if her imagination had created the grisly idea or if it was what it appeared to be. Rico yanked her hard, and she turned her gaze to the dark ground again.

Eons later, he pulled her to a stop. As she caught her breath, she took in her surroundings. They were in a small clearing. Moonlight peeked between the trees, spotlighting its center, but the edges lay in shadow. A strange shape, half in and half out of a gloomy corner caught her eye. It was a mountain of branches. It looked as if a deluded beaver had built the Taj Mahal of dams where there was no water. She was afraid of it, but she didn't know why.

Rico walked slowly toward the mound, dragging her after him. He yelled into the dark, "I brought her."

A bolt of fear shot down her spine. Who was he talking to? Who wanted her? And for what? No one answered him, so her questions went unanswered as well.

As they drew closer, the shape of the dam-thing became clearer. It looked like a car covered by tree limbs. Was someone inside it? Fiona was shaking hard, whether from cold or fear or both, it was impossible to tell.

"Did you hear me?" Rico said.

She gazed at him but could see he wasn't addressing her. A bar of metal shone silver in the dim light. He reached out a hand, grabbed it and pulled.

29

DEVON

Devon thrust his wrists into the fire, but had to draw them out a second later. Black blotches appeared before his eyes, obscuring his vision. Nausea rose into his throat. A cold sweat broke out on his forehead.

Sometime later, he opened his eyes and stared at the pocked white ceiling of the cabin. He'd passed out. He was dehydrated after his vomiting attack. His limbs and face were blazing with fever, and the pain must have become too much.

He pulled at the tie, thinking it might be malleable enough to stretch from the few seconds he'd had it in the heat, but it was no use. In the time he'd lain on the floor unconscious, the plastic had hardened again.

He struggled against it and felt the hard ridges shave his blistered skin. The black spots and nausea returned, and he had to stop. Devon squeezed his eyes shut. The tears that had gathered in them slid onto his cheeks. He'd never felt so helpless in his life.

His wife, his beautiful, courageous wife, had been dragged into the night by a murderer, and he couldn't help her. He was never there when she'd needed him. Wasn't that the story of their lives?

He hadn't been there when she'd gone into labor with Caleb. He'd been in court and had only made it into the delivery room when she'd begun to push. He hadn't been there when she'd gotten the news that a corpse had been found in the upstairs bedroom of her father's house. He hadn't been with her in the courtroom during her half brother's trial. She'd said she didn't want him there, but he should have gone anyway.

He'd told himself, and anyone who'd asked, that she didn't want him there, which was true. It was also true that he hadn't wanted to go. He'd been too busy sorting out someone else's family drama.

Facts dropped into Devon's heart like leaves from a fall tree. Each memory, each admission alone wouldn't convict him, but the pile was great. The truth was he liked *the idea* of being a husband and a father. He liked showing up to social occasions with Fiona on his arm, showing off his adorable son. He liked the way his wife and son made him feel, the way Fiona took care of him. He'd thought all those things were love.

They weren't.

Love would have been there the moment she'd gone into labor, would have rushed home when the body was found, would have sat in the court room next to her and held her hand.

This trip was a perfect example of his selfishness. He'd thought he was being such a splendid example of a father, taking his son away for a weekend. He hadn't wanted Fiona along, not because he'd wanted to give her a break. No, the truth was he'd wanted to prove what a great dad he was. It was a joke.

A roar, half anger, half grief erupted from his mouth. He strained at his ties again, embracing the punishing pain.

A small shadow appeared in the hallway. "Daddy?"

Devon choked back his anger. He tried to make his voice calm and steady. "Hey, Caleb."

Caleb came closer but stopped on the other side of the puddle of vomit. "Are you sad, Daddy?"

Devon almost said no, but he stopped himself. He was too tired to keep up the charade, too tired to lie. "Yeah. Yeah, I am, buddy."

His little boy skirted around the mess, sat on the other side of him, and rested his head against Devon's chest. "Why?"

"I'm sad, and I'm mad because I'm all tied up."

"Did Rico do that?"

"Yup," Devon said.

"I don't like him."

"Me either."

They sat that way for a long minute, then Devon had an idea. "Caleb?"

Caleb sat up and looked at his father.

"Can you go into the kitchen and get the box of matches on top of the stove for me?"

His son's brow furrowed. "I not allowed."

"It's okay, just this once because Daddy's asking you to."

Caleb thought this over for a moment, then popped up and slid across the floor in his footie pajamas. Devon heard the scrape of a chair across linoleum, a grunt, and his son appeared again carrying the box of wooden matches.

"Good job," he said. "Now take one out of the box."

Caleb slid the box open and carefully pulled out a match. He held it out to his father.

"I can't take it from you, son. You're going to have to light it for me." Caleb would have to light it and hold it against the plastic tie at his wrists, not easy tasks even for an almost four-year-old.

The child's eyes grew wide. "How?"

"You see that white tip on the end?"

Caleb nodded.

"You just rub it across the bricks here, and it will light up."

It didn't. The first four matches broke against the fireplace as Caleb attempted to do what his father said. Now there were only three left in the box. The seedling of hope that had sprung up inside Devon began to wilt. "Better hold off there, buddy." He leaned against the bricks and thought.

As they sat in silence, Caleb picked up one of the match heads that had broken off and threw it into the fire. It flared for a moment, then was engulfed in the larger blaze. He gazed at it with surprised eyes, picked up another piece, and threw that into the fire with the same results.

"Caleb." Devon heard the excitement in his own voice. "I have another idea. You'll have to be brave, but I think you can do it."

"Brave?"

"Yes. Did you see how the match head flared in the fire?"

"Yeah."

"I want you to hold onto one of the long matches and put just the tip into the fire. We can light the match that way."

Caleb pushed his lips to one side of his face and slowly turned his head from side to side. "I don't think so."

Devon kept his voice calm. "It'll work, Caleb."

"I scared."

The movie of Fiona being dragged from the room that had been replaying in Devon's mind, played again. "For Mommy, Caleb. Mommy needs us, and I can't help her unless you help me."

Caleb stared into the box for a long moment, then picked up each of the matches one by one, examining them. After what seemed an eternity, he chose a match that looked exactly like the others to Devon. He pinched the far end of it in his chubby fingers and moved it toward the fire.

It lit with a whoosh of flame. Devon was about to cheer when Caleb dropped it into the fireplace, his lower lip drooping crookedly. "I sorry."

Devon glanced into the box. Now there were only two matches left. "It's okay, buddy. We can try again, but you'll have to be really careful this time. Can you do that?"

Tears welled in Caleb's eyes, but he took another match from the box. He put it in the fire more quickly this time, and when it flared, he pulled it out and held it at arm's length.

"Good job, buddy." Devon pivoted so his hands were in front of his son. "Now hold the fire on the plastic tie. Can you do that?"

A second later Devon felt heat against his skin. He waited for a moment then began to gently work the tie. He felt it loosening.

Too soon, Caleb dropped the match on the wood floor. "It burned."

The tie had stretched far enough for Devon to slip his hands out as far as his thumbs, then they stuck. "We have one more match," he said. "Let's do it again."

Caleb swallowed and grabbed the last match with solemnity. They went through the same ritual, and this time the plastic tie stretched and broke. Devon whooped, pulled his wrists free and threw his arms around his son. "We did it."

Caleb was grinning now. "Let's get Mommy."

Daddy has to get his feet free first," Devon gazed around the living room searching for some-thing to sever the ties. His gaze fell on his jacket hanging on a hook by the front door. His pock-etknife. He'd forgotten about it until this moment. "There's a knife in my jacket pocket." He pointed. "There, by the front door. Can you get it for me?"

Caleb trotted to the where the jacket hung. It took him several tries before he was able to pull the coat down so he could reach into the pockets. He returned a moment later with the knife held in front of him like a torch. Devon took it, pulled it open, and ran a thumb along the edge—not sharp, but rough now, after cutting snowman arms.

Two minutes later, the ankle tie split and Devon was free.

He gazed at his child. Fiona would want him to take Caleb and run. She would want him to leave her if he could save their son.

He couldn't do it.

He wouldn't do it.

"Come with me." He reached out a hand, took Caleb into the bedroom, then upended the boy's suitcase onto the bed. He pulled a pair of snow pants, a thick sweater, and thermal socks from the jumble of clothes. Then he limped into the living room and took Caleb's jacket, hat, mittens, and boots from the front hall and brought them back with him.

"I'm going to go find Mommy," he said. "While I'm gone, I want you to put all these clothes on. Can you do that?"

"Yes," Caleb said.

"Put your boots on, too. You need to be ready to go out in the snow as soon as we get back."

The solemn expression returned to Caleb's face, and Devon got a glimpse of the man his boy would grow into. "Okay," Caleb said.

"Lock the door behind me."

After Devon heard the lock click, he shuffled to the living room, put on his own boots and jacket, then headed toward the kitchen. A streak of red was smeared across the stove front and on the floor next to it. He stopped for a moment, the color a stark reminder of the danger he was facing. He'd heard what he'd thought was the dog's death. Apparently not.

The knowledge that Crackers was alive and had escaped gave him hope. Not a big, brass band kind of hope, just a single flute song of hope, but it was more than he'd had before.

Devon thrust the small pocket knife into his jacket pocket again. It was a feeble weapon compared to the butcher knife Rico carried, but like the faint melody of hope within him, it was something.

The mud room door opened and slammed closed like a bellows fanning chill air into the house. Devon shut it firmly behind himself and walked out into the freezing night.

30

FIONA

Rico leaned into the car and addressed someone in the back seat. "She's here. Just like you wanted."

He cocked his head to one side as if he were listening to a response Fiona couldn't hear. He straightened and began to shift the branches that covered the car until he uncovered the door handle for the rear seat. With more shuffling of branches, the door opened with a loud creak. He looked at her. "Get in."

Fiona couldn't move. The paralysis of a nightmare had taken over her limbs, and they refused to obey. Not that she wanted them to get inside the car. No, she wanted them to run, fast and far in the other direction, but her body wouldn't cooperate.

"I said, get in," Rico repeated.

Adrenaline hit her like a shot of whiskey, she reconnected with her feet, turned, and ran. In two long strides, Rico was on her, knocking her to the ground. "I don't think so."

He lifted her to her feet and dragged her toward the car. Panic, blind and thoughtless, surged through her. She fought with fingernails and teeth, twisting in his grasp with all her strength, but his grip was a steel trap.

He placed a hand on her head and shoved her down into the backseat of the car like a cop making an arrest, then slammed the door shut. She hugged the door, terrified to see who or what was in this tiny space with her. Every boogie man from every childhood terror paraded in front of her eyes. She expected claws to rip her from the door, teeth to tear her apart, but nothing happened.

Minutes passed in cold silence. Finally, Fiona pivoted on the seat, still pressing herself against the door, and gazed around the car's interior. Her pulse began to slow, her breathing grew regular. There was no one there. She was alone.

She pushed herself away from the door and leaned over the front seat. Nobody there either. There was nowhere else to search. She was the only person, alive or dead, in the vehicle. What had Rico been playing at? Had he been trying to scare her?

"She's all yours," she heard him holler at the car.

Steven King's *Christine* floated through Fiona's thoughts. Did Rico believe the car had thoughts, a personality? Was he offering her as a sacrifice to a gas-guzzling god?

He was delusional. That was the answer to all her questions. Rico was delusional.

This understanding brought both fear and hope. Fear, because delusional people were also unpredictable. Hope, for the same reason. She had no idea what he'd do next.

He might march away, leaving her at the car's mercy, in which case she could wait ten minutes and leave. Or he might... Might what? The only way to know would be to enter into his delusion, and that would be as terrifying as it was impossible.

Metal screeched behind her, and she spun in her seat. The car windows were completely covered in pine needles. She was blind to the outside world. Rico must be getting something from the trunk. A moment later, she heard a thump. He'd closed it.

Her pulse was thudding in her ears. She inhaled and exhaled deeply, trying to still it. She needed to hear what he was doing. A long moment later, she heard a splash, as if he was throwing water against the car. Why... *God, no.* She smelled gasoline. It wasn't water; it was gas.

Fiona reached for the door and yanked at the handle. It wouldn't budge. She was locked in. Childproof locks maybe.

She threw herself at the front seat, toppled over it, and reached for the driver side door. The handle lifted and the door popped open, then stopped. She pushed again. It didn't budge.

He'd barricaded it with something.

Liquid splashed against the passenger side of the car. The smell inside grew stronger. Fiona flew into a frenzy. She battered the door with her hands, pushed herself away from it, and kicked it with her feet until the interior fabric and plastic ripped and dented. The door remained shut.

The locks. Why hadn't she thought of that? She pressed the child-proof lock button and darted to the passenger side of the car. It wouldn't open. She fell over the seat into the rear of the car and tried both doors. No good. He must have done something to the locks.

She climbed up front, pushed every lock button again and again, but heard no responding click. He'd jammed them somehow. Only the driver side door was unlocked, but it only opened a few inches.

Think. She had to think. What could be holding the door closed? If she knew, she might be able to work it free.

She lay on the seat, brought her face close to the opening, and peered through. One end of a thick tree limb had been dug into the snow and dirt outside. The other end was propped against the door. All she had to do was knock it aside.

Her gaze skittered around the interior of the car. What could she use? The vehicle was new and very clean. It had none of the detritus of motherhood that she toted around. No sippy cups, no children's books, no toys or crumbled Goldfish.

She dropped to the floor and searched under the driver's seat. Nothing. She moved to the passenger seat and saw a dark, oblong shape in the far recesses of the space. She reached under the seat but couldn't grab it. She shoved her arm forward, scraping her skin on the seat adjustment bar. This time, she felt fabric brush against her finger-tips, but that was as far as she could reach.

Fiona jumped to the rear seat, thinking she might be able to grab the item from there, but there wasn't enough room between the seat back and the floor for more than a finger. The object was too fat to fit.

She climbed up front again, flattened herself on the floor, and thrust her arm as far under the seat as she could. She felt like a vet she'd once seen in a video who had shoved an arm inside a cow to deliver a calf. The long metal bar on the underside of the seat dug into her shoulder painfully. She grimaced, just as the vet had done, but she pushed until she could just pinch the fabric between the pointer and middle fingers of her right hand. The grip was tentative, but she had it. She sucked in her breath and drew the object toward herself, inch by inch.

The odor of gas was so strong now her eyes began to tear. She squeezed them shut. Without her vision to guide her, the thing got stuck on the bar, and she lost it momentarily. She flapped her hand around, found it, gave one last pull, and the passenger seat gave birth to a compact umbrella. She held it up, tears cascading down her cheeks from both joy and gasoline fumes.

Fiona shoved the umbrella through the crack in the driver side door and whacked at the air. In it's compressed state, it was too short to reach the branch. She brought it inside, elongated it without opening the top, then shoved it outside again.

It bounced against the branch this time, but she didn't have enough leverage to knock it down. She hadn't heard the sound of sloshing gasoline in at least a minute. In fact, she hadn't heard anything outside the vehicle. A vision of Rico snapping on a lighter played in her mind. She had to get out of this car, and she had to do it now.

As she pulled the umbrella back to try again, her elbow struck the seat adjustment lever. *The seat adjustment lever.* Of course, she hadn't been thinking straight. She grabbed the lever, slid the seat back as far as it would go, thrust the umbrella through the opening and whacked the branch with all her strength. It hit the ground with a thud, the door swung open, and Fiona fell onto the snowy dirt.

She lay there for a moment, catching her breath and listening for Rico, but heard nothing. Where was he? She slid onto her stomach and pressed herself onto her knees, eyes scanning her surroundings.

His booted feet were planted behind the vehicle, his stance wide. The car hid the rest of him from view, which was good. If she couldn't see him, he couldn't see her. Fiona crept on hands and knees toward the front of the car and the dark shadows beyond. Maybe he wouldn't notice she was gone. Maybe he would light the car on fire believing she was still inside.

Everything in her wanted to stand and run as fast as her exhausted, wounded body would go, but she resisted the urge. Slow and silent were her best hope of escape.

Seconds seemed like hours as she put one knee in front of the other, inching her way to the dark woods. When she reached the tree line, her shin hit a pine cone that had been hidden by the snow. It cracked loudly in the quiet night. She froze.

Several long seconds later, she continued her crawl. He hadn't heard, or he'd assumed it was a passing animal. Either way, he hadn't come to investigate. Once Fiona passed five large pines, she felt safe enough to stand.

The escape had led her to the wrong end of the trail. The cabin was on the opposite side of the clearing. Keeping the car on her left, she moved as quietly as she could back the way Rico had dragged her.

Every footfall echoed in her ears. The crunch of ice, the swish of fabric against fabric, her breath, all sounded like the opening of an orchestral moment to her ears, but he must have been so intent on what he was doing he hadn't noticed.

The farther Fiona got from the clearing, the lighter she felt. She was almost giddy at her escape. She'd heard people describe the joy that comes when they faced death and defeated it, but she'd never experienced it until now. Happiness bubbled inside her like an open bottle of champagne.

Logically, she knew this was foolish and premature. Her would-be killer wasn't far behind, he was still armed, and he would return to the cabin eventually. *He'll think I'm dead, though.* She grinned at the thought. As far as Rico was concerned, she'd be a ghost. She jogged forward, anxious to find Devon and Caleb and get away before Rico discovered the truth.

She replayed her victory moment, the swipe with the umbrella that gained her freedom, and stumbled on a tree root. The umbrella—she'd left it lying in the dirt. She'd also left the car door open. He'd be sure to see those things, then he'd know.

The fragile joy she'd felt disappeared as quickly as it had come. He would come after her. He might be tracking her right now.

Fiona shot a glance to the right and another to the left. She needed to get off the trail, hide in the woods. He'd expect her to run straight to the cabin. She had to do the unexpected. Defying every bit of advice she'd ever heard about hiking in the woods, Fiona darted off the path and into the brush.

Her plan, if it could even be called a plan, was to find a vantage point where she could watch the path. He'd return to the cabin for Devon and Caleb. Even in his psychotic state, she was sure he'd do that.

She searched the ground for a downed tree limb. She hefted one but discarded it, then settled on another. It was the right weight, heavy but not too heavy. The branch would serve as a walking stick as she climbed uphill, deeper into the woods. Later, it would become a weapon. The hunter would become the hunted.

31

DEVON

The trail of prints in the snowy ground told a story. A man's large feet and the dragging steps of someone smaller. Fiona's. His wife's. Resolve seeped through Devon, hardening him cell by cell.

He followed the prints across the field behind the house and into the woods. The last time he'd gone this way, he'd been dragging the sled with Bob's body on it. The memory brought a stab of fear. *Not Fiona too, please.* Devon couldn't allow his imagination to go there.

He walked more quickly, stumbling over roots and rocks until his eyes adjusted to the forest gloom. He couldn't see the footprints any longer, but where else would they have gone? He'd seen their steps leading to this trail, and there weren't any branches heading off in other directions.

Up ahead, he saw an opening in the trees. It was the place they'd buried Bob. He slowed. What if Rico were there with Fiona now? Devon slid behind a pine and mentally mapped his course forward.

He moved from tree to tree with as much stealth as an out-of-shape, middle-aged, suburban lawyer could, which was to say, not much. However, even with the crunching and thumping and fumbling, nobody burst through the brush and attacked him.

When he reached Bob's final resting place, Devon rested too. The moon lit the small clearing, and he could see that it was empty. No Rico. No Fiona. No visible prints.

He wrapped an arm around his ribcage, squatted, and peered at the ground the way he'd seen Native American trackers do in movies. He didn't know what he was looking for. Bent twigs? Scuffs in the snow? But he looked because he hadn't a clue what else to do.

He was about to rise, his thighs burning, when he noticed something. A single heel print. At least he thought it was a heel print. He duckwalked closer. Yes. His pulse rose with excitement. He measured it with a thumb and pointer finger, held his hand stiff and measured the distance against the span of his own heel. Smaller. It was smaller.

It had to be Fiona's. He stood and, his thighs beginning to tremble with the strain of squatting, hugged his ribs more tightly. Thing was—this print was headed toward the cabin.

He pivoted and looked behind him hoping to see another clue, but there was nothing but darkness that way. Had she escaped? Had Rico released her? Or was this an old print from another day or another person?

If he was an experienced woodsman, he would know these things. He'd have noticed the particular marks her shoes made and be able to tell them from other shoes. He'd be able to calculate how long the print had been there based on weather conditions or whatever, but those things were outside his pay grade.

Which way? The question burned a hole in his brain. He faced forward again. The path was shadowed in this direction too. No heavenly beam pointed the way.

Devon didn't know how long he stood in indecision before he remembered Caleb. Caleb was in the cabin. The cabin lay in the same direction the boot print faced. He didn't know what lay ahead, only what lay behind. He turned and walked the way he'd come.

Failure. The word rang through his mind. He'd failed. He hadn't been there for Fiona yet again. The pain in his side seemed to increase with every intonation of the word. He had to get back, had to rest before the pain took him out again.

Devon was so immersed in his inner agony, he almost missed the faint thump, thump, thump of heavy footfalls behind him. It had started so low and steady it seemed a part of nature, like the steady hammer of a woodpecker's beak. Then an exceptionally loud crash—the breaking of branches, the crushing of pinecones—startled him into awareness. He ducked off the path, into the deeper woods, and hid. Seconds later, Rico ran past him.

Shockwaves washed up and down Devon's body, immobilizing him. The man disappeared quickly, but a long second passed before Devon realized he should follow. He moved into Rico's wake, no longer aware of his own body, his pain anesthetized by the hormones racing through him.

When he came to the edge of the woods, he paused. Rico charged, head down, bull-like across the field. He'd be able to see Devon if he turned, but he was too intent on his prey to look back. Devon stepped from the shelter of the trees and trotted after him.

Rico pounded up the three steps to the cabin, threw the mudroom door open and entered. Caleb's brave face and wide eyes flew into Devon's mind. His son was behind that door.

He picked up his pace, but the cabin seemed to move farther away the faster he ran, his ribs shooting arrows of pain through him. What seemed an eternity later, he grabbed the handrail of the small flight of steps and hauled himself up.

The warmth and smells of the cabin wrapped themselves around him as he entered: coffee, maple syrup, hot dogs, and something foul hidden under the more pleasant scents. He padded softly through the kitchen, noting the coppery odor of Crackers' blood and the more pervasive stench of vomit when he got to the doorway.

A glance at his old prison filled him with dread. He'd reached the lowest point of his life on that floor by that fireplace. He wouldn't go there again, not that low. He'd die first.

Devon pulled the knife from his pocket and snapped it open. It was small, but it was sharp. If he thrust hard enough—

A slam. The splintering of wood. A child's cry.

Rico must have kicked down Caleb's door. A second later, he heard Caleb's cries growing louder.

Surprise was Devon's only hope of success. Resisting the almost irresistible urge to rush to Caleb's rescue, he ducked behind the sagging couch. He would ram it into Rico as he passed. Not an elegant, thought-out scheme, but it was all he had.

Rico entered the living room and strode past the couch. Caleb squirmed under his arm like an angry cat. As the two moved into the kitchen doorway, Devon sprang forward, knife held like a lance in his extended hand.

It ripped through Rico's jacket, bounced off something beneath, and came away clean. It accomplished less than Devon had hoped, but it did cause Rico to stumble over the threshold and drop Caleb.

"Run," Devon shouted at his son.

Caleb hesitated, his face white in the gloom.

"Run, damn it," Devon yelled again. This time Caleb obeyed, his feather-light steps fading as Devon faced his enemy.

Rico didn't speak. He seemed beyond words, a beast driven by instinct and emotion. His lips drew back to reveal yellowed teeth. The steel glinted in his hand.

This was what Devon had thought himself superior to. This kind of man. He'd joked with colleagues about the low IQ of the criminal mind, but that low IQ had a much bigger, much sharper knife. At this moment, Devon would happily trade a handful of IQ points for a better weapon.

Rico didn't charge as Devon had expected. He crouched and circled to the right, every muscle and sinew sliding into place as if his body had its own intelligence. Devon attempted to mimic his movements, but he was injured and inept.

He'd never given much thought to his own death, not even when one of the partners at the firm died of a widowmaker. The man exercised and ate right and died on the trail in his running shoes. Devon had been shocked, of course, but the shock wasn't personal. He was secure in his own mental superiority, as if somehow being smart was a shield against the inevitability of death. It wasn't.

He stumbled into the couch and righted himself. Rico didn't react, just continued his slow revolution around the foyer, eyes glinting in the light streaming through the front windows. Was that a smile on his face? Yes, Devon was sure he'd seen a smile. The man was enjoying this the way a cat enjoys torturing a mouse.

The smile made Devon's purpose clear. His job was to give Rico as much pleasure as possible. His job was to prolong his own death. Embrace torture. Because the longer he suffered, the more time Caleb had to get away.

Fiona and the dog were out there somewhere. Devon imagined them finding Caleb, then running through the trees to the main road, flagging down a car, and being driven to safety. He would die a happy man if that happened.

Rico feinted, the knife lashing toward Devon. He sprang back, and it whistled past. Three more slow steps to the right, front foot stepping over the back in a complicated dance, and the knife sliced the air, missing him again.

The process was repeated, but this time the knife sheared through Devon's jacketed arm and nicked the skin beneath. He felt blood, warm and sticky, wet his shirt. They circled again, and again Rico struck after three steps—a slice to his head this time. Blood matted Devon's hair.

Did the man realize how methodical he was being? Three steps, strike, three steps, strike. Was he aware of the pattern? Devon didn't think so, but he decided to test his theory.

One step, two, and Devon lashed out with his pocket knife. It did no physical harm, but Rico stopped his dance, confusion clouding his eyes. He *had* been unaware of the pattern, or at least thrown by the change in it.

That information was costly. The confusion cleared, Rico's eyes narrowed, and he lunged. Devon skipped back, surprised at his own nimbleness. He'd surrendered to his survival instinct, and the results were startling.

Rico retreated and resumed his grapevine step. An idea struck Devon. Could he lead Rico across the living room to the bookcase? One of the cabin's many wooden bear lamps burned dimly on its surface. It would be a better weapon than his pocket knife.

He stepped in time with Rico, dancing back on every third step, sometimes allowing himself to be cut, sometimes avoiding the blade. The white-faced man opposite him seemed to move through a dream. Devon didn't want to wake him, just lull him and lead him.

Devon counted footsteps and knife thrusts rather than seconds and minutes. He no longer measured time by the planet's revolutions, but by their revolutions. Every circle led them closer to the bookshelf where time would end for one of them.

One, two, three, and this time it hurt. Really hurt. The knife sank deep into Devon's side, opening the old wound, the one Fiona had bandaged. He gasped as the dreaded black spots clouded his vision and sweat sprang out of the pores above his upper lip. He couldn't pass out. Not now. The lamp glowed in his peripheral vision.

So close. He was so close.

Rico's nostrils flared, his jaw clenched, and he lunged again, plunging the knife into Devon's upraised arm. Pain, searing and impossible to ignore, burned through him. He was done. He couldn't dance any longer.

But he'd given Fiona and Caleb time, precious time. He hoped it had been enough. As he fell to the floor, he grabbed the cord of the lamp for support, which it didn't give him. Instead, he felt it tip off the shelf. The spots spread into a solid curtain behind his eyes, he heard a distant crash, then the lights went completely out.

32

FIONA

Fiona trudged uphill, growing warmer from the exertion. So warm, her shirt grew damp. It was a relief not to be cold, but she was concerned about what would happen when she stopped moving. The sweat would freeze. Hypothermia was a real possibility, considering her lack of jacket, gloves, and hat. She wore jeans, a long-sleeved cotton shirt, and a sweater—not enough to protect her in below-freezing temperatures.

She'd stopped twice during her trek to gauge her vantage point, but each time, trees had blocked the view of the path. The third time was the charm. Not only was there a high stump to sit on, but she also had a clear view of a stretch of the trail and the field behind the cabin. It was possible for Rico to see her if he glanced up, but she'd take her chances. She could duck when she heard him coming.

Fiona climbed onto the stump, pulled her knees up to her chest and wrapped her arms around them, trying to make herself as small as she could to maintain her body heat. She began shivering before five minutes had passed. In ten, her teeth were chattering. Her plan had a gigantic flaw. She was freezing.

She stood, did twenty jumping jacks, then sat. It helped for a minute or two then the cold soaked through her clothes and pores and into her blood stream again. The cabin with its thin trickle of smoke coming from the chimney called to her. She wasn't sure how much longer she could take this. What was taking Rico so long?

Of course, she may have missed him. It was possible he'd come this way while she was climbing. Fiona felt suddenly foolish. How had she believed this would work? Even if she was able to sneak up on him, he was strong, and he was wary.

She marched around the stump slapping her arms with her hands, feeling hopeless. She must have missed him. She picked up the stick from where it leaned against the stump and revolved it in her hand. Why hadn't she brought her gun?

Because she never travelled with it, that was why, but the thought of it lying in her bedside table at home almost made her weep. She'd never used it other than for practice shooting at the range. Never had a need. The irony of this moment hit her hard.

Fiona began to move downhill. She would peer in the cabin windows before entering. Maybe she'd still be able to stage a surprise attack. Throw rocks at the windows, and when he came out to investigate, throw rocks at him.

Another dumb idea, but she was too cold to think clearly. Her blood felt slow and viscous, her brain oxygen deprived. She had to get warm.

She hadn't gone two yards before she heard the sound of someone running. It was him. It had to be. Fiona crouched behind a tree and watched. A moment later, Rico appeared through the trees.

His shoulders were hunched. His feet pounded the earth. Anger and purpose were in each stride. He was looking for her. She was suddenly glad she hadn't gone to the cabin immediately, no matter how cold she'd been.

Fiona began to slide downhill, her feet slipping on ice and the moldering leaves beneath. Afraid he'd hear her descent, she stopped herself with the walking-stick-slash-bludgeon, hobbled to a tree, and hugged it.

Rico hit the field and broke into a sprint. She was about to follow when the breaking of a branch behind her made her freeze. It was an animal, it must be, but not a small animal.

With all the terrifying things she'd faced in the past twenty-four hours, an animal seemed the least of her worries, but there were bears in Big Bear.

Another branch broke, and the sound echoed in the cold air. Afraid to turn, afraid to see what was sneaking up behind her, she hugged the tree more tightly. She'd heard you shouldn't make eye contact with bears. If she didn't move, perhaps it would amble on and leave her in peace.

The thing was coming closer. Fiona gripped her stick, readying herself to turn, but before she did, a happy whine broke the still air. A dog.

She spun to see a black dog, fur matted and shining with frozen blood. "Crackers?" The dog yelped, a joyous sound. Fiona ran to him, sank on her knees and buried her face in his fur while he tried to reach it with his tongue. She'd never been so happy to see another being in her life.

"I'm so glad you're not dead," she said to him over and over, alternating between hugging him and smoothing his coat.

When he calmed down, she looked into the dark depths of his eyes and spoke to him the way she'd talk to Caleb. "We have to go down there. I know you don't want to. I don't want to either, but Devon and Caleb are in there. We have to help them."

Crackers cocked his head as if he wanted to understand, and she remembered. He was a trained search and rescue dog. He probably did understand that his services were required even if he didn't know who they were searching for.

Fiona pushed herself to her feet with the help of her stick, turned toward the cabin, and started downhill. "You coming?" she said over her shoulder, but she hadn't needed to. Crackers was right behind her.

It took longer to get down the hill than it had to get up. She had to sit and scoot in several places so she didn't fall, and twice she had to circle around especially steep areas.

The dog trotted ahead, nose to the ground. When she lagged, he waited for her to catch up. Fiona had the feeling he didn't want to lose her any more than she wanted to lose him. There was strength in numbers, even between species.

When they finally hit level ground, she paused, eyes searching the open expanse of white in front of them. Once they left the trees, they'd be visible, but Fiona couldn't see any other way to reach the cabin.

She took two deep breaths and pushed ahead onto the open ground. She hadn't gone ten yards before the back door of the cabin flew open and a small figure shot out. Caleb descended the stairs one at a time, holding tightly to the rail, but began to run as fast as his stubby legs would go when he hit the ground.

Crackers gave a single bark and darted toward her son. They collided about five yards from the cabin. The dog knocked him over and gave him the same wet greeting Fiona had received.

With tears freezing on her cheeks, she followed and reached her son less than a minute after Crackers had. She pulled him into her arms and hugged him to her. For a moment, she forgot where they were, and why they were there. The surge of joy was so great she never wanted it to end. Then she remembered Devon. She sobered and held her son away from her so she could look into his face. "Where's Daddy, Caleb?"

Caleb pointed to the cabin.

"Is Rico there, too?" It was a pointless question. Fiona had seen him racing toward the cabin.

Caleb ran a mittened hand under his nose and nodded. "I no like Rico."

"Me, either," she said. Fiona looked around her. She needed to find shelter, someplace safe and warm she could leave Caleb while she returned to the cabin for Devon. She searched the tree line. There was shelter of sorts in the trees, but no warmth.

She turned, examined the cabin, and noticed a small door beneath the stairs. It appeared to be made from plywood but was painted the same brown as the house. She hadn't realized the cabin had a basement.

"Come on." She pulled Caleb toward the house, and they ducked under the stairs. She yanked on the metal handle of the little door harder than necessary. It popped open and almost slapped her face.

Inside was a crawl space, not a basement. The floor was dirt, but it seemed slightly warmer than the outside world. She crept inside and smelled freshly cut wood. When her eyes adjusted to the dim light, she saw why. At least a half-cord of firewood was tucked against the far wall of the low eight-by-eight space.

Crackers ducked inside and sniffed every corner. When he was done, he wagged his tail in approval. Fiona drew Caleb into the space. "I need you and Crackers to stay in here and be really quiet. I'm going to go find Daddy. Okay?"

"It's dark," he said.

"I know, honey, but you have the dog. He'll keep you safe."

Her son looked doubtful, but Crackers curled up against the wood pile. "Go sit with Crackers," she said.

Caleb hugged his mother, then crawled farther into the shed, leaned against the dog, and stuck his thumb in his mouth.

"I have to close the door," Fiona said.

"Okay," Caleb said in an unhappy voice.

Fiona took one last look at her child, crawled into the cold again, and shut the door behind her.

33

DEVON

The world returned in a pinpoint of light that grew until the inside of Devon's eyelids glowed maroon. He opened them slowly and wondered where he was. The room was illuminated by moonlight streaming through a window, dim but enough to see by. He turned his head to gather more information and winced. A click and a pinch sent a jolt into his shoulder. Something was out of place.

The sight that met his eyes confused him—a head of filthy black hair, matted with blood. As he examined the rest of the body, memories returned like the scenes of a movie slowed to single shots. Rico with Caleb under an arm. A small knife bouncing off the man. A long dance. The cord of a lamp.

Devon shot up into a seated position, then waited for the room to cease its revolutions. When it did, he saw the bear lamp laying two feet away from Rico's head. It must have hit him on its way down from the bookshelf. Was he dead? Or was that too much to hope?

He didn't appear to be breathing, but… The command Devon had given his son earlier echoed in his mind: *Run, damn it.*

Devon hauled himself to his feet. His entire body hurt, his arm, his side, his ribs, his lungs—probably from the broken ribs—his head, his neck. He looked at the lamp, then at Rico. He saw himself lifting it high overhead and bringing it down on the man's head one more time for good measure. But, no. It wasn't in him.

The bear. He stared at it for a long moment trying to retrieve something from his battered brain. Something to do with a bear. Something that... He pivoted. He couldn't believe he hadn't thought of it until this moment.

The shortest distance to the hallway was over the downed man, but Devon couldn't make himself step over Rico. He'd seen one too many thrillers where the dead villain sprang to life as soon as the hero was within grabbing distance. Instead, he limped around the coffee table through the dried vomit and hobbled into the hall, past Caleb's room and into the larger bedroom.

His pack still leaned against the wall where he'd left it. It was probably gone. Rico had removed almost everything that could be turned into a weapon, but Devon began removing things from inside the pack anyway, searching.

He found the bear spray in a side pocket. He'd forgotten where he'd hidden it and had almost given up, but there it was. Relief spiked through him. Okay, maybe relief was too strong a word. It was more like a lessening of dread. The spray was a good weapon. If it could take down a bear, it could take down Rico.

He chose not to think about about the fact that it had been there all this time, that he could have disarmed Rico the first day. That kind of thinking wasn't productive, not at the moment. He'd beat himself up when all this was over.

Devon retreated from the room, walked quietly through the house, and slipped out the front door. It was fully night now. A half-moon brightened the snow in front of house and made eerie shadows with Caleb's snowman. Caleb. His son was his first order of business, but which way?

Devon descended the porch steps, looked up and down the dirt road, thinking his son may have taken the main drag, but changed his mind and rounded the house instead. Caleb would've headed for the woods. He felt sure of it.

The snow was littered with boot prints in all sizes and going in all directions. It was impossible to read. As he reached the end of the house, he paused. If Rico came to, what would he do? Would he head out the back door? He'd been carrying Caleb that way.

Devon felt a stab of regret. Perhaps he should have killed Rico, but he wasn't a murderer. If Rico was dead, Devon was responsible since he'd been the one to grab the lamp cord. He'd certainly wished Rico was dead. However, wishing and dumb luck weren't against the law. Murder was. Killing a man who was knocked out cold was murder in any court of law.

Devon flattened himself against the cabin and peered around the corner. A person was posed to climb the back steps, one foot on, one foot in the snow. It took him a moment to recognize the person. He'd never seen her like this before, wild eyes, tangled hair surrounding a face smudged with the war paint of dirt and blood.

"Fiona," he rasped.

Her head snapped toward him, and the heavy-looking branch she held flew to her shoulder like she was readying herself to hit a home run.

"Fiona, it's me," he said with more strength.

"Devon?" She dropped the stick and ran at him. Her hands found his face, felt it all over as if she'd gone blind. Once she was convinced it was him, she kissed his eyelids and cheeks and lips.

Tears welled into his eyes. When she was finished with his face, she threw her arms around him, or maybe he threw his around her. He wasn't sure, and it didn't matter. The embrace didn't last long.

They pulled apart and spoke at once.

"Where's Rico?"

"Did you see Caleb?"

Fiona answered first. "Caleb is safe. Where is Rico?"

"In the house. He was unconscious when I left him. We need to go while we can," Devon said.

She gave him a quick nod, grabbed his hand and dragged him around the back of the house. She darted under the steps and opened the door to the woodshed. Crackers and Caleb emerged together.

Fiona raised Caleb onto one hip. "I think I left my keys in the car." She spun and headed around the other side of the house.

Caleb's legs wrapped around his mother's waist. He was getting so big. Too big for her to carry for long, but Devon couldn't take him from her. He didn't have the strength.

They reached the car. Crackers ran to the rear door on the driver's side and stared at it as if willing it to open. Fiona tried the driver's door, but it was locked. She set Caleb on his feet and peered into the window. "Not there. He must have taken them."

Devon turned to view the cabin. "I could go—"

"No." Her voice was sharp. "Nobody's going in there. We walk. Town isn't that far." She picked up Caleb and stomped toward the road. The dog gave a last longing look at the car and followed. Devon did the same.

When they reached the road, he took her arm. "Not the road. He'll see us if he comes after us. Besides, it's a shorter distance to the lake that way." He jutted a chin toward the trees on the far side of the road.

Fiona gazed in the direction he'd indicated, then at him again. "We won't get lost?"

"The lake is a pretty big target."

34

DEVON

The first five minutes of the hike weren't bad. Devon took the lead through the thinly treed area. The land sloped gently and was easy to navigate. Ten minutes later, he struggled through the underbrush, holding back branches so they didn't slash Fiona and Caleb.

There was no path, and the trees grew wherever they pleased. Manzanita bushes and other flora he couldn't name huddled in the spaces between them. Devon had to veer right at times and left at others to find a way through the increasingly densely packed brush. Before long, he lost all sense of direction.

He stopped. Fiona, who'd seemed lost in her own thoughts, walked into him. "What's wrong?" There was fear in her voice.

"I don't know where we are."

"I thought you said the lake was up ahead."

"Where's up ahead?"

Fiona set Caleb down and stretched her back. "The way we're walking."

Caleb toddled to his father and held up his arms. "I can't, buddy. Daddy's injured."

His son dropped his arms and sat on a rock next to Crackers. He seemed to have reverted to more childish ways, but Devon guessed that was to be expected in the circumstances. Children were malleable. That's what everyone said, but they still felt fear and stress, and it took its toll.

Fiona straightened. "We're lost. That's what you're saying."

"I don't know. We've made so many detours, I'm all turned around."

His wife closed her eyes and inhaled deeply through her nose. She was taking Pilate's breaths. Not a good sign. It generally meant she was trying to pull herself together, so she didn't scream.

"What are we going to do then?" she finally asked.

Devon lifted his palms skyward then let them fall.

Fiona mimicked his movement. "That's all you got?" She sounded angry now.

"That's all I got," he said.

"Okay, I'll pick a direction." She turned in a slow circle. "Let's go… "She stopped and pointed. "That way." Sarcasm saturated her words.

She held out a hand to Caleb. He took it, and she began threading her way through the bushes. The dog bounded behind her. Devon took up the rear, thinking hard.

He knew she expected him to have a logical solution to their problem. That was his role in the family—Mr. Logical. He did the research. She intuited. But there wasn't anything to research here in the woods. He had no GPS, no phone. He couldn't even see the stars.

Stars.

He tripped over a tree root. "Fi, stop."

She spun around, anger, exhaustion and fear printed in the lines of her face. "What?"

"If we could find a clearing, we could look at the stars."

"And?"

"Then we'd know which direction we were going."

The tension left her expression. "I saw the Big Dipper and Orion's Belt earlier, but they move, don't they?"

"Yes, but they'd still give us the general direction."

"Okay. Okay, that makes sense. There was a small clearing a little way back, wasn't there?"

"Yeah. This way." Devon turned and retraced their steps. They walked longer than he'd thought they'd have to, but the clearing didn't materialize. He kept on, primarily because stopping didn't seem to be an option.

After about fifteen minutes, the trees thinned a bit, and black sky began to show in larger and larger patches. This must be the clearing; it had just been farther back than they'd thought. He walked faster, encouraged. "Just up ahead," he called over his shoulder. A moment later, he burst through the trees and onto a dirt road.

35

FIONA

Fiona hurried after Devon as fast as Caleb's legs could hurry and stepped onto the road after him. "Where are we?" she asked.

He looked at the sky without answering. She followed his gaze and saw Orion's Belt. "Orion. So which direction?"

Devon massaged his forehead. "The lake has got to be on the other side of those trees." He pointed the way they'd come. "I'm guessing this road runs parallel, or almost parallel, to the road the cabin is on."

"Or it is the road the cabin is on," she said without emotion. She had no emotions left, she was depleted, freezing, and exhausted.

"It can't be." Devon tried to sound confident, but she heard the doubt in his voice.

"Either way," she said. "I'm not going into the woods again. I can't. I'm not even sure I have the energy to walk on the road."

"If he comes looking..."

"I thought you said this wasn't the road the cabin was on," she said.

"I can't be sure."

Frustration threatened to break her. She wanted to scream, stamp her feet, lay down in the road and cry, but she didn't do any of those things. Instead, she lifted her son onto her hip again. "If we see a car, we'll hide."

They stumbled down the snow-covered road in the direction of the lake. At least, they believed they were headed to the lake. They passed two houses, a log cabin like the one they'd rented and an A-frame. Nobody had been home at either. There were no lights, no cars in the driveways, but to be sure, Devon had banged on the front doors. Apparently, the snowstorm had kept many skiers and vacationers away from the mountain. Maybe the news stories about escaped cons had kept them away as well.

Caleb lay his head on her shoulder and gradually grew heavier. He'd fallen asleep. Fiona's march became a shuffle under his weight. She wasn't sure how much longer she could carry him, but when she put him down, she felt the bite of cold in the air. She needed his body heat.

She glanced at her husband. He looked like one of the walking dead. His brown skin had an ashen sheen. A line of blood ran along the side of his head and hardened into rivulets on his cheek. He held his rib cage with one arm and a red rose, the blossom of yet another wound, decorated the other. He needed medical attention, soon.

They'd walked—or perhaps staggered was a better word—for at least fifteen minutes when they heard the engine. Devon grabbed her arm. "A car," he said.

They hobbled off the road, slid down a step bank, and huddled against the snowy berm. Caleb cried out in his sleep but didn't wake. She shushed him, her eyes scanning their surroundings for the dog.

Crackers wouldn't go far without them, but she didn't want the driver of the car to see him. She was about to call out, when he trotted through the brush and scooted between her and Devon.

The rumble of the engine grew louder, and the beam of headlights lit their hiding place. They stayed still until the crunch of tires could no longer be heard, then Devon stood and offered his good hand to Fiona. She refused it, not wanting to break open any of his wounds.

"That could have been help," he said.

"Or it could have been Rico."

He acknowledged her comment with a tilt of his head. "No way to know."

Fiona had to wake Caleb and pull him up the bank by the hand. She couldn't manage the steep climb with him in her arms. He sleep-walked through the process and nestled into his place on her shoulder again as soon as they were on the road.

"How much farther do you think it is?" Fiona asked.

"Can't be more than a few miles." Devon's voice held pain.

A few miles sounded impossible. She had to get her mind off the distance. "What happened back there?" She was referring to the time he spent alone in the cabin with Rico.

"I bought you time."

They continued on in silence for a long minute, but the details weren't forthcoming. He didn't want to talk about it, at least not yet.

Devon broke the silence. "Where did he take you?"

"He had a car way out in the woods."

"Was he going to drive off with you?" Devon asked.

It was her turn to watch her words. One day, she'd tell him about Rico's delusion, the smell of gasoline, the umbrella that had saved her, but not now. "I don't think so," she said.

Devon must have sensed her reluctance to talk about it, either that or it took all his concentration just to keep moving. He stopped asking questions. It was a relief, although now she had nothing but the endless road ahead to think about.

Another mile passed, and Fiona's foot hit something hard. She stumbled, and Devon put out a hand to stop her from falling. She leaned against him for a moment to regain her balance. When she stepped away, she examined his face, taking his measure. He was a study in self-control. How much longer could they go on?

"Look," he pointed to the ground. "Asphalt."

Hope, as tiny and tired as a mouse newly released by a playful cat, limped into her heart. "We've got to be close, right?"

"Yeah, we've got to be."

They moved quickly across the blacktop. There were more houses here, but all were dark and without cars in the driveways. Fiona paused, an idea forming in her mind. "Maybe we should break into one of the cabins?"

Devon didn't stop, just shot the reply over his shoulder. "It's illegal."

She strode after him. "I think this is an extenuating circumstance."

He halted so abruptly, Fiona almost walked into him. He spun to face her. "How?" he asked.

"What do you mean how?"

"How do you intend to break into a locked cabin? Do you have any tools? Crowbar handy?" His voice was laced with anger.

She'd never broken into anything in her life and fumbled for an answer. "We could break a window," she finally said.

"And what would we do when we got inside? What's your plan?"

Fiona set Caleb down. She didn't have the energy to hold him and argue at the same time. "They might have a phone."

Devon shot his palms toward the night sky. "Nobody has landlines these days."

"How about a computer? Internet connection?"

"Who leaves computers in their vacation cabins?"

Fiona stared at him. His jaw was set in a stubborn line. He didn't know what he was saying. He was hurt, exhausted. She'd have to do this herself. "Watch Caleb." She stomped toward the closest house.

It was an extended A-frame with a small front porch. Fiona opened a bug-filled screen door and grasped the handle of the wooden door behind it. It was locked as she'd expected. She moved to the picture window next to it and peered inside—too dark to see anything.

She stepped down from the porch and searched the ground for a rock. Her gaze wandered to Devon and Caleb. They'd collapsed onto a fallen tree that lay next to the road. Devon's good arm encircled his son. He really wasn't going to help her.

Fiona kicked harder than necessary at the snow until her foot rammed into something hard. She dug through the ice with half-frozen fingers and unearthed a baseball-sized rock. After pulling her sweater sleeve over her hand, she gripped the rock, climbed the porch, and smashed it into the picture window. The sound of tinkling glass was her reward. She pulled long shards from the frame, then climbed through the opening into the house. Two minutes later, she climbed out again. Devon had been right. There was no landline and no computer.

They didn't speak when she returned to the road. She lifted Caleb onto her hip, and they set off again. Soon, they reached a true neighborhood. Paved streets crisscrossed one another, homes came in regular intervals. Fiona searched the sky for tendrils of smoke, for lights, but saw nothing. It was graveyard quiet, and she was too deflated to break into another home. The lake now glittered with promise in her imagination, an oasis in this desert of fear.

Get to the lake. The words became a chant. Her feet marched to their rhythm. Suddenly, the road bent left, and her imaginings became reality. Just ahead, between a stand of trees, black water sparkled with moonlit diamonds.

"Look." Devon pointed, with something like excitement in his voice.

That excitement carried them the distance. What seemed seconds later, they stood on a sandy beach and looked across the water and ice of Big Bear Lake. Fiona laughed and set Caleb on the ground. He plopped onto his bottom, too drowsy to share in his parents' happiness.

"Look, Caleb, the lake," Devon said.

"Why we here?" he answered in a sleepy voice.

Cat claws descended on Fiona's hopeful mouse. Why were they here? Nobody was fishing or boating at—what, 1:00? Or whatever time it was. There was no more help here than there'd been in the empty houses. She sank down beside her son and rested a cheek on his head. Devon seemed to have the same revelation at the same time. The joy faded from his eyes, and he sank onto the sand as well.

Fiona wasn't sure how long they sat there staring at the ice floes, but it was long enough for cold fingers to creep under her clothing and run up and down the length of her, long enough for lethargy to nibble on her ear.

Her chin struck her chest, and she bolted awake. "We can't do this," she said. "We can't stay here." Rico wasn't the only danger in this night. Hypothermia was just as real and just as deadly.

Devon gazed at her through cloudy eyes for a moment, and she watched understanding dawn. "Right," he said and pushed himself to a standing position. "Let's head to town."

They walked along the beach, passing vacation mansions and boat docks, but it was eerily silent. Fiona felt as if she were marching through an apocalyptic landscape, as if the world had fallen off the grid while they fought with Rico at the cabin.

"Where is everyone?" Devon said.

"The roads up the mountain are bad, foggy, icy. There will be people in town—full-time people."

Town assumed the mythic status the lake had held earlier. If they could just get to town. They trudged without speaking, needing all their energy to put one foot in front of the other. Fiona heard a car passing on an invisible road to their left. There were people out there; they just needed to find them.

Up the beach, she saw a parking lot which signified the end of this stretch of lakeside trail. They'd have to take the road after this. It would be easier walking, but the fear that Rico would find them was always present.

They approached the small lot with caution, but it appeared to be empty. It was a strange thing to want to find people, yet be afraid of every passing car. As they rounded a stand of snow-covered bushes, Fiona saw a lone car in the corner of the lot. It was a Lexus. Her Lexus.

"Devon!" She grabbed his arm, trying to stop him from lumbering into the open, but it was too late. Another arm snaked out from behind the brush and wrapped around his neck. Devon grunted and fell against Rico.

36

I found them wandering like refugees at the shore of the lake. My head still throbbed, but purpose muted the pain. Chuck had talked to me. At least, the thing that had lived inside him had talked to me. I wasn't sure which was which anymore. All I knew is, he wanted what he wanted, and he wasn't going to leave me be until he got it.

We were in our cell at the jail, and he was droning on and on about the injustices of his childhood. I'd tuned him out, the way I'd always done, but in the middle of one of his diatribes, he stopped talking, jumped off his bunk and screamed.

It was an uncanny, jawless scream. No words, mouth as big as a snake getting ready to swallow a rabbit, eyes white. I can tell you, it got my attention.

I put my hands over my ears, but the sound reverberated through my head, every hit causing a bolt of pain. "What do you want?" I tried to make myself heard over the noise.

He turned his white eyes on me, and two words grated through the air, "My sister."

It was the first time he'd spoken to me in words since I'd dispatched him to the next reality, and it was terrible. His voice was sandpaper on my skin, and I had the feeling that if I didn't do what he wanted, that sandpaper was going to rub everything off me until there was nothing left but bones.

I wanted to tell him I'd tried, but somehow, she'd escaped. I couldn't make my mouth form the words, though. I was paralyzed like a rabbit before a snake.

I dragged my eyes open, and I was in the cabin staring at the ceiling. I'd been given another chance. I'd been reborn for a purpose.

And that purpose walked before me now. I grabbed the father first. He was injured but, still, I believed he could cause the most damage. A second later a sharp pain shot through my leg. It was the damned dog.

I stared at it for a second, wondering what other horrors this night would bring. I'd been sure I'd ended that mongrel's life, but I'd been sure I'd ended Chuck's life as well. The living and the dead danced together under the moon.

I kicked the animal off, tightened my grip on Devon's windpipe, and heard the wheeze I'd been hoping for. "Call off your dog or I break his neck," I said to the woman.

She did. The dog didn't like it, but he obeyed her.

"We're going back to the cabin," I said. "We need to have a talk."

Her face, already white in the gloom, grew deathly pale. "Let's talk here."

I squeezed Devon's neck harder. He wheezed again. The boy cried out as if I'd hurt him.

"All right, all right. Stop that," she said. "We'll do what you want to do."

"Get in the car."

She glared at me through cat's eyes—Chuck's eyes. I shuddered, reached for the door handle with my free hand and opened the back door. "Get. In."

She set her son down without ever taking her eyes off me. "Release my husband."

I smiled at that. "After you get in."

"What do you want from us? I told you I'd give you money, everything we have, as soon as the banks open. Why not take the money and run?" She gestured toward the road. "Have you noticed how many empty houses are all around us? You could hide out in a mansion. You don't need us."

Irritation crept over me with spider legs. She was talking, talking, talking, just like her brother. I needed her to shut up. I raised my free hand to the arm around Devon's neck. I'd break his neck right in front of her.

Before I could apply any pressure, a fog appeared before my eyes. A second later, the burn started. A searing, corrosive pain filled my eyes, my nasal passages, my mouth. My hands released their hold on Devon and flew to my face. I dropped to my knees, gasping for clean air but found none.

37

DEVON

Headlights lit the road. Devon squinted through irritated eyes, stepped into the path of the car and waved an arm. They'd been hiding for so long it felt wrong, but logic had to override emotions. He'd used emotion and instinct to do what he'd had to do for his family. He'd sprayed a man with bear spray, inhaled quite a bit of it himself, possibly killed Rico, considering the man's compromised health, but now it was time to re-enter civilization.

The car slowed, then pulled to a stop. The window lowered, and a voice came through the opening. "You been in an accident?"

Devon walked closer and peered inside. The man behind the wheel appeared to be in his forties. He had heavy jowls and a forehead that creased deeply with apprehension.

Devon realized how they must appear, covered in blood and dirt with the smell of pepper spray on their clothing. He gestured to Fiona. She walked into the light carrying Caleb, Crackers at her side. The man's tension relaxed.

"It's a long story," Devon said. "But we need help. Can you drive us to the police station?"

"The hospital," Fiona said.

"I can wait," Devon answered her.

The man paused, then they heard the click of locks. "Get in," he said.

Fiona, Caleb, and Crackers clambered into the back seat. Devon climbed into the front. Heat blew through the vents and began to thaw his frozen body. It was heaven.

The man made a three-point turn and drove toward town. "What, ah, what happened to you folks? You look like you been through a war."

"I guess you could say that," Devon said. "But I think we need to talk to the cops before we share the details with anyone else."

"Understood," the man said, sounding very much like he didn't understand, but the rest of the drive was made in blissful silence.

The sheriff's station was located in a low, beige and brown building. The windows glowed like beacons in the blackness. Devon thanked their driver and he and his family spilled into the cold night air that seemed even colder now because of the warmth they'd left behind.

They trooped inside and made their way to the front desk. It was manned by a sleepy looking deputy. The sleep left his face as Devon crumpled to the floor.

38

FIONA

Fiona woke between clean sheets with an IV in her arm. It would have been sheer luxury, but anxiety gripped her almost at once. She turned her head, saw a small form in the next bed and relaxed again. They were all in the hospital. They were all safe.

Her fluids had been dangerously low, but other than that and a few bruises, she was fine. Devon, on the other hand, had been rushed into surgery. She'd dozed in her bed until being told the surgery went well, then she'd allowed herself the luxury of falling into a deep, dreamless sleep.

The events of the night before shuffled into her mind, and she struggled to put them into some kind of order. After Devon passed out at the Sheriff's station, chaos erupted. Medics charged through the doors, deputies arrived in twos and threes, and everyone asked questions. Endless questions. What had happened to them? Were they injured? Where and how had they been injured? What year was it? Who was the president? Where was Rico?

Fiona went through the story many times with many uniformed people, while another ambulance and several patrol cars were dispatched to the lake in search of Rico. After much cajoling, Caleb allowing himself to be carried away by a female paramedic, while other medical professionals assessed Fiona's condition. Crackers was leashed by the desk deputy and taken to a local vet for examination.

Then there was the ride down the hill to the hospital in Arrowhead. The warmth of heated blankets and hot tea. The cold of stethoscopes and probes. The relief of being washed and enveloped between smooth sheets.

A nurse, pretty and brown, popped her head in the door. She made Fiona think of the squirrels that leaped from tree to tree here. "You're awake," she said.

Fiona nodded.

"Hungry?"

"Famished."

"Good. Breakfast is on its way." The nurse crossed to Caleb's bed. "You hungry, little guy?"

Caleb yawned and stretched and smiled at her. "I like pancakes."

"I'll see what I can do." She looked at Fiona. "The food isn't gourmet, but it is edible."

After an edible breakfast, Fiona and Caleb were released. The business of signing forms saved her from having to think about what would come after the forms. She had no car, no wallet, no cell phone, and nowhere to go if she did, but when she walked into the hospital lobby, two deputies were waiting for her. One large and male, name of Connelly, one petite and female, name of Jones.

Although the deputies solved her current dilemma, their presence also made her uneasy. She didn't believe it was common for the police to provide taxi service. They must need her for something. After asking about her health, Connelly confirmed her suspicion.

"Rico Del Monaco wasn't at the lake when we arrived last night."

Despite the warmth of the hospital lobby, Fiona shivered. "He wasn't there?"

"We were hoping you'd be willing to come back to the cabin with us—walk us through what happened," Jones said.

Fiona had no desire to see that cabin ever again. However, their things were there. She needed her purse and a car to get home, if they'd let her take one. "Sure."

Jones handed her a puffy jacket. "You didn't have one last night." She smiled. Fiona slipped it on. It was too big, but the extra yardage was comforting.

"Our people are at the cabin, and we have roadblocks on the 18 and the 38," Connelly told her on the way outside. "He can't leave the mountain without being seen."

"Did he take my car?" Fiona asked. Not that it mattered. They had their lives, that was the important thing.

"No. We found it at the lake. It'll be towed into the station," Connelly said.

"Then where did he go? He was in bad shape," Fiona wondered out loud, but the question was rhetorical. If the police knew where he was, he'd be in custody. Connelly and Jones didn't bother answering.

She followed them out the hospital doors to a waiting vehicle. They must have taken the car seat from her car, because it was belted into the back for Caleb. Connelly got behind the wheel, Jones in the front passenger seat, Fiona and Caleb in the back.

"We're hoping you might be able to help us figure out how he disappeared," Connelly said without taking his eyes from the road.

A vision of mounded branches appeared in Fiona's mind. "He had a car."

Jones and Connelly shared a look.

"The Audi at the cabin is registered to you and your husband," Connelly said.

"Right. That's Devon's. Rico had a car hidden in the woods."

Jones reached for the police radio. "What make and model?"

"I don't know. It was covered in branches."

"Where exactly was it?"

"I'd have to take you there. I don't think I can explain it."

There were many things Fiona wanted to tell them about her trip to the car in the woods, but Caleb was watching the world pass outside the window, as alert as a chipmunk.

As if Jones read her mind, she said, "We have someone, a search and rescue volunteer, at the station to watch Caleb. Is that okay with you?"

Caleb turned his head toward his mother, his lower lip beginning to droop.

Fiona placed a hand on his leg. "You'll have more fun."

"I want to stay with you." His voice wavered.

"MaryBeth is a really nice lady, and she has cookies and puzzles," Jones said.

Caleb narrowed his eyes. "What kind of cookies?"

"Oreos," Connelly said.

Caleb pondered this for a minute. "Okay." The rest of the ride to the station was passed in silence except for the occasional squawk of the police radio.

The volunteer was a sweet-faced twenty-something. Caleb took her hand and headed to an interview room without a backward glance. Fiona watched him go with more reluctance, but he couldn't go where she was going. She returned to the car with the deputies.

They pulled up to the cabin ten minutes later and parked behind two county vehicles. It was a very different tableau than the one she'd left behind the night before. Boot prints obliterated Caleb's snow angels, the snowman was toppled, and crime scene tape crisscrossed the front door. She exited the car and hesitated.

"You up to this?" Jones asked, but Fiona got the feeling it didn't much matter if she was.

"Yeah, sure." Unreasonable fear prickled up and down her arms as they climbed the porch steps, and she was glad Caleb had stayed at the station. He may have to revisit the events of the past few days at some point, but it would be in the safety of a child psychologist's office, not here. Not here where the nightmare took place.

A horrible perfume of vomit, blood, sweat, and smoke met her as soon as she entered. Two men and a woman in paper booties and jumpsuits were inside. The crime scene team, she supposed. One picked invisible things off the couch and placed them into plastic bags. Another wandered down the hallway. The third squatted on the floor near the fireplace, taking photographs of the blood-stained floorboards.

"Have you found the neighbor?" Fiona asked as she donned the booties Jones handed her.

"Yes. Well, we found the grave, but we're waiting for the medical examiner before we fully exhume the body," Connelly said. "We were hoping you could walk us through the events as they happened here in the cabin, then take us to the car."

Fiona dragged her gaze from the deep brown patch on the floor. "You know Rico was here with my family for two days before I arrived? He'd already killed the neighbor when I got here."

"We'll question your husband when he's up to it." Jones clicked on a tablet. "Just tell me what you know."

Connelly retreated through the front door, and Fiona walked Jones down the hallway. She pointed out the room Caleb had been held in and the door Rico had kicked down, then moved to the master bedroom. She paused in the doorway. Her aborted attempt to seduce him played through her mind like a bad movie, and her cheeks burned. She opened her mouth to tell Jones about it but shut it again. There was no point in putting herself through that.

They returned to the living room. She told Jones and the crime scene techs about the events she'd experienced there. Her throat constricted when she described how Devon had been kicked and beaten. Had these things really happened? It seemed like fiction now, with the authorities surrounding her, taking notes and discussing the events in their rational, unemotional voices.

She strode toward the kitchen when the questions petered out, wanting to get this over with, wanting to get her things, her child, her husband and return to the normal world. She had a suspicion, however, that normal as she'd known it no longer existed. Her hope was that she'd gained the freedom and wisdom Gwen had told her about. Fiona had certainly faced a demon, maybe not the demon she'd expected to meet, but a demon nonetheless.

When they entered kitchen, Fiona saw the blood smear on the stove and floor and pivoted toward Jones. "How's Crackers?" She'd almost forgotten about him.

"Is that the dog?"

"Yes."

"He's okay. You can pick him up when we're done here."

Fiona pointed to the stain. "That's his blood. Rico stabbed him when he was trying to defend me."

"Lucky he wasn't killed," Jones said.

"He's tough."

Jones gave her a tiny smile. "I think you all are."

A lump formed in Fiona's throat. "I can take you to the car now if you want."

Jones disappeared for a moment and returned with Connelly. "Ready?" he asked.

Fiona gave him a quick nod and headed through the mudroom into the outside world. She narrated events as they traversed the path through the woods, pointing out where she'd climbed off the trail to find her lookout, and the spot where Crackers had found her. The feeling of unreality that had come over her in the cabin persisted. It was as if she were peering through a picture window at someone else's life.

They skirted the gravesite. It was full of crime scene investigators, a woman Fiona assumed was the medical examiner, and more deputies. Their presence was comforting. *I'm not alone.* She repeated that phrase to herself like a mantra.

Another mile or so up the trail, they came to the clearing where the car had been hidden. Fiona stopped at the edge of the trees, unable to take in what she was seeing. The deputies halted alongside her. The mound was gone. Instead, the ground was covered in a carpet of pine boughs. The smell of gasoline pinched her nostrils.

"He came back for it," Connelly said.

"He covered it in gasoline." Fiona's voice rose. "He locked me inside and splashed gas over the whole thing." The horror of the experience broke the surreal pane of glass that had been protecting her. It had been real. He'd planned to burn her alive.

Jones placed a hand on her shoulder. "He never lit it."

Connelly squatted next to the boughs, rubbed needles between his fingers then brought his hand to his nose. "The branches must have absorbed the worst of it."

He stood and turned to Fiona. "Did you see anything about the car that might help us? The color of the vehicle? Or an insignia on the steering wheel?"

Fiona shut her eyes and forced herself to relive those terrible moments. The steering wheel had been in her way when she'd tried to knock down the branch holding the door shut. It had been black, padded leather or faux leather. Had there been a logo? She seemed to remember something embossed in the center, but what? She'd been so terrified, so intent on getting out, she couldn't remember.

She opened her eyes. "The interior was black leather or faux leather. I remember that."

"Good. That's good," Jones said. "How about the shape of the car. How big was the mound of branches?"

Fiona stepped over the boughs on the ground. "It went from here"—she walked to where the rear of the car had been—"to here." She turned to look at Jones. "I'd say a mid-sized sedan."

"How about the color?" Connelly asked. "Could you see anything between the branches?"

"It was getting dark," Fiona said, but again she squeezed her eyes shut and tried to imagine the scene as it had been. She remembered Rico reaching for the door handle of the car and pulling it open. When he did, the driver's door had been exposed, but she'd been on the wrong side to see the paint.

The inside of the door was black, as she'd told them. She focused her mind on the edge of door where a rim of paint might have been visible, but it blended into the evening. Blended. Why had it blended?

Her eyes popped open. "I think it was green. Not like a neon green, but like an army green, or a khaki green."

"Great," Jones said. "That really helps. It's an unusual color for a car. We might be able to peg the make from that."

"One more question," Connelly said. "Did the car seem new or old?"

"Neither," Fiona answered without pausing. "There wasn't a new car smell, but it was clean. No scratches on the upholstery."

"Great," Jones said and made more notes on her tablet. As they tromped back to the cabin, she called in the information on her Walkie-Talkie. Fiona felt ridiculously proud of herself for remembering as much as she had and for helping the police. Something bordering on happiness blossomed inside her.

When they reached the neighbor's grave, the feeling faded as quickly as it had come. Through the trees, she witnessed two medics hoist a full body bag onto a gurney.

39

DEVON

Devon jockeyed into the driveway next to Fiona's car. He'd been liberated from the hospital that morning, and the Big Bear police had released their vehicles the day before. He'd already made appointments to have both cars detailed. He wanted to wash every trace of Rico from their lives. Fiona left the mountain with Caleb after lunch, but he'd had to handle insurance paperwork with the hospital. He'd followed several hours later.

Home had never looked so good. The front yard was trimmed and leaf-blown and wholly suburban. Nothing wild about it. The windows glowed the gold of electric lights and so did their neighbors' on either side. Cars filled the driveways and parked along the street. There were people everywhere.

The smell of the ocean, not pine forest, met his nostrils as soon as he opened the car door. He eased his aching body outside, readjusted his sling, and walked up the front path.

Crackers met him at the door and gave him a subdued wag. He was still wearing the "cone of shame" from the vet. Fiona popped her head out from the kitchen doorway. "You made it." She strode forward and kissed him. "I was worried."

"Nothing but ibuprofen today. The drive was fine," he said. "Where's Caleb?"

"He fell asleep on the way home. I put him in bed."

Devon entered the living room and gazed around him. He felt as if he were returning home after a tour at war. He walked to the fireplace, so different than the one at the cabin, and ran his hand along the smooth wood mantle. He stared at the painting above it—a Laguna Beach scene with Bird of Paradise in the foreground and tiny sailboats scudding along on a gray-blue sea in the background.

He sank into a deep green easy chair and picked up the framed photograph from the table next to it. It was of Fiona and him on their wedding day. Red ringlets fell around a plumper, younger-looking Fiona. He, on the other hand, was leaner. But they both radiated joy. Would they ever be that happy again?

"Hungry?" Fiona leaned against the wall. He hadn't heard her enter.

"No. I'd love a glass of wine, though."

She disappeared into the kitchen again, and he set the photo down. The room was the same as it had been when he'd left, but it felt different. It seemed bigger, cleaner, more open.

He'd dreamed about the cabin last night. He'd smelled the stifling, smokey air, felt the dark wood walls close in around him, and when he tried to wake, something held his arms and legs immobile. When he finally roused himself, he was sweating. He had a feeling he'd be dreaming about the cabin for a long time to come.

"Here you go," Fiona handed him a glass of wine and folded herself onto the couch with her own glass. "Good to be home."

"Yeah." It was the understatement of the century, but he didn't have the energy to expound.

Crackers joined them, whacking the cone on the coffee table. Fiona laughed, leaning down and untangling him. Her laugh made Devon ache inside. It was so clear and beautiful. How had he never before noticed how wonderful her laugh was?

"Olivia should be here soon to get him," she said. "I'm going to miss him."

"Me too." Devon took a sip of wine and let it fill his mouth and nose with sensation before swallowing. "Let's start looking for a puppy this week."

Fiona sat up straighter. "Really?"

"Yup."

She pinched her forehead. "Have you made up your mind about the breed?"

He waved his wine glass toward Crackers. "The Crackers breed. I want one like him."

"Me too."

They sat in silence while they finished their wine. Words seemed inadequate for the first time in his life. He wanted to soak this moment in through his pores, to let it flow through his blood stream and heal the places the doctors couldn't reach. He was home with his amazing wife and his beautiful boy. They'd walked through the valley of death and come out the other side, alive if not unscathed. It was a miracle.

A knock jarred him out of his revery. Crackers hoisted himself to his feet, gave a half-hearted woof, and padded toward the door. "He's going to protect us with every last ounce of energy he's got, isn't he?" Devon said.

"No need this time. Wait until he sees who it is."

THE HOUSE FELT empty after Crackers left with Olivia and Brian. Their reunion had been emotional and touching. Devon watched it with awe. How had he never realized how strong the bond between dog and owner was? How had he never realized that dogs weren't things you picked out like new cars or pieces of furniture? Dogs were family.

He ate a bowl of soup, not because he wanted it but because Fiona said he should, and she was probably right. Then they got in bed. He lay under the electric blanket he'd always taken for granted and stared around his bedroom with the same sense of wonder he'd felt in the living room. This was his bedroom. His bureau. His armchair. His bedside table. His lamp. It was as if he had to convince himself.

He rolled over on his good side to view *his wife,* and froze, all warmth and wonder fleeing. "What are you doing with that?"

Fiona sat up, propped against the headboard, her gun in her hand. "He's still out there."

"He won't come here."

She turned her gold-brown eyes on him. "What makes you think that?"

"Why would he?"

"He wants me."

Devon rolled onto his back with a grunt and gazed at the ceiling. "He turned you down once."

"That's not what I mean." She sounded angry, and he hated that their peace was broken. "He wants to kill me. I think he believes it will atone for killing my brother."

Devon pondered that. Rico had grown more and more unpredictable during the time in the cabin. When he'd first arrived on the doorstep, Devon had believed him to be harmless. As the days progressed, he realized how wrong he'd been. But irrational? He wasn't sure about that.

"You didn't see him in the woods," Fiona said. "He opened the car door and spoke to someone. I was terrified. I thought he was throwing me inside with a crazy person."

"How do you know he thought it was Chuck?"

Fiona seemed to think about that for a minute. "I don't, for sure. He said, *She's here, just like you wanted.* It sounded like someone had been asking for me, but there wasn't anyone there."

Devon turned his head on his pillow and stared at her. "Didn't mean it was Chuck. It could've been some long dead relative, or a demon from his imagination."

She lifted a shoulder and let it drop. "But it wanted me."

"Or a woman. Any woman."

Fiona bit the inside of her cheek. "Maybe, but maybe not. Either way, I'm loading the gun."

"Do you think that's safe?"

"I'll put it in the bedside table. Caleb never goes in there."

"Unload it in the morning?"

"Right. I'll unload it in the morning."

They turned out the lights, and each sank into their side of the bed. They didn't make love or even cuddle up together. It was enough to know the other was there. Devon drifted off, feeling safer than he had in what felt an eternity. They were stronger together. He knew that now.

40

FIONA

Fiona woke, but why? The house was a silent hug around her. Maybe she was no longer used to the quiet. It was such a contrast to the noisy motel where she and Caleb had stayed while Devon was hospitalized.

She'd rented a car, and they'd spent the last two days visiting him, walking through the shops in Arrowhead Village, playing at the shoreside playground, and making phone calls. Lots of phone calls. She'd called Olivia, Devon's parents, and Gwen. She'd spoken to the owner of the cabin, who'd called her after the police had interviewed him. She'd called two of her Pilates instructors to ask them to cover her personal training clients. She'd sworn everyone who now knew the events of the past few days to secrecy.

The police didn't want the press to know about the home invasion until they'd captured Rico. They were already getting hundreds of phone calls—false sightings of the escaped convict. It took too much manpower to eliminate them all. She supposed the cops were afraid of starting a panic as well, but they hadn't taken her into their confidence.

It had been such a relief to be off the mountain and back in her own bed she'd been sure she'd sleep like a brick. Apparently not, and now that she was awake, her bladder was singing. She threw the covers back and slid from bed. The trip to the bathroom brought her fully awake. Too awake to return to dreamland without checking on Caleb first.

This was something she'd have to talk to her therapist about. Seeing her son in danger had flicked on an emergency switch inside her. She was having a hard time turning it off. Putting him to bed in another room, even his own room, had been difficult. She felt like she was missing a limb whenever he was out of sight.

His Winnie the Pooh nightlight shone through his open door, creating a patch of light brown on the dark floor of the hallway. No sound came from within. Good. He'd had nightmares while they were in the motel.

Fiona pushed the door open, took a step inside, and everything inside her froze. The curtains fluttered at an open window. She'd shut that window. Locked it.

"Hey there."

Her gaze shot to the bed. A pair of eyes glittered like obsidian in the dark room.

It was his voice. His hateful voice. "What are you doing here?" She whispered so she wouldn't wake Caleb, so her child wouldn't feel the same fear she felt, the fear that had frozen her where she stood.

"Came to get you," he said.

She didn't know why she'd asked. The inevitability of this moment had been obvious to her as soon as she'd heard Rico wasn't by the lake when the cops arrived. Truthfully, she'd feared something like this would happen the first time she'd seen her half brother sitting next to his lawyer in the courtroom years ago. He'd turned his head to look at her, and she'd glimpsed a nightmare world in his eyes.

"Why? You have money." The questions were useless, but she needed to connect with him, to get him away from Caleb. "You beat the roadblocks. Why don't you head for the border?"

His glittering gaze dropped to the floor, and he became a shadow sitting on the edge of her son's bed. "I want to, but I can't. He won't let me."

"Who? Who won't let you?"

The obsidian glint returned. "You know who."

"Chuck?"

"That's right."

"He's dead."

A growl came from across the room. Her heart raced, pumping adrenaline through her limbs. She prepared herself to fight, but realized he was laughing. A deep rumbling laugh. "That's a good one," he said.

"He is," Fiona insisted. "The police told me. His body is at the morgue."

"Oh, I know. I was the one who put him there."

"Let's talk about this in another room," she pleaded with him. All she could think about was putting distance between him and her son. If Devon heard them and brought the gun in here... No, that couldn't happen.

"I'm not leaving without you."

"Fine, fine. I'll go. Just come away from Caleb."

He didn't move. After a long pause, he said, "There was something evil in him."

Fiona's fear became frustration. "You think I don't know that? He murdered at least two women, maybe four."

Rico continued as if she hadn't spoken. "The thing left Chuck for a time. I guess it couldn't use him while he was in Quentin."

She didn't know what he was talking about and struggled for a response that would get him to walk out of the room with her. Before she could think of anything, he spoke again.

"He was different on the inside. Smaller. Sadder. But it came back when we broke out. He looked at me with the same eyes as Hal."

"Who's Hal?"

"My mother's boyfriend." Rico turned his head to the window, and the eyes flickered out. "The evil thing... you can't kill it. I think it just moves on to somebody else if you kill the person it's living in."

The conversation had taken a turn Fiona didn't understand with her mind, but a more primitive part of her understood just fine. The primitive part of her screamed, *Run*.

She couldn't run, though, not while Rico sat on her son's bed.

"Can we talk about this in the kitchen? I'll get you coffee or something to eat." Her voice sounded like a stranger's, calm and hostess-y. Not like her at all.

"There's nothing to talk about," he said.

"I want to know about the evil thing." She didn't, not even a little bit.

"You'll know more about it than you want to know very soon." He stood.

It's what she'd wanted. She'd wanted him to stand, to walk out of this room, to leave her little one behind, but suddenly he seemed so tall. He was a childhood boogie man. A terror. It took all of her self-control to turn her back to him and walk slowly into the hallway.

She heard the creak of floorboards and knew he was following her. She didn't turn, didn't look behind her. She continued forward, one foot in front of the other. When Fiona reached the kitchen doorway, she made a right. His hand stopped her. "No. We're leaving," he said.

She flinched away from his touch but didn't turn. "You still haven't told me why you need me." Fiona allowed her voice to rise to normal decibels. Now she wanted Devon to hear her, wanted him to wake, to understand what was happening.

Rico sighed. It was an unexpected sound. It made him seem vulnerable and human. "The evil needs a new person. It's going to take me if I don't give it someone else."

So that was it. He was insane. Certifiably insane. She'd thought it was the case when he spoke with someone who wasn't there at the car that night, but she'd thought maybe it had been his guilt talking, that maybe he'd hoped killing her would resolve his remorse over Chuck's death.

"If you kill me, won't it need someone new?" She played his game in a loud voice. *Devon, get the gun.* She sent a silent plea into the bedroom.

Rico tapped something against his leg as he thought about her question. It glinted like his eyes had done earlier. "I can't be sure, but I don't believe so."

The knife. It was so close. If Rico heard Devon coming, if he knew they had a gun, he'd put it to her throat. She had to keep him talking, find logic where there was none.

"Why?" she asked. "You say it left Chuck when he was in prison because it couldn't use him there. It left him again when he died for the same reason. If I'm dead, it can't use me either."

He grabbed her arm again. "Listen," he hissed. "I've seen this thing my whole life. I've seen it in jail. I've seen it on the outside. There are different ways to make it happy. I'm hoping killing you will satisfy it."

Fiona forced herself to gaze into his eyes instead of down the hallway toward the bedroom. "Then you'll be just like Chuck."

"What do you mean?"

"It used him. He killed to make it happy, but it didn't work. He had to kill again and again, and in the end, it trapped him." She spoke as loudly as she could without making him suspicious. "Killing me won't help you escape from it. You'll play right into its hands."

Light from the front door's sidelights shone into the foyer, and she could see him clearly for the first time that night. He looked terrible.

His skin, always pale, was now gray. A purple bruise covered his left cheek. His hair was crusted and tangled and there was panic in his eyes. He was as terrified as she was, maybe more so. His fear gave her hope.

"Don't let it use you. Resist it," she said.

"Resist it?" He asked the question as if it had never occurred to him.

Her hope grew bolder. "I can help you fight it," she said. "Turn yourself in. They have doctors—"

"No." He almost shouted the word.

She'd gone too far. She shouldn't have mentioned turning himself in. "Okay. Okay." She raised her voice as high as his. *Devon, wake up. Devon, get the gun.* "Don't turn yourself in. Run. Get away from the cops. Get away from it."

He tossed his head back in frustration. "You haven't heard a word I've said."

"I have," Fiona said. "Leave, and it'll stay with me. I'm Chuck's sister, right?"

He brought his head down slowly and met her eyes, but he didn't speak.

"I saw it, too," she lied. "When Chuck was on trial for the murders.

It looked at me through his eyes. I think it wanted me then, wanted me alive."

He inhaled and exhaled deeply, the sound whistling through his nose. "I don't want to kill you," he finally said.

Something jumped inside her, but she tamped it down. Maybe they wouldn't have to shoot Rico, add another death to the number her family had already accumulated. Maybe he'd just go away. She had to be calm, sympathetic. "I know you don't. You're not like Chuck, not like—" What was his mother's friend's name? Hal, that was it. "Hal," she said.

"I'm not. I never hurt a woman."

"I could tell that about you." God help her, she put a hand on his arm. She'd learned the power of touch through her years of teaching Pilates. He seemed to melt under its warmth. "I have some cash, not a lot, but a few hundred. I'll get it for you."

She began to move away, but he grabbed her hand. "I got money."

"What do you need then? You want to take one of our cars?"

"No." He didn't release her hand.

Her heart began to thud again. What did he want? She thought she'd convinced him to go. Why didn't he do it?

"Did you really see it?" he finally said.

Fiona nodded slowly, not trusting herself to lie again. She'd never been a good liar, although it seemed she was getting better.

"So you know I'm not crazy?" he continued.

"You're not crazy," she said.

He dropped her hand, and she rubbed hers on her pajama bottoms as if she could rub the insanity off. He moved to the front door but paused and turned with his hand on the knob. "I hate to leave you with it."

She forced a smile. "It's okay. I'll handle it."

He turned toward the door again, and a shot rang out.

41

DEVON

Rico dropped to the floor, gripping his leg. Fiona's head snapped toward Devon, who stood at the far end of the living room, her gun in his hand.

"What did you do?" she said in a hushed voice.

What did he do? He'd saved her, that's what he'd done.

"He was leaving," she said.

Devon looked at the gun in his hand. "I didn't know."

Fiona rushed to the bedroom and returned with a phone pressed to her ear. "Yes. Yes. Please hurry." She disconnected.

They stood there staring at Rico, not moving, for a long moment. Blood was gushing from the wound in his leg, the pool growing beneath him. A vision of Bob, the nice neighbor, lying in a puddle of red injected itself into Devon's mind. Rico deserved this.

Fiona spun, ran down the hallway, and returned a moment later with a bath towel. She dropped to the floor next to Rico and began to wrap his leg. Devon could see she was attempting to create a tourniquet, to stanch the flow. He didn't help her. He didn't understand why she was doing it. Wasn't it better to let him die? They'd never have to fear him again if he was dead.

"I'm sorry. I'm sorry." She repeated the words over and over.

Devon walked to the couch and sank onto it, his thighs suddenly weak. He set the gun on the coffee table and watched his wife cry over the wounded man on his foyer floor.

Sometime later, Devon was unsure how long it actually was, a siren howled in the distance. Within minutes, it screamed on the street outside. He roused himself from the couch, walked to the front door and opened it to the paramedics and the police.

Fiona backed away from Rico and let the professionals take over. She was covered in blood. His blood, not hers, so that was okay. Small arms wrapped themselves around Devon's leg. He looked down to see Caleb's wide eyes peeking around him at the scene on the floor.

He turned his body to block Caleb's view. "Let's go back to your room, buddy."

When Fiona found him, he was sitting on the side of his son's bed. Caleb had crawled beneath the blankets with a teddy bear, and Devon had stroked his back until he'd fallen asleep again. "The police want to talk to you," she said.

"Who's going to stay with Caleb?"

"I can."

Devon left his son's room and marched into the living room to face a long stream of questions that ran into the river of endless inquiry he'd experienced since Rico had come into his life.

THE SUN WAS up by the time Devon returned from the police station. The house was quiet. Fiona must have cleaned up because the blood stain was gone from the foyer floor.

He was exhausted but knew he wouldn't be able to sleep. Not yet. Instead of heading to the bedroom, he walked to the kitchen and brewed a pot of coffee. He wasn't done answering questions, he knew that. He'd seen them in his wife's eyes and knew she'd seen the betrayal he'd felt in his. He poured a cup of coffee and sat at the kitchen table.

His mug was half empty by the time she appeared in the doorway. She was wrapped in a terry bathrobe and rubbed her wet hair with a towel. Her eyes were red and ringed with dark circles. Her face was drawn, and she had a large bruise on her clavicle. They were war wounds, and he thought she'd never been more beautiful.

Fiona moved to the cupboard, took out a mug and filled it from the coffee pot, then she took the chair opposite him. She cradled the warm cup in her hands. Neither spoke.

After a long silence, Devon cleared his throat. "I heard him from the bedroom. Heard his voice."

Fiona gazed at him and sipped her coffee, inviting him to continue with her eyes.

"I didn't think. I reacted. I got the gun. I saw him. I fired."

"That's it?"

"That's it."

She nodded. "He was insane, you know that?"

Devon blinked. "You'd have to be to do the things he did."

Fiona shook her head. "No. That's not what I mean. He was delusional. He believed Chuck had an evil spirit living inside him, and since Chuck was dead, it needed a new host."

"At what point did that particular delusion occur to him?" Devon couldn't keep the hint of sarcasm from his voice. "He seemed pretty sane when he forced me to try to clean out the bank accounts. Bob's death, albeit terrible, had a certain logic to it."

Fiona leaned away from him. "I don't know when. Before he took me out to the woods, I guess."

"So you're saying the devil made him do it?" Sarcasm saturated Devon's tone now.

"He thought so."

Devon rose and refilled his cup. "So you feel bad for him? You think I shouldn't have shot him?"

"Yes and no. Yes, I feel badly for him. No, I don't think you did the wrong thing. I prayed you'd get the gun and come."

He returned to the table with a full mug. "Thank goodness."

"Why are you angry at me?" Fiona asked in that disconcerting way she had of changing the subject.

"I'm not angry at you. I'm angry at Rico, at the fact that he forced me to resort to violence."

"It sounds like you're angry at me."

He stared at her, emotions pinging around inside him like a pinball, lighting things up and ringing bells. He struggled to make sense of it. "I guess I expected gratitude. I expected to feel like a hero. Instead, I feel like I put down a sick dog everybody loved."

Fiona rose from her chair and pushed herself past his resistant arms into his lap. "Sorry."

Sorry. The simple word dropped like an ember into his cold gut. Its warmth spread through his body. He lifted his good arm and wrapped it around her. "I hope he makes it."

"I think he will. I think they got here in time." She rested her cheek on his head. "You know, when we were standing there watching him bleed out after you shot him?"

"Yeah."

"I wanted him to die."

"You did?"

"I thought about killing him a hundred times when he was in the cabin with you and Caleb."

"So why did you try to save him?"

"He said the thing that had my brother, the thing that made him kill people, wanted me."

"Dead? Or alive?"

"He thought it was dead at first, but I convinced him it wanted me alive so it could use me."

"You believe that?"

"Not in the same way he did, but I did think maybe I was like him."

"Who? Chuck?"

"Yeah. We shared half our DNA. There is a genetic component to psychopathic behavior. I've worried about it for a long time."

Devon pulled away so he could look at her. "That's not you, Fiona. You're filled with light, with goodness."

Her lip lifted on one side, and he saw Caleb in her face—their son's crooked frown, upside down. "You don't know what goes on in my head sometimes."

"I don't know a lot of things about you." She opened her mouth to speak, but he interrupted. "My fault, not yours. I learned something through all this: I need you. Not just to take care of our kid and help me impress people. I need you to be my friend."

She frowned. "I am your friend."

"Then I need to be yours." He pulled her close again, and they sat that way until fatigue dropped onto his eyelids, weighing them down.

Fiona stood. "Let's get some sleep while we can."

He let her lead him into their bedroom.

42

DEVON

Devon entered the kitchen and glanced at the wall clock—5:25. He'd been home early every night for the past month. It had to be some kind of record. Fiona didn't even seem surprised anymore. "Hey, babe." She lifted her face for a kiss. He obliged.

She and Gwen sat at the kitchen table, half empty glasses of iced tea and a plate of cookies in front of them. He walked to the cupboard and grabbed a clean glass. "What are you up to, Gwen?"

"She's trying to talk me into telling our story to a woman who's writing a true crime novel about recent crimes in our area," Fiona said.

"No, I'm not." Gwen turned her gaze on Devon. "I'm simply saying that I learned the hazards of giving the press complete control over the information the first time around. It almost broke up my marriage."

Devon poured a glass of tea and leaned against the counter. "How's that?"

"As far as the press is concerned, the more lurid the better. Abby isn't like that," Gwen said. "She has her own story."

Fiona lifted a cookie from the plate. "Then why doesn't she write that?"

"She is." Gwen gazed out the window as if collecting her thoughts.

"However, while she was doing background research, she discovered a link between several crimes that have occurred in our area over the past five years."

"That's the part that bothers me." Fiona waved her cookie between Gwen and herself. "Our stories are connected, but I don't see what any of the other crimes have to do with us."

"Except for in our case, the criminals aren't the connection," Gwen said. "It's the victims that are linked."

"How many crimes are we talking about?" Devon asked.

"Seven. Well, eight if you count Amy McKee's," Gwen said.

"I didn't hear about that one," Fiona said.

"It's what created the association in Abby's mind. Amy McKee moved into a fixer in Capo Beach. While she was remodeling, someone kept breaking in at night and drawing pictures from Dante's Inferno on the walls."

Devon pulled up a chair next to his wife. "Okay, that's weird."

"Then Amy gets a job at Saint Barnabas and meets Art," Gwen said. "And I find a body in your listing. Next, Olivia, whose son goes to Saint Barnabas, gets a job with you and runs into a stalker."

"I know," Fiona interrupted her. "Then Abby, who knows Olivia from school finds a dead body at the Mission. Rosie Ring happens to be decorating the house next door to Olivia's father's, and she too has a run in with a murderer." Fiona recited this in a bored voice.

"Exactly." Gwen's eyes brighten. "Then Honey, Rosie's best friend, finds a dead body out in Black Star Canyon; her daughter has that horrible experience at Sunset House; and now, you two."

"Coincidence." Fiona bit a chunk off her cookie.

Gwen pushed back into her chair as if distancing herself from Fiona's opinion. Devon saw both women's points of view. It was an odd set of circumstances. However, there didn't seem to be a causal relationship between the crimes. He tried to imagine convincing a judge that the events were linked but couldn't. It was all too circumstantial.

"What does Abby think?" he asked. "What's her angle, other than locale?"

"She doesn't know." Gwen turned her palms up. "Something

supernatural, maybe? The people who lived in Amy McKee's house before she moved in held seances and black masses there. They believed the barrier between earth and hell was thin in many places in Orange County, that being one of them."

"You see?" Fiona turned her gaze on Devon. "It's crazy."

Prior to his experience with Rico, Devon would have agreed with her. Now, he wasn't sure. Logic had betrayed him more than once during those terrible days. He was learning to listen to his gut. His gut was interested in Abby's theory.

"Did you know that the years between 1970 and 2000 are called the serial killer decades? There was a rash of horrendous crimes all across the country, although California had more than its fair share," he said.

"Your point?" Fiona said.

"Crime does seem to come in waves sometimes. Perhaps"—he held up a hand to stop the argument he saw building in her—"perhaps, there are forces at work we don't understand."

"There were a lot of sociological reasons for the serial killer trend." Fiona's voice rose. "The 60s' free love movement encouraged people to abandon long-held cultural ethics. Many of the killers had dads that came home from war with PTSD. They saw violence early, were attracted by it, and freed from societal constraints. It was a recipe for disaster."

There was something evil inside Chuck. Devon couldn't get Rico's words out of his head. He knew Fiona heard them as well, which was why this conversation had her so worked up.

"Maybe." Devon inclined his head. He didn't want to fight. Not with her. "And maybe there was something else going on as well."

"What? Like demons?" Fiona's words dripped with sarcasm.

Gwen broke in. "Abby isn't saying she believes the stuff about demons. She's simply pointing out that there was a trend."

Fiona snapped her head toward Gwen as if she'd forgotten she was there. "There *was* a trend? How do we know it's over?"

Ah, that was the problem. Fiona was afraid. Devon placed a hand over hers. "It's over for us."

They sat in silence for a long moment, until Caleb's voice broke the tension in the room. "Mommy."

Three pair of feet padded into the kitchen—Caleb's two, and Sophie's four. The German Shepherd Chow mix would be as tall as Caleb soon. She'd become his constant companion since they'd brought her home from the shelter three weeks ago.

"Can I have a cookie?" Caleb eyed the plate. Sophie gazed at it with rapt attention as well.

Fiona handed Caleb a chocolate chip cookie, while Devon retrieved a biscuit for the canine half of the duo.

Gwen stood. "I didn't mean to upset you. I'm just finding the process of talking with Abby cathartic." She put her purse strap over her shoulder. "If we can find meaning in the things that happened..." She shrugged. "But maybe there is no meaning. Maybe it was random."

Fiona reached out and took her friend's hand. "I'm sorry I overreacted. I guess I'm still raw. I'll think about it."

"Think about what?" Caleb said.

"Think about"—Devon grabbed his son, turned him upside down and carried him to the living room couch—"tickling you." And he did.

43

FIONA

A week later, Fiona found Abby sitting at a table outside the Dana Point coffee shop where they'd agreed to meet. Abby stood and waved when she saw her coming. She wasn't what Fiona had expected. Perhaps because Abby was a school librarian with an interest in supernatural things, she'd imagined an older woman given to flowing caftans and too much costume jewelry. But Abby was young, slight, and pretty, and had the most unusual brown eyes flecked with gold.

"Who's this?" Abby held out a hand to Sophie when Fiona drew closer. Sophie sniffed and wagged her tail—a good sign. If the woman was deranged, the dog would know, wouldn't she?

"This is Sophie," Fiona said. "We've only had her a few weeks."

"She's beautiful." Abby petted the chow's head. "Carlos and I have been thinking about getting a dog."

"Don't think. Do it," Fiona said. "We thought about it for much too long."

Small talk reigned as they ordered drinks, and Fiona found herself liking Abby despite herself. However, an awkward silence fell as soon as they settled themselves at the table again. Abby blew in her coffee, sipped, then cleared her throat. "Gwen says you're a little concerned about the book."

She was direct. Good. Fiona had found it difficult to be anything but honest since the events of last month. "I am. I guess it's the whole supernatural element that has me worried."

Abby gave her three slow nods. "When I was living at the Mission, my view of the unseen world changed."

Fiona felt her jaw tense. She'd heard about Abby's bizarre scheme to live like a medieval mystic then write a book about it. It was one of the reasons she hadn't wanted to talk to the woman, but Gwen had assured her Abby wasn't weird. The jury was still out.

Abby held up a hand. "But that's not what the book is about. I don't know what the link between these crimes is, and I don't plan to speculate. What I want to do is present the facts, the viewpoints of the victims—or should I say victors—and allow the reader to make up their own mind."

Fiona liked the term victor rather than victim, but she wasn't entirely convinced this book was a good idea. "Gwen said something about thin places between Orange County and hell."

"That's what some people believe. I don't know." Abby drew her shoulders forward in an almost apologetic gesture. "I do know I felt the presence of entities I couldn't see when I was at the Mission, but whether they influence peoples' behavior or not, I have no idea."

Fiona sipped her tea. She liked Abby, but she wasn't sure if she trusted her. The last thing she needed was for her family history to be part of a sensational series that read more like fiction than fact. She'd been humiliated enough for one lifetime.

She set her cup down. "Why are you writing this book?"

Abby wove her fingers together and rested her chin on them. "That's a good question." She paused. "I guess it's because I want to understand why people do the things they do. The events that took place in your life, Gwen's life, my life, they can all be explained on a practical level—that the crimes were financially motivated."

"Yes, and no," Fiona said. "Rico wanted money in the beginning, but eventually it was something else."

"Something else?" Abby gazed at her intently with those gold-flecked eyes, and Fiona wished she hadn't spoken.

"No." Fiona waved a hand. "You go on. What were you going to say?"

Abby dropped her hands to her lap. "I believe crime, at least these crimes, all have something in common besides where they happened and to whom."

"What's that?"

"They're multifaceted. They each have an obvious motivation, like money. But there are less obvious motivations as well. Those are the ones that interest me."

There was something evil inside Chuck. How many times had that phrase reverberated through Fiona? How many times had she woken up in the middle of the night in a cold sweat, wondering if the *thing* was after her? But there was no *thing*. There was no evil entity stalking her. "What if things are exactly as they appear? What if the motives behind the crimes are simply greed or lust or pride?"

"Then they are," Abby said and smiled. "I don't have an agenda, Fiona. I'm not trying to build a case for a particular sociological or supernatural influence. I would simply like to understand what drives one person to kill another. There are easier ways to get money."

"And you believe you will understand if you write these stories?"

"Better than I do now."

Fiona couldn't argue with that, but the idea of putting herself in the mind of a murderer to better comprehend him made her shudder. Abby was more courageous—or more something—than she.

"I have another motive for writing the book," Abby said.

"So you're multilayered, as well," Fiona said.

Abby laughed. It was a nice, transparent laugh. "I guess I am."

"What's your other motive?"

"The experience I had changed me." Abby leaned back in her chair. "These kinds of things do. I want to examine that change, put it under a microscope, figure out what occurs in a decent human being's soul when they're pitted against an evil one."

There was that word again, *evil*. Fiona hadn't believed in evil until

Chuck came into her life. Now, she knew it was real. "Either it makes you stronger—"

"Or it kills you," Abby finished for her. "Honestly, I hope reading stories about victors, people who made it through terrible things, will help others who are dealing with lesser problems."

"My dad," Fiona said with a hitch in her voice, "used to read about people who were imprisoned by the Nazis in World War II whenever he got frustrated with life. He said it put things in perspective." She hadn't said anything positive about her father since she'd found out about his past sins. That needed to change. She didn't want Caleb to grow up with the familial shame she'd been living with.

"That's a great philosophy."

"I think so."

Abby reached down and patted Sophie. "Will you consider letting me interview you?"

Fiona gazed at the sky. It was clear and blue, only a few white clouds bobbing along on the breeze like ethereal sailboats. It was time to set aside the past. To forgive the sins of her father, to destroy their impact on herself and future generations. Maybe telling Abby her story would put it in perspective. And if it could help someone else, well, that would be an incredible bonus.

She brought her gaze to Abby's golden flecked eyes. "Okay, let's do it."

AUTHOR NOTE

The Seven Deadly Sins series has been a real education for me. Each of the books, although they can be read as standalones, built upon the last both in my understanding of the world and my understanding of how to write a page-turner.

I admit, I experimented with plots stolen from movies, books, and newspaper articles. *A Margin of Lust*—the first in series—was inspired by the movie *Pacific Heights,* which held a special horror for my husband and me since we'd recently become landlords when it was released. *The Key of Greed* was my take on Gothic horror in the vein of *Rebecca. The Sanctity of Sloth* was a nod to *Rear Window* and *The Girl on the Train. The Color of Envy, A Pinch of Gluttony,* and *The Scent of Wrath* were all pulled from real life—with added mystery and mayhem of course.

This last installment in the Sins was inspired by a Nevada Barr book I devoured years ago, *Destroyer Angel*. That story was about a canoe trip that went horribly wrong. In my mind, there's nothing scarier than a vacation gone bad.

I chose a cabin in Big Bear Lake, a town in the San Bernardino mountains, for my characters' getaway for one primary reason. There's no snow in the flat lands of sunny So Cal, and I wanted snow.

My books loosely follow Dante's ideas about where and how each of the seven deadly sins are punished. You can read more about that in *The Origin of Sin*, a prequel to the series. According to the *Inferno*, the Prince of Pride—Lucifer—is imprisoned in the center of hell in a frozen lake.

I loved the idea of adding ice and cold as both a metaphor for pride's effect on our souls and to create some of the same feelings of isolation and desperation that *Destroyer Angel* evoked.

If you enjoyed reading the story as much as I enjoyed writing it, please leave a review on Amazon, Goodreads, or wherever you purchased it. And please stay in touch. There's always a free story on GretaBoris.com for those who join my reader community.

Best,
Greta

ALSO BY GRETA BORIS

The Origin of Sin (prequel)

A Margin of Lust

The Scent of Wrath

The Sanctity of Sloth

The Color of Envy

A Pinch of Gluttony

They Key of Greed

VISIT US AT

WWW.GRETABORIS.COM

WWW.FAWKESPRESS.COM/NEWSLETTER

FAWKES PRESS

CPSIA information can be obtained
at www.ICGtesting.com
Printed in the USA
LVHW031251151221
706194LV00004B/273

9 781945 419836